THE OLDEST SOUL

ANIMUS

TIFFANY FITZHENRY

Printed in the United States of America

First printing, 2015

ISBN 978-1-944216-00-9 (Paperback)
ISBN 978-1-944216-04-7 (Hardcover)
ISBN 978-1-944216-01-6 (Kindle)
ISBN 978-1-944216-03-0 (epub-iTunes)
ISBN 978-1-944216-02-3 (epub-Nook)

Hierarchy Publishing, LLC
1029 Peachtree Parkway, #346
Peachtree City, GA 30269
www.hierarchypublishing.com

Cover design by Vanessa Mendozzi
Formatting by Polgarus Studio

I dedicate this book to the most inspiring daughters in the world, for all your love and patience. And to my husband, my soul mate, for your unwavering support and for believing in the beauty of art and dreams.

"You don't have a soul, you are a soul. You have a body."

—C. S. Lewis

PREFACE

"I'm lucky to be a part of it, you know," she nodded, looking for my agreement. But I sat still as a stone, studying her as she swabbed my skin with alcohol. "It's actually really interesting!" she gushed to fill in the gap left by my silence. I could tell the young lab tech was doing her best to try and reassure us both. "A few drops of blood Evelyn, that's all we need."

But despite her efforts, Payge (according to her nametag) couldn't hide her nerves as she sunk the cold steel needle into the crook of my elbow. And when the dark red fluid crept from my vein into the vial, I saw the glimmer of fear in her eyes. Not of needles, or of blood, or even of me this time. It was her fear of what she was doing, of what it meant. A fear buried deep, microscopic in its appearance, invisible in her knowledge of its presence, like undiagnosed cancer, but immense for what it could do inside her. Monstrous.

"It's Eve," I told her. "And it's fine," I managed. For her sake. Hoping she'd think back on my words later.

"Almost done. Then you'll be free to go," she seemed proud to tell me, her smile genuine. And of course I would. Why wouldn't I be? Everyone else was …

"Oh, Payge," I remember thinking. "What will this do to you?"

I'd never thought much about what it would be. You know, the thing that would finally divide the world in half. The singular obsession that would polarize humanity to the point of no return—but if I'd had to pick something, a cluster of circles discovered deep within our DNA wouldn't have been my first choice.

Payge liked me. She'd only known me for about ninety seconds, but it was easy to tell. What was harder to understand was why, and to try to exist in a normal way knowing it wouldn't take me two minutes to get her to jump out the window or cut her own wrists or stab me in the chest if I wanted.

People either liked me or they didn't, *deeply*, and almost instantly. At first I rejected it, perfect strangers feeling entitled to having an opinion either way.

I'm learning to accept it.

She smiled down at me as she removed the needle and softly compressed a cotton square onto the injection site. This time, I smiled back.

It was true that all they needed was just a few drops. The ugly lie this poor girl didn't know she was telling was that once she got it, I would be leaving here; I might never see the outside of this building I realized, and fought to stay calm, as she skipped out of the room with my blood. The blood they didn't even know they were looking for. *Until they found it.* The blood that would change everything.

"Back in one minute, literally!" she promised, as if I'd be timing her.

And so I was hardly surprised when she walked back in the room, forty-five minutes later … pale as a ghost.

PART ONE

FINDING EVE

CHAPTER 1

I was nine when my grandfather said to me, "Eve, if you've worked the question and come to your answer, the only way to be sure you're correct is if the answer leads to at least two more questions." One day soon, he said, I would start to search for questions more than answers. That "people like me" always did. It was at that moment when I realized I wanted my grandfather to live forever. Looking back, it was at this precise moment that I believe he began to die.

Now, eight years later, we're both in heaven; only it looks a lot like Rugby, North Dakota, 58268. Total land area, a magnificent one point nine square miles. Elevation, a wonderful one thousand, five hundred, and forty-nine feet above sea level. Population, two thousand, eight hundred, and seventy-six small-town souls, plus the future resident thriving inside the pregnant woman I see from time to time at Higgins

Market. I can tell by the way she tilts her head and smiles with her eyes across the produce that she's curious, and a little worried frankly, to see such a young girl seems to do the household shopping; best guess she thinks I'm about twelve. My seventeen-year-old body is stubbornly slight. My flat chest and sharp hipbones ruthless evidence of a currently square shape. Only as developed as it absolutely must be for today and not an ounce more. I try not to let it bother me.

I stay focused on positive things, like Rugby, which happens to be the geographic center of North America. If you dropped a pin from the edge of the atmosphere down to the exact middle of the combined area of Canada, Mexico and the United States, it would land right in the center of Rugby. People around here, those over forty anyway, tend to be obsessed with this fact and I admit I share their enthusiasm, while kids my age think it's nothing more than a sarcastic punch line that sums up everything they find lacking in Rugby's remote and rural life. We may not have a stoplight and we may have to drive an hour to the nearest movie theater, but hey, they joke, at least we're the geographic center of North America.

I couldn't agree more. But then again, I invent alternative computer languages for kicks. I enjoy tinkering with unsolved mathematical theorems and have an unhealthy fixation on a nineteenth-century poet … I began to suspect a long time ago that I was different from the other kids.

It should come as no surprise that I was elated to discover the monument, the one that rises out of the ground at the miraculous spot at which this geographic center point exists. A fifteen-foot-tall stone obelisk, congratulating ourselves on this "achievement," under which I always seem to find myself sitting, well-worn copy of the complete works of Lord Byron in hand, to bask in the cozy idea that I am in all directions as far from an ocean as North Americanly possible. If I close my eyes and sit there long enough I start to feel like I can see for hundreds and hundreds and hundreds of miles, in front of me, behind me and on both sides. I see nothing but the sure footing of solid land and I feel safe, even if it's just in my mind.

I've never been a fan of oceans. Maybe *that's* why Rugby suits me. I've lived everywhere and anywhere you can imagine; on every continent, and in every corner of the globe, yet I'm somehow certain that this tiny place has been patiently waiting for me. In fact, on a frigid night last February, less than twelve hours after my grandfather, Cian (key-in), and my brother, Shamus, and I first arrived in Rugby, snow whipping across the rugged plains, I said without thinking, "I'm staying here." I say, "without thinking," because Cian has been known to take certain things that come out of my mouth a bit too seriously. Sometimes it's hard to tell if we're just chatting or if I'm making an unintentionally binding declaration, but since we've never lived in one place as long as we've lived here,

I suspect this time it was the latter.

So yes, Rugby is heaven on earth, at least to me. My little land-locked slice of paradise sparingly populated with small town people who take pride in silly things.

Hell on earth is trying to wake up Shamus. I'm about to begin school for the first time in my life, eleventh grade, and not that I expect his enthusiasm—I don't—but consciousness would be appreciated.

We both know things are changing and in our own ways we're both scared. Too bad we don't have each other to lean on.

"Shamus," I say into his room from the safety of the doorway and can't help but wonder what it would be like if he were a good brother. A different person.

"I heard you!" he roars through clenched teeth from somewhere deep inside the mess of bedding he's tangled in, his irritation teetering on rage, and I flinch at the pillow he flings at me. It falls a bit shorter than usual this time, at least a good yard from my feet, on top of a pair of jeans. There is not a clear spot of carpet in his room, every inch littered with the debris of laziness and drunken abandon.

"Please, Shamus. Ten minutes," I say in a firm tone but somehow sound like I'm begging. I'll be late. I already know this.

As his lanky frame rolls over, his swollen eyes strain to open. If I leave now he won't get up and I won't get to school.

I wait, preparing to hold my ground; uncertain whether he's going to jump up and lunge at me, feigning the threat of bodily harm, or scream something disgusting or hurtful. I pray for the cruel words: I'm not worried about my feelings; my mind is a fortress Shamus can't infiltrate but my body is small. Vulnerable.

For more than a minute nothing happens. It's excruciating. I know I can't say anything more until he speaks first or he'll be completely lost to his wrath so I concentrate on matching the inhale of my breath with the exhale; the length, the depth, the rhythm. But as the next minute of quiet stillness passes I grow increasingly uneasy, like how seeing the clouds gather and sky turn green sounds the alarm in your brain, telling every cell in your body that a tornado is about to descend.

His eyes finally focus in my direction. They instantly radiate with malice. I concluded a few years ago that the hatred he feels toward me is etched in his DNA. There's no other way to rationalize the unprovoked wildfire inside him that my mere presence stokes with oxygen. He snarls at me like a lion bearing his teeth and my pulse quickens. I change my stance, turning my back leg outward, shifting my weight in case I need to break into a sprint.

He begins shaking his head. Then he does something disturbing. Something I've seen many times before. He smiles. Wide-eyed, like a certified lunatic. Then his maniacal smile breaks into an unsettling laugh, wild and hearty, a hyena now. His cackling mirth is devouring any shred of sanity in him, and it's not for show. I know what that looks like. This laughter is real. Each time he does this a certain Byron quote cycles through my mind: *Nothing can confound a wise man more than laughter from a dunce.* Then, per usual, just as abruptly as his uncontrollable fit started, it stops, and his face and eyes turn dead. It's the kind of dead you can't fake, and it always reminds me that he's not a dunce; he's a depressed and sociopathic mental patient. All he's missing is the hospital.

"You actually want to do this," he says, his body now listless as a sloth. I let down my guard; he's too tired to hurt me.

"Yes," is all I can manage, adrenaline vacating every cell at once. *Yes,* I want to do this. I want to go to school. To be an average girl who lives in one place, goes to high school and has friends. Is that so difficult to imagine? Is it so hard for Shamus to understand? That as it turns out, I didn't know what *wanting* something really was until the idea of going to school occurred to me. Until the thought sprang into my mind in mid-July, a sudden flash flood, a bucket of cold water in the face. And I've thought of almost nothing else since.

This is pretty much how I operate. I would assume that by now my brother would know that. Shamus, of all the repressed and unhappy people, should be able to comprehend a desire for things to be different. But as he rolls back over to face the wall grumbling something under his breath, I remember that my brother lacks all rationality, he isn't a reasonable person. Sometimes I think that his whole purpose in life is to provide obstacles for me, points of impasse, without any route to resolution. An audible exhale at his disconnected state concludes my protest. What else can I do? Then, as if he's making an announcement for the entire world to hear, his words building like a storm: "There's something wrong with you, Eve." His menacing voice, projecting off the walls, like thunder through a canyon, sends a chill down my spine.

Hunger, or maybe dread, drags me into the kitchen against my will, breaking my momentum with Shamus, ensuring several more minutes of delay. Food is a bother, a constant nag. I gulp cold, unfiltered cider from the large glass jug until my stomach begins to hush, then smear butter on a slice of soft white bread and eat as I pack two apples and another slice of bread in a sack and glide quietly to my grandfather's bedroom door.

The wooden door is a knotted, unstained pine, the knob is black, plain and unpolished. I think of knocking, but don't. I think of my grandfather and how, to the world, he appears … just elderly … fragile and weak. They never look at him long enough to notice that his cheeks are pink with life. They disregard the old man shuffling around the neighborhood and never learn that his hands are as strong as those of a man in his prime. They certainly don't take the time to look into his eyes, which are as clear and lucid as my own. Of course, for his part, it doesn't help matters that his clothes look about a century old, and that something in his quietness makes him seem distinctly unapproachable.

Fragile and weak, senile, frail ... irrelevant ... I almost have to laugh. Only Shamus and I know the truth, that Cian is as far from senile as humanly possible. And weak? In their wildest dreams they couldn't imagine the ferocity of his strength, and if people knew, I don't think they'd like it. *Humanity isn't crazy about the truth,* Cian teaches me whenever the lesson applies, *even if deep down, it's what they want.*

The truth is that the man, who goes practically unseen, is the answer to the question that humanity has asked since the beginning of time: when bad things happen, is it part of some mysterious plan or is chaos to blame?

Both. The answer is both. But only the waker can correct what chaos disrupts.

Our grandfather is *the waker.* Modern humanity has never known they had one, and has never known a time without one. I marvel, daily, at the irony of it. Death, the one thing man cannot conquer. My ancient grandfather, seemingly useless to society, is in fact the most vital man on the planet.

No one on earth is more pivotal, more powerful.

But he is aging, rapidly, and one day soon he will die. Everyday, I see him dying more and more before my eyes. I'd be lying if I said I wasn't terrified. What happens when he dies? "No," I tell myself, shaking the thought from my mind and enter his room without knocking.

The room is so small, seems to be getting smaller. In one corner, his bed with the soft blue cotton cover sits neatly made. It's the size of beds used some time ago, smaller than a twin, like children's furniture of today. It's "what he prefers." Though I've never seen him in it. Beside the bed is his night table, a wooden relic of undisclosed origin, the ornately engraved door on the front, locked, a key for which I have never seen. I've repeatedly asked where it's from, and when. How he got it and from whom and what on earth is inside? But his answer is always the same: a smile.

The room appears empty but as I turn I know my grandfather is behind me and I know I will see that smile. I haven't yet figured it out, but before I can wonder at its power, his smile whisks me away, like it always does. My anxious energy melts. The tiny room melts. Life and earth melt. It's just my grandfather and me and for the moment we're standing in a vast desert. It's sweeping with silence and vacant as space, bathed in burned yellow light and soothing as a hundred thousand sunrises. I wonder if my eyes are open or closed back in the tiny bedroom in the modest white house on East Gate

Drive as I marvel at the endless golden dunes surrounding us. I look down at my bare feet in the powdery amber sand.

There's something wrong with you, Eve. I watch, as the words Shamus said to me are pushed into the cloudless sky above, each word dissolving as it rises, like an ecosystem ridding itself of a poisonous gas.

"Promise me something, Eve," Cian asks, his voice strong and tender. He takes my small hands, cradling them in his larger ones.

"Anything," I say, and now we're standing in the middle of his room, space and time unbroken. We're back, or maybe we never left. The sky and the dunes are gone. But so are Shamus's words, once they dissolve they're gone forever. Now all I can think about are my grandfather's hands, and wonder why they've always been so comforting to me. When I was younger I used to imagine I could curl up in them, as if I was the size of an apple, and just rest there for as long as I wanted. Right now his hands are warm and I detect the subtle tremor that's recently taken up residence in him. I know, as always, he's been out walking since well before dawn but lately his aging body is struggling to keep up with his inexhaustible mind and indestructible spirit. In the silence I wonder what he wants me to promise. Stay true to myself? Work as hard at school as I have worked learning with him?

"You won't be an island any more," he asks, combing a wisp of hair away from my eyes and I feel a bittersweet mix of sadness and anticipation. He'd taken to calling me "a happy little island" for the way I thrived despite our isolated life. The way I even loved it. It's all I've known.

"Okay," I promise.

"One more thing. Please, find some trouble, and get into it. It's okay to be a little reckless," he says, odd advice to give a teenager on her first day of high school. But I can tell that he means it. This is the same simple tone he uses when he teaches me anything for the first time. We are eye to eye, his are the same bright emerald as mine but they shimmer, almost transcendentally, like silver moonlight reflecting onto a pair of secret gem-green coves. Our height is precisely identical at this moment, which gives me a thrill.

"If I must." And if he's telling me to, I know that I will.

"Nothing would please me more."

"You won't be here when I get back?"

There is no answer. Not so much as a nod. There's never any answer to this question. My asking the question *is* the answer. I'm only comforted by the fact that for now, at least, he still has work to do.

He hugs me tight, the same way he always does. My grandfather is needed—by whom, only he knows, and so he goes, my brother always his one companion, his heir apparent I fear. I've learned to understand the process. I've studied it since I can remember, never talking about it to a single soul. But like I said, things are changing.

CHAPTER 2

Shamus's car is a twenty-year old four-door Subaru Outback. Steel grey. He does nothing to keep it running. If it needs oil, it could sit for weeks in the driveway, engine seized in protest. If it gets a dent or a ding, he doesn't get it fixed. Except for once, when he was probably too drunk to even walk home and he drove into a tree with such force that the damage had to be fixed or the car would never drive again. The body shop mechanics talked for weeks about how my brother should have never walked away from that accident. They couldn't wrap their heads around how he survived, but I knew, and walk away he did, with a DUI and a loud introduction as a lowlife drunk to our new small town. If I ever choose to mention this incident Shamus would erupt in a millisecond. I never mention it. Not because of his volatility, but because I never seem to find myself in the mood to discuss the fact that I believe he did die. That I'm pretty certain the master of his own demise had been scooting ever closer to death's door for some time and that he'd finally done it. That it was all his fault, but it wasn't his fate. I never bring it up because then I would be admitting out loud what we both know that means. That there's something else my older brother is meant for, something critical to the history or survival of humanity. I don't dare say it out loud; because anytime the thought so much as crosses my mind I shudder.

Shamus has seen a lot, I sometimes remind myself. Maybe I'd be the same way, I even give him. Maybe when Cian was young and trying to cope with the reality of who he was—*what* he was—he was a bitter and toxic shell of a man too. Or worse, maybe not.

"Anyone who voluntarily elects to attend high school is automatically the most detestable, most despised person on campus, just so you know. People aren't going to like you." That was my benediction as he drove through McDonalds for two egg sandwiches.

"Shamus, couldn't you just drop me off and get breakfast after?"

I was already twenty minutes late. Walking into class on your first day when everyone has been together since kindergarten is bad enough, but walking in twenty minutes late is a recipe for the kind of trauma that haunts a person for a lifetime.

"Of course I could," he says, his best imitation of sweet, smiling stiffly as he drives up to the second window and reaches out for his food. "I'm sorry, you didn't want anything, right? Oh course you didn't, you probably couldn't eat a thing this morning, you must be so nervous." He studies me for a reaction. Finding none he goes on. "How selfish of me. You just want to get to school ... but school starts so early. I don't think you'll ever be on time. You should just drop those first couple classes now. Can you drop classes in high school?"

"No. That's only college," I tell him as if he doesn't know that.

"That's right," he sighs, taking a few minutes to slowly unwrap one of his McMuffins with an exaggerated carefulness, like it's some delicate ancient artifact that will turn to dust if he moves too quickly. "That's right, in high school you just fail them," he adds nonchalantly, his car still in park, as if time has ceased to exist.

For my brother attempting to anger me is his blood sport of choice, and not just because he hates me, it's even more than that. It's because so far it's been impossible for him to do. When it comes to my brother, my one and only sibling, I feel a lot of things—sadness, fear, anxiety, even love. But no matter what he does or says, my anger is never triggered. It's almost unfair, I often think, to rob him of all the power he could have if I would just get on the roller coaster of rage he's been offering me my entire life. It's not that I don't want to ride it; it's more like I don't have a choice. I just never have. Even now, while logically I'm aware he's trying to provoke me and that any little sister worth her salt would be spitting nails by now, the only feeling I'm hit with in this moment is another bucket of cold water in the face—*I want to learn how to drive, and I think it's time for me to have my own car.*

My desire is reinforced when Shamus chooses to drop me off not curbside, but at the adjacent street corner about a hundred yards from the front doors.

"Thank you," I say with the smallest hint of sarcasm, as I exit.

"Hey sis, don't mention it. You don't know this kind of stuff because you've never been to school, but it's the cool way to get dropped off. Trust me." What Shamus doesn't seem to be able to process, despite my many hints, is that I gave up trusting him around the time I turned six. But it's probably for the best. He would go berserk if he had any idea how flat his words fell around me, like smooth round stones just laying at my feet. Stones, I imagine using one day, to build something new. By the look on his face he imagines I'm thinking, *how would you know, asshole? You've never been to school either!*

I'd just walk away but feel the sudden need not to leave him wondering.

"I'm sure it is, when you've arrived on time," I start, and he waits for it … an outburst, some kind of protest, even mild agitation. "Thank you, Shamus," is what I end up saying and close the door softly to which he peels off and speeds out of sight.

Once in the front office, I immediately note the clock. It's eight fifty-five and this whole moment has the feeling of standing on a cliff at the Grand Canyon in a windstorm. I've heard people talk about having bad dreams, where they show up to school naked. I've never had this dream, probably because I've never been to school. And though I'm pretty sure this isn't a dream, I still look down to check my body for clothes. Jeans, green Converses, T-shirt, my lucky belt … I'm good. I also remember and am soothed by the fact that I already know my schedule by heart. Literature, which is likely over, then Geometry, then Biology, Religious Studies, World History …

"O'Cleirigh? Evelyn Raine?" asks the tall woman behind the counter, approaching me warily like I'm a Bengal tiger.

"*Eve*, yes." I answer, and she tears around her large book-filled workspace like a whirling dervish, moving franticly and groaning often. Either I've already annoyed her somehow or something else is seriously overwhelming this woman.

"Your last name is rather odd, you know. Anyone ever tell you that?" she stops to commiserate with me, like I can help it. I know it's odd. And yes, people have mentioned that. Just about every single person who's ever tried to say it read it or write it has mentioned that very thing, I want to tell her but take mercy.

"Yeah, it's ancient," I inform her, beginning the soliloquy I've orated before about how it's the oldest known surname in the world, but she's already over it.

"I have never seen anything like this." She waves the papers in her hand at me. "Your entire schedule has been changed. Every last class! And at the last minute, of course. It's a good thing you're late, I've just finished rearranging everything. You'll need a whole different set of books too," she reminds herself and goes into overdrive. She flings my freshly printed schedule on the counter and I look at the still warm small slip of paper as she sets about swiftly gathering those books. AP French 4, Accelerated Calculus II, Intro to Organic Chemistry …

"Wait, why?" I ask her as a man enters the office and walks over to me.

"I couldn't tell you Hon, I haven't the slightest. *Mr.* Envoy will explain all of that," she tells me with a friendly wink, her emphasis on "mister," as she heaves the last in a long string of enormous books onto the counter between us with a thud.

"*Eve*," the man starts, like we're old friends, even though I've never seen him before. His black mustache the only thing on his face darker than his eyes. "*Dr.* James Envoy," he presents himself to me, emphasizes the "doctor" and giving the woman an annoyed look for not using it. Which, by her smug expression, was intentional. "That's all, Penny. I'll let you know if I need anything else," he says to which she theatrically rolls her eyes. Not discretely.

"I'm sure you will," she mumbles loud enough for him to hear. He decides, rather painfully, to let it go and instead in an overly dignified voice he informs me that we will be spending a few minutes together getting to know one another and that since meeting with him for educational counseling is an excused *privilege*, even though I was late, *almost an entire hour late*, I won't have to get a tardy.

"You're welcome," he suggests smugly. "Come on, this way." He starts walking and I follow, still yet to say a single word, though I'm already certain he's a man that doesn't notice things like that. Doctor James is actually a few credits and one lengthy thesis paper shy of his doctorate, he feels it necessary to explain to me, however dismissively, en route to his office. Technically making him still *Mister* Envoy, like Penny said. So this is what I chose to call him, after which he and I sit very quietly in his office, staring at each other.

He looks me over in a way I'm all too familiar with. Scanning for certain outward signs, searching for fresh layers of newly minted self-awareness that manifest during the teenage years as a confusing and often painful clash of vanity and insecurity before ultimately distilling a lasting "identity," based mostly on feedback. People like him don't even know they're doing it, but they look for this hyper ego knowing it creates a sort of lullaby for the consciousness, to generate their own feelings of authority, superiority, or both, and I can already see his distress. He can't locate mine at first glance so he glares awkwardly, to which I simply return unbroken eye contact. Most adults, but especially *professionals* like Mr. Envoy, can't put their finger on it and I feel for them. From what I can gather their minds keep circling around the idea that I don't quite look seventeen. Something tells them I'm younger while something is telling them I'm older, much older. But it's even more than that. Just being with me very often flips alarms in people's brains. Which alarms and why they're flipped is something I don't know. Trust me, if I could shut them off I would.

Sitting here, watching him study me, I realize that the principal, whom I met a week ago, Texas transplant Mrs. Billings, tipped him off about me, though I'd bet a thousand-acre cattle ranch she struggled to articulate what she was tipping him off about. I'm unsettling. Especially, it seems, for those whose jobs it is to place children neatly into certain folders and bins.

"No one knows much about you," he charges, as if I was the last person seen holding someone's missing cat.

"I've been here for five minutes," I say, bordering on defensive. "I assume over time that will change." He looks me straight in the face as he flips intensely through a stack of papers on his desk.

"Your birth certificate mystifies me."

"Well, it's in Bambara, which I can safely assume you don't speak and have likely never seen in print before, so … don't be so hard on yourself," I say without any particular inflection. Though it's not my goal, the simple truth and my encouragement only agitate him further. It looks like Mister Envoy can tend to feel uncomfortable when faced with the fact that there are things he doesn't know. I attempt to help.

"You see, French is the official language of Mali, where I was born, but Bambara is also widely spoken. Actually, thirteen of the indigenous languages of Mali have the legal status of 'national language.' Isn't that something? You actually got off kind of easy. It could have been in Xaasongaxango!"

He takes a deep breath, a slow inhale of equal parts condescension and exhaustion, followed by an audible exhale of blasé, designed to tell me that I am not special, he's met a million students just like me, that he knows exactly how to handle all this, and to assure us both that he is still the most intelligent person in the conversation. In reply, I clear my throat just once and raise my eyebrows ever so slightly saying that I have my doubts about, well, all of it. Frankly, I have my doubts about *you,* mister.

"This is a nice talk we're having," I remark in reference to our wordless yet contentious exchange. Then he does the most amazing thing. He gulps, hard. His eyes dart around the room and for a hair of a second I see something remarkable. Fear.

Fear of *me.* Fear, as unmistakable as a giant purple elephant stampeding through the room. Though I can tell, as he regroups, he's already convinced himself that I didn't see it, that there was no elephant at all. This game of communication charades he's playing is not something I'm used to, but it certainly feels like something I need to figure out, and quickly.

He dials up the aggression considerably. "Your records are spotty at best. In fact, Eve, 'spotty' is too generous a word to describe the holes in your educational history." Here's where I'm supposed to feel frightened by my obvious intellectual shortcomings. He takes a beat wherein I suppose he'd like me to elaborate on the unimpressive nature of my traceable education. I take a beat wherein I choose not to.

"You did exceedingly well on your entrance testing," he adds, almost an accusation.

I shrug. "I feel like I guessed, mostly." He raises his eyebrows at me and I realize that's not quite true. "Maybe 'guess' isn't the right word …"

"On which part?" He thumbs the pages again, looking for bubbling that resembles Christmas trees, I assume.

"On all of it," I say plainly, he looks up from the pages of results like his feelings are hurt. "I had never taken a test like that, or any test before. Answering so many questions, one right after another, I felt kind of … weird. Like I was half asleep or something."

I'm remembering the inactive sort of feeling as I notice an

unpleasant look taking over Mr. Envoy's face. I try to describe it more accurately for him.

"Honestly, I didn't put much thought into it," I say. Like, *any thought* … at all.

"Didn't put much thought into it, huh?"

"No."

"You prepare in any way?"

"No. I just walked in and took the test. It's a placement test. I assumed preparation would sort of defeat the purpose."

"Let me see if I have this then. You've never taken any kind of standardized testing or testing at all for that matter. You don't have any record of any kind of formal education that I can find and you didn't prepare. Oh, and you feel like you guessed."

"Right. I'm sorry, is that a problem?"

"Yes. It's quite a problem … we have quite a problem if you expect me to believe you," he sits back in his chair, like a prosecutor who'd just exposed a hostile witness's perjury.

"Excuse me. Why would I lie? How would I?" Does he think I secretly went to Harvard as part of some bizarre plot to become covertly brilliant, all just to arrive at this awkward and problematic moment?

He turns quiet, and seems to be contemplating whether he wants to tell me something or not. Finally: "No one in this county, *or in the state*," he whispers, to keep it from all the people who aren't in the room, "has ever scored what you did."

The obvious conclusion, "I guess they don't know as much

as I do," doesn't sit well with Mr. Envoy. His face twists further. He's shaking his head. As his aggravation turns back to anger he narrows his eye on me.

"Are we going to have a behavior problem, Ms. O'Cleirigh?"

It's definitely a threat posed as a question. Again, not the kind of thing I'm used to hearing from an authority figure. I think hard about how I'll answer. I notice a strange part of me crop up that wants to answer for his sake, give him what he's looking for and diffuse this awkward situation we find ourselves in, the one where I don't feel inferior to him. I could shake my head no and look at the ground, ashamed of myself, or carrying on as if I were. Then a bigger part asserts itself, one that isn't concerned at all with giving this man the answer he's looking for to a question that he choose to ask, out of fear, in an attempt to make himself feel dominant.

This other part is only concerned with the truth.

"Are we going to have a behavior problem?" I repeat the question, take a deep breath and remember what my grandfather told me this morning, *to find some trouble and get into it.* I have never been in any kind of trouble, in any form, in my entire life. But whether it's the power of suggestion or simply a warning shot across the bow from my grandfather, I suddenly realize that today, I'm in brand new territory. I decide to double down on Mister Envoy's worst fears and go with the truth. "Are we going to have a behavior problem?" I restate, emphasizing each word carefully.

"*That's my question*," he says possessively, claiming the words for himself.

"About that, I'm just wondering can a statement really be a question and also a threat, you know, at the same time? If you make a threat but you keep calling it a question, because of phrasing or intonation or semantics isn't it still a threat more than it will ever effectively be a question? You know, if you had to pick one," I quiz him, like I would be free to ponder anything of the sort out loud with Cian—"Never mind," I say, staring at his livid expression. "My first instinct was to tell you no, we are not going to have a behavior problem. But I decided not to lie."

"Thank you …" he says, trailing off, realizing he spoke before he processed.

"I'm quite sure that we are. That we will. Whichever way you want to say it. I think they're both correct. You get the point I'm sure. You're very educated."

At the news of my impending inevitable trouble-making the non-doctor's blood pressure visibly rises before my eyes; his ears turn a hot, purple-red, then the crimson spreads to his cheeks and the corners of his mustache quiver downward as his lips purse tight together.

"Is that a threat?" he demands. Really? Is he joking?

"I'm just answering your question. See how it's so confusing?"

Watching Mr. Envoy's head preparing to explode off his body, I feel compelled to tell him one more thing I know to be true. Something my grandfather started to teach me when I was maybe three. That *suffering is optional.* But the timing feels a bit off.

At a total loss, Mr. Envoy told me to go to class but not before citing me for being late, my very first tardy, what little act of retribution he could muster. I look down at the pink slip in my hand and wonder if this is the only trouble my grandfather was hoping I would find. Now I know the feeling of being reprimanded. What worries me is it's not as bad as I thought, depending on the source it even feels right, and what troubles me further is that I'm certain my grandfather was referring to something more than a late pass, even a late pass given simply out of spite.

I struggle down the deserted hallway, arms filled with new textbooks for my fancy new classes, pink slip tucked halfway into my massive Organic Chemistry book, my new schedule shoved into my back pocket, and a map of the campus clenched in the hand I'm using to secure the top of the pile of books I'm struggling under. I can barely read the room numbers as I pass but know I'm in the one hundreds and need to get to the five hundreds. Five-twenty is my homeroom, where locker seven awaits. That could be far and as I falter under the books' weight likely matching my own I wonder if I overplayed my hand with the one administrator who even knows my name at this place. A place I actually want to be. Then I start to wonder about wanting to be here as my thoughts turn to Shamus. I start to think that maybe he was right when the sound of a bell shrills through the halls; chasing the thought from my mind and in an instant I'm a pinball being knocked around for amusement and what feels like possibly points as well. I stumble, get spun around, and am about to go down when I hear a voice, a voice that by now I know nearly as well as my own.

"Give me those." The heavy books levitate from my arms into his much larger ones and our matching green eyes meet.

"Hi, Roman," I say, lacking the enthusiasm he always seems to expect.

CHAPTER 3

Turns out, Roman and I have every single class together, except homeroom. "That's a coincidence," I suggest, and can't figure out if it's a good thing or a terrible thing as he escorts me to Mrs. Silver's homeroom under the watchful, almost disapproving, glare of a good half the people we pass, which I note, is dissolving a portion of the self-assurance I carried into Mr. Envoy's office.

"Not exactly," he explains. "How many classes a day do you think they need for the subjects you're taking? Sure it's the only high school for fifty miles but still, how many kids here do you think will get beyond French 2 when this state doesn't even require a language credit? And Accelerated Calculus, there are going to be four students in the entire class, including you."

Roman and I go way back, as far back as possible to be

exact, to the first moments after I arrived in Rugby.

Cian, Shamus, and I had traveled for several long days through what would later be hailed as the winter storm of the century across the Midwest. This was the final day of the storm, and the worst. It was February thirteenth. I know this because the lady across the aisle on the Greyhound bus kept feeling the need to repeatedly inform me that it was almost Valentine's Day until she finally fell asleep.

As we drew closer and closer to Rugby, over the final few hours of the journey, I grew hungrier and hungrier. Pains of starvation like I had never felt before consumed me as I sat on the dark bus, not so much as the glow of a single reading light in the whole cavernous space. The "interior illumination system" was "on the blink," the driver explained when we first boarded, and by this late hour, it was complete and utter darkness, "like being in the womb," he had jokingly warned us, and he was barely exaggerating. The blackness combined with the floating sensation of the road beneath us and the constant hum of the diesel engine lulled almost all the passengers into a fetal kind of sleep but only seemed to cause my senses to heighten, metabolism to accelerate, and ravenous appetite to steadily increase.

When my feet finally sunk into the deep powder as I stepped off the bus in Rugby, a single picture had hijacked my mind—a massive hamburger. Even the grave frostbite warnings being announced on a continuous loop were barely white noise compared to the screams of my fixation.

As we stood waiting in the luggage line I couldn't help rambling incessantly, giving an audible play-by-play of my intensifying pangs, trying to describe the uncanny exactness of my craving. I carried on and on. I felt myself being annoying, and still I couldn't seem to stop.

"We get it, you're hungry," a man waiting just in front of us mumbled under his breath, which gave me momentary pause until the next hollow churn of my stomach.

As he often did in the presence of our grandfather, Shamus kept quiet. But he hadn't been on a decent drinking binge in days and there was no mistaking the pained scowl he wore. He wanted to hurl me headfirst into the side of the bus and leave me lying limp on the salt-covered asphalt, a mess of metal and glass and blood. Instead he was storing the pent-up aggravation in his infinite databank of hatred.

"Eve, I haven't seen you this hungry in your entire life," Cian remarked as a Greyhound employee extracted our suitcases from the belly of the beast, his gentle way of suggesting I consider giving it a rest. But in an unprecedented lack of self-control I continued rambling on about me and every little thing I thought or felt, my faint wondering at his words, *You've been with me for my entire life?* shuffled to the back of my mind.

We set out from the bus depot and within just a block found a motel. Shamus and Cian were still checking us in, both too tired, or too tired of me, to eat, as I ventured back out into the arctic wind, snow pelting my body.

I was on my own.

Through the blinding blizzard I spotted a diner just about a block away, its neon sign still visible in the near whiteout, and it beckoned me.

I'd been in Rugby less than ten minutes as I sat alone in a sticky vinyl booth at the Green Owl, still trying to thaw the icicles enwrapped around my bones and impatiently waiting for a server to come take my order. It was just past midnight and by now the emptiness I felt inside my body was causing a whistling in my ears. I was working on convincing myself to stay in my seat while imagining tearing through the kitchen doors like a wild animal that smells raw meat. That's when I first spotted Roman. He came striding through the swinging doors as I fixated on them, wavy sand-colored hair, black T-shirt and a bright white apron around his waist. His intense eyes, I could tell from across the room, were the same rare color as mine, and seemed already focused in my direction, even before he could have seen me waiting.

He strode toward me, long arms swinging at his sides, small twist of his chest with each casual but deliberate step. Watching him cover the space between us was like seeing something spectacular in a setting far too ordinary. Like a fiery comet blazing through a grocery store.

When he reached the table, for a brief second, he just

stared at me, an indistinct look on his face, one I couldn't translate. Then he crossed his arms and cocked his head, letting an enchanting smile gently steal his face by first making his square jaw push his wind burned cheeks upward, revealing perfect pearl-white teeth. When this smile reached his eyes they wrinkled at the corners, and what looked like two warm glowing nightlights, affixed somewhere at the bottom of vast emerald pools, slowly lit, shining out from some mysterious place deep underneath.

"Hi," he said, soft and easy, but in a way that made the tiny word feel like it contained within its two letters all the words of the English language.

"Hi," I replied, the minute word again filling all the space around us.

"My name is Roman."

"Eve," I tell him.

"*Eve.*" He repeats, with a strange little smile, nodding his head slowly.

Just then it occurred to me that I was there to eat, that he was there to take my order, but what I had planned to get had completely vanished from my mind.

"I am not entirely sure what I want," I told him, and with that news, it seemed, he took a seat across from me, scooting into my booth and propping one elbow on the table to support his tilted head at the temple. We talked for several minutes, the conversation light. Surprisingly *effortless.* Once our knees even touched in what I'd later determine wasn't an accidental bump. The entire time his expression was warm and welcoming, and utterly engaged. Everything else about him, from his body to the way he moved, had a precision, was streamlined, sleek and chiseled.

When he got up to head to the kitchen and retrieve the burger I had finally remembered I wanted, he smiled back at me over his broad shoulder.

"Happy Valentine's Day, Eve," he said with an easy tone, like he was rolling the sentence down a soft grassy hill, but as the words reached me all the tiny hairs on my arms stood on end, electrified, then the current coursed through my entire body at once, like I was standing ten feet from a lightning strike when it scorched the ground.

"Thanks," I whispered, a few seconds after he was gone, once I was blinking and breathing again.

That's how I met Roman Alexander Davidson, raised in Rugby since he was five, born in New Zealand in 1999. The same year I was born. Even though we were born on different continents, on opposite corners of the earth, as we talked we discovered that we were also born in the same month. December. For some reason I couldn't get over the shock of this fairly mild coincidence, although I don't think Roman thought much of it. When I asked him what day he was born, thinking I'd probably pass out on the spot if he said the 21st, he never even answered as the conversation naturally drifted to other things.

I'd be lying if I said I wasn't left more than a little bewildered by our first exchange, but in retrospect, meeting Roman that night, no matter how enchanted the moment felt, was all foreseeable. There's just one place to find a hamburger, or any food after midnight in Rugby and there's one hotel, The Green Owl and The Cobblestone Inn, which have been on the same block for over a hundred years. And as for the sort of paralyzing, almost unearthly nature of our initial encounter, I've come to understand that Roman has the kind of personality that could disarm a bank robber, on top of what I knew right away, that he happens to be a spectacular looking human being. *Spectacular.* And I'm a seventeen-year-old girl who's hardwired to desire him, genetically speaking, of course.

To this day, Shamus refers to him by descriptive words only, never any effort to hide his incredible contempt. "Oh look, it's muscles," he'll announce. Or mock me when I walk in the house—"I bet you saw wavy hair today." Shamus also seems to think it should bother me that Roman has a way of crossing paths with me most days. It doesn't. I don't think seeing a boy like Roman every day would bother any girl. Aside from his always cheery, often witty, and endlessly engaging nature, he's just about the closest thing to a textbook example of a boy whom girls find attractive: one to two inches over six feet, sun-lightened brown hair that's a little wild and just on the side of unruly, mysterious clear green eyes with no limit to their depth, a sharp square jawline that traps your eyes if you're not careful, impossibly copper skin that stays tan through winter, and shockingly soft hands. This last part I know because since that very first time we met he seems to be able to find a reason to touch me. It's always innocuous enough but there is no getting around the fact that it's unlikely I need a hand on my shoulder as I enter a classroom, that kind of stuff.

There's just one thing I haven't been able to explain away about Roman Davidson, something I haven't been able to find a folder or bin to fit into; there doesn't seem to be a compartment in my mind remote enough to store this, where it's completely out of sight, where I could somehow deny it was happening. You see, from the first second I laid eyes on him, Roman had been flipping a lot of alarms in my head. Which alarms and why, I don't have a clue. But he has an answer to every question I ask him so if I get curious enough I'm fairly certain he could explain it all to me.

As I attempt to fit all of my oversized books into the small square locker, which I'm growing positive is spatially impossible, I note the unmistakable feeling of eyes on me. Something tells me not to turn to see whose they are, and I keep trying to jam my books into my locker. I know they're not Roman's—he's lingering outside Ms. Silver's room, waiting to walk with me to our next class. Besides, I've felt him staring at me before. This is a much different feeling—it almost hurts. I focus on my books and try to forget that someone is burning a hole into the back of my skull. I hold up the largest, Accelerated Calculus II, and it strikes me, in this moment, with the burning stare burrowing into my cranium, I can't say what exactly calculus is at all.

It does occur to me, however, that I shouldn't be putting this book in my locker; it's for my next class. My first real class, ever. I thumb a few of the pages without really looking at them and feel a wave of nausea start in the bottom of my stomach and a flash of heat on the back of my neck. Do I really know this stuff? Am I going to be able to do this? I imagine Shamus's face, as if he's somehow here to witness this moment, and I see his maniacal smirk. Just outside the room, I can hear the unending stream of greetings and flirting that seems to envelop Roman when I'm not at his side.

"It's you," I hear, and instinct tells me that the "you" refers to *me*. I turn and a girl sitting in a desk nearby has her distinctive caramel eyes trained in my direction. "There were rumors that you were going to grace us with your presence but I never believed them." She stands and takes a few steps toward me, easily five inches taller, not including the knot of thick brown hair tied in a flawless bun on top of her head. Her stature is imposing; she's probably twice as strong as me (maybe three times?), and who knows how much faster. Just looking at her I know she could run me down in seconds and kill me with her bare hands. We both know it. She sums me up with her eyes and seems to laugh to herself, "Get ready to watch your back, *Evelyn.*"

Before I can formulate a thought, I see Roman striding toward us.

"Phoenix, leave her alone," he orders, looming over her and suddenly it's as if I'm standing between two skyscrapers. She backs away, almost imperceptibly, but the instant she does I feel the real tension isn't between her and me. It's between her and Roman. "And she prefers Eve," he states plainly, but his words seem to echo in the most unnatural way. I do prefer to be called Eve, of course, but it's not something I recall ever mentioning to him, and why did his voice sound so strange? I can't be the only one who noticed but neither of them seemed to.

Phoenix gives me a good and thorough once over with a face as expressionless as a slab of cement.

"Welcome, Eve," she manages with a tiny bow of her head, giving Roman a jaded look before turning to leave but keeping her eyes locked dead on me. When she finally departs I exhale, and it occurs to me for the first time that I have lived my entire life in a completely controlled environment. Until today, contending with a manic unstable sibling was my only real adversity. And since his provocations never affected me, I was free to be blissful. But my cage had already been rattled by the time I got into this room, and Phoenix just ripped it to shreds, exposing me, leaving me ripe for any savages who want to come and finish me off, to completely plunder the last scraps of my apparently delicate confidence.

Once Roman and I are back out in the hallway, swimming upstream through throngs of glaring students, I ask in a low voice, "Okay, do I want to know who that is? What I did to make her hate me so I can never do it again?" Hating the insecure words and the sound they make traveling from my lips to his ears.

"She's not that bad, and trust me she doesn't hate you. Nothing could be farther from the truth actually," he says, almost to himself and I have less than zero idea of how that could be possible. "But look, I'm not going to sugarcoat it," he says, stopping to turn toward me. "There are people here that don't like you."

I look at him in disbelief. How? I just got here. Is he kidding?

"*Really* don't like you," he warns and I can tell by the way he's intending for his eyes to pierce right through mine, that he isn't kidding. What's worse is, I know he's right. I've felt it since the moment I got here, I admit to myself as I pass one blatantly hateful stare after the next, all of them unprovoked and aimed unmistakably at me. Their obvious disdain appears automatic.

But why? And why so immediate? Is it something in how I look? How could a small, hardly developed girl with average brown hair no makeup and making no attempt to get noticed cause an instant and hateful reaction, or any reaction … unless … there's something wrong with me … Used to my brother's hatred, I had been considering this in a dispassionate manner, but the thought is a trigger. A hidden trip wire. And all at once I'm bum-rushed by Shamus's words: *There's something wrong with you, Eve.* Like an invisible demon sweeping down the hallway and snatching me up and carrying me back to Shamus's doorway. I hear his voice, how it thundered, low and sinister. I see him clearly, lying in his bed, his dark hair, made darker by days of sweat and oil, matching the hollow blackness of his eyes. The same chill ices each vertebra like a cold serpent slithering down my spine.

My face gets hot then instantly flushes. It seems my blood remembers how adrenalin drove it out to my limbs this morning and decides to repeat the drill, switching to a position of high alert because it too knows Shamus's insults have never come back into my mind like this before. Once Cian takes me to the mysterious golden dunes, once the insidious words float away and disappear, they've always stayed gone. What does this mean? As I try to process the thought for the first time, nausea bubbles up from a place I've never felt. A place so deep inside my body it almost feels outside my body. I must be actually turning green from the crushing tsunami of digestive acid pooling behind my jaw because Roman grips my elbow and bicep with his hands.

"Whoa, hey, are you okay?" He studies my reddened face for a cause. A cause I can never let him see. What was I thinking coming to school? I'm a freak show!

"I'm fine," I lie, gently taking back my arm. What would I say? Even if I wanted to tell him about the fear that's crushing me from the inside out, the fear that something significant just shifted between Shamus and me, there's no way to easily bring Roman up to speed on my peculiar family dynamics. How my brother is a monster, a monster I fear would initiate a rein of terror unlike anything in history if given the chance, and how my grandfather, *oh who by the way can wake the dead*, mitigates the damage Shamus inflicts by taking me, somehow, to another realm or something, to dispose of the dark words my potentially world-endingly powerful sibling has spewed at me since I can remember. That deeply, secretly, I believe that *Shamus* is terrified that he won't be the one to inherit Cian's gift. That he somehow knows it will be me, so he wants nothing more than to destroy me and that he plans to destroy my mind first and worry about killing my body later.

Obviously, I can't share a single word of this with Roman, particularly if I want him to speak to me ever again. So I say nothing. But Roman, clenching his jaw, clearly isn't satisfied with nothing.

"I'm fine," I insist, drawing out the words for emphasis, but see that he knows better. He knows I'm lying to his face.

He levels me with his eyes and I realize instantly there's a difference between reading someone's mind and knowing what they're thinking. I can't read his mind, but I know exactly what he's thinking. *Oh, you're fine? Oh, okay. Are you kidding me? Something is wrong, and it's obvious.* And he's right. Too bad there's no way to even begin to explain what's wrong, so instead, I don't tell the whole truth, which is to say I lie, again:

"I'm just a little worried about being disliked by what looks like half the student body. Fair enough?" Then, for good measure, I deflect, "I mean, a little sugar would have been all right. It is my first day of school, you know. Ever." I've noticed that when you make something sound like someone else's fault they become all distracted. It's not nice, but it works.

He raises his eyebrows as if he's saying, *Um, nice try. You do realize that I know you're not telling me everything.*

"And I don't do you any favors by lying to you," he says, having projected his first thought before verbalizing the second, impervious to my trick.

I take a deep breath. It's what I always do when I feel like I'm losing my mind. Then I take another breath and try my very best to pretend that aside from my acute and seemingly baseless social problems, everything else is normal. That I'm a normal girl who isn't concerned about the resurrection of someone's words in her mind and what it might mean and that there's nothing odd about Roman and me. We are just two normal teenagers getting to know each other in a normal way. Becoming friends. He isn't projecting his thoughts while I follow along seamlessly. No, that isn't happening. And he doesn't know stuff about me that I've never told him before. Nope, that wouldn't be normal and everything is normal here. Of course, I don't actually believe it, but right now I cling to my fantasy like I'm clinging to a cliff over a ravine. I grasp and claw at normalcy. Too afraid to ask myself why I think being normal can save my life.

"I just mean, you know, if Phoenix is my only shot at a friend, I'm obviously in trouble," I say, committed to the normal lie with everything I have but hearing the transparency in my voice and feeling dangerously exposed.

If I were to verbalize the look on Roman's face, he'd be saying, *I see you. I see you hiding in there. Do you want to come out now or would you like to keep hiding?*

There's something so inherently sad, pitiful really, in knowing that you're not functioning normally, knowing things are obviously and definitely amiss, seeing other people knowing it too, and yet you continue to fake it, desperate to appear like everyone else, for your pathetic sense of self, and never even considering stopping. Even when your life looks like it's being held together with toothpicks. Right now, this is me. This is my best attempt at holding it together. And these are my toothpicks. Please act like you don't see them.

How do you like my imitation of normal? Isn't it convincing?

He decides to indulge me: *Why yes, it is. It's very convincing;* his smiling eyes tell me before he even opens his mouth.

"So, Phoenix—I'm the one she dislikes," he offers, a lifeline, a welcome distraction. And like any phony, I'm grateful.

"Yeah, I did sense that," I say, masking my relief quite well, like the professional liar I feel myself becoming.

"And you would be correct. It hasn't always been this way with her and me. Things are kind of tense for us right now ..." he says, trailing off.

"And why is that? What, some kind of lover's quarrel?" I wonder to myself but realize I said out loud. "Sorry ... I, ah ... just forget I asked you that."

"No, it's fine," he insists, like he's about to tell me.

"No, I shouldn't have asked you that," I say, feeling no right to that information and wondering how I let the question escape from my mouth.

"You can ask me anything, Eve," he starts, casually at first. Then turns to me, "Anything. I want you to know that," he urges, no attempt to conceal a new earnestness in his voice.

I know I can ask him anything. He's told me that, in one way or another, just about every time we've ever talked—another likely abnormal conversation piece of two people just getting to know each other. But the odd thing is, I do have questions, loads of them, more with every passing minute.

Like, what day was he born on in December 1999? Did he feel what I felt at the moment we met? How did he know I don't like to be called Evelyn? How does he manage to cross paths with me everyday? Why did he protect me from Phoenix? Why did his voice echo when the three of us stood together? I want to ask him everything and I have no doubt he has all the answers. The problem is, my questions very likely have answers that I don't want to hear, answers that don't solve problems but open doors to new ones. Answers that confirm the mysterious and long suspected freakishness buried just under the surface of who I am. I don't want anything to do with any of these answers. I don't like how he echoed what Shamus said, how he actually somehow knew that people weren't going like me. How Shamus knew that is the kind of thing I'd rather not have an answer to at this particular moment, thank you very much. The answer to a question like that might cause me to hyperventilate in the bathroom for a fairly substantial amount of time, when all I want to do is go to class.

"Tell me you understand. That you know, you can ask me anything," he repeats with calculated clarity, his shimmering green eyes locked on mine, like he's asking how many fingers he's holding up to see whether I have a concussion.

"I know," I tell him finally, but don't ask about anything on the growing list of things I don't understand. Right now I just want to be a high school student.

I try to regroup, yet again. He's watching me as I grip the straps of my backpack, focus my attention straight ahead, and he seems to get the hint.

"With me and Phoenix, it's a long, and very complex story," he starts, and I grimace. "I'll tell it to you sometime," he says, kind of gently.

"Sure, sounds wonderful. I'll let you know if I actually stick around long enough for that *sometime* to get here."

"Oh, well in that case, I'll just tell you now. How's that sound?" he teases, knowing it's the last thing on earth I need or want.

"Yes please, a lengthy and complex story sounds delightful right now."

"Great, I'll make it the extended, overcomplicated version," he jokes, his eyes twinkling, and we both laugh a little. It feels good, *really good.*

"So let me get this straight," I say. "Phoenix likes me but has a strange way of showing it, while other people hate me for no reason that I'm aware of. Everyone loves you but Phoenix hates you and people get mad when we are together. It makes perfect sense," I add, heavy on the sarcasm.

"It makes perfect sense," he affirms, sounding more confident than he has any right to in response to the ludicrous statement I just made. "It's like, having all the same classes seemed to be an odd coincidence at first but as soon as you really thought about it for a second … it makes perfect sense."

"That's a very different thing, Roman, very different. This is ... there's no logical reason why people who I've never met don't like me. I don't understand," I almost whine, all my self-pity on full display.

"Neither do they," he says, and I can see that he wants to tell me more but stops himself as we both note a gang of girls glaring at me, almost violently, and suddenly, I think I get it. Shamus was trying to torment me this morning, to make me feel insecure, that's all. *I* let him get in my head. There's nothing wrong with me, I realize, as I notice for the first time how Roman is practically glued to my hip, walking in lockstep, shadowing my every move, fixating on me like I'm some china doll that might shatter or vanish at any second, and I wonder how I could have been so naïve?

"Look, Roman, you're a great guy," I start tepidly. He smiles at me.

"Thank you, Eve."

"Yeah, I wasn't done. You've always been beyond friendly to me, for no apparent reason, and now I see how, you know, popular you are, and realize how, you know, unpopular I am," I venture, guessing this is how high school works. "If you want to keep your distance at school, I get it. I'm completely fine with it." I add, looking for a way to save him from me and also save myself from everyone else.

"I'm not going anywhere," he vows.

"How did I know you would say that?" I give up, for the

moment, abandoning my efforts to grasp or fix any of it.

"Something's going on. I think the bell should have rung by now," he says, looking around. I shrug as we continue on our way. What do I know? It's my first day. And judging by the groups of teachers gathered, talking in the hall, which Roman remarks is "weird," I don't think we need to worry about being late.

After a few seconds, an easy quiet comes over us.

"Look Roman, I'm used to being alone," I share into the silence. "I'm really fine that way. *Really*. I've spent a lot of my life more alone than you can probably imagine."

There is so much I want to tell Roman. The way he's listening, he wants to know more, there isn't anything about me that he doesn't want to know. I can feel it.

But I have to be careful. A big part of me wants to tell Roman everything about my life. If I'm being honest, for the six months I've known him I've been restraining myself from absolutely pouring my heart out. From dragging him completely into my world. But I won't let myself. For some reason, I want to feel what it's like to have something normal. My world isn't normal, has never been anything close to normal, and I want to lie to myself a little longer and pretend that it is. I need to hold back the truth, to protect our budding friendship from it, though it's agony. Every second I'm with him I fight a compulsion to tell him everything.

The halls are almost empty now as we stand outside our

class, trying to finish what we're talking about before going in. Still no bell. Still no teacher.

"I know it sounds strange, but, my life, if you knew more about me, it … it hasn't been average. It's … different." I say, feeling him out, deciding whether I can say more.

Roman is quiet for a moment, seeming to roll this over in his mind.

"Well," he starts, followed by a pause so pregnant I'm about to forcibly induce labor when he announces finally, "Today, you learn to swim," with some trumped-up enthusiasm to mask the faint but distinctly ominous bend in his words.

"What?" is all I can muster, as most of my ability to communicate confusion is busy creating all the frown lines between my eyes and on my scowling forehead.

What is he talking about? Is he talking to me about swimming?

"Didn't I ever mention?" I say. "I don't swim. *Even as a metaphor.*"

"You will. Because you're not an island any more, Eve," he tells me with kind eyes, casually shaking his head. An unnerving notification at best. At worst, a premonition of the impending inescapable fulfillment of my deepest fears and the very words Cian said to me no less than an hour ago.

And just like that, my allotted time for lying to myself expires, and the ridiculous fantasy of my life ever being normal goes up in smoke.

CHAPTER 4

Like a typhoon, an unfamiliar anger wells up inside my stomach as Roman motions toward the open door of our classroom. I storm in, livid, and throw my books on one of the desks. But since my particular textbooks are so unusually huge, because all of my classes are so freakishly advanced, the weight of them causes the desk to dip instantly forward, the connected seat to levitate and the whole thing to topple to the ground in one calamitous crash. I stare at the mess for a minute—books flung open and strewn everywhere, some pinned under the overturned desk, pages torn. It looks a lot like how my day feels. It looks a lot like the messy end result of this knee-jerk instinct to join the ranks of the everyday teenager: an ugly and confusing mess. I've yet to even attend a single class and already I'm fairly certain that high school is nothing more than a wasteland of confusion and pain. A wasteland that turns to a house of horrors as Phoenix's commanding voice startles me from the back of the room.

"Nice one, Evelyn," she shouts. I jump at the boom of her words and sight of her looming in the last row, eyeing me with arms crossed. The way her long legs end in combat boots that rest atop the desk beside her.

I drag my intimidated eyes off Phoenix, forcing my attention back to my mess. As I pick up the books and fix the desk I start to wonder, *was* it so unreasonable? Was it completely foolish for part of me to think that by starting a more average life, my life would become *more average*, that maybe I could even have something *normal,* like a friend! But it's clear, crystalized by his last remark, that there's nothing remotely normal about the relationship between Roman and me. On top of that, my merely attempting a task as simple as *being average*, as going to high school has only made everything that's glaringly different about *whoever or whatever I am* flare up, an apparent allergic reaction, a bizarre response to standardized tests, to exchanges with administrators, to meeting new people, to having a conversation with a boy I'm getting to know, and it's time to find out why. As soon as I'm done with my tantrum and mourn the loss of Eve the average high school girl who lives in one place and has friends, I resolve to finally ask Roman about everything. *Everything.* Including why he doesn't seem to be at all confused by my sudden irate display, why he's trailing in behind me, giving me space, which is exactly what I need.

On the opposite end of the annoying spectrum there's our calculus teacher, Ms. Speakman, who blows into the room like she has somewhere else to be, launching right into her *accelerated* lecture on Implicit Differentiation, just about the very last thing I need right now in this new constant state of fluster I've adopted. When I pictured what school would be like, I never imagined myself feeling this way, insecure, unfocused, aggravated and disoriented. I never imagined myself feeling so angry. But I am. And this tiny woman who looks to be in her fifties with a neat bob haircut and square glasses, who flies through one high math concept after the next, has no clue that I can't focus right now, that I can't possibly pay attention, that I need a few minutes to process Roman's comment, the one that broke the proverbial camel's back, before I can actually compute numbers.

You're not an island any more, Eve.

His words hit me like a brick over the head. There's no chance it's a coincidence, an innocent play on words that just happen to be the same words Cian said to me this very morning, and a hundred times before that. It's not. I know it's not, and I accept that that's incalculably abnormal and I move on, determined, now, to find out what it means.

Today, you learn to swim.

If he was trying to be cryptic, he would have picked an analogy that didn't involve my worst fear, my lifelong arch nemesis of a pastime. But he wasn't. He was trying to be obvious. Well, point taken. Duly noted, sir. I get it. It appears you know me. More than is possible, in fact. Just like how he knew to tell my best friend Phoenix that I preferred Eve. His voice was the same each time. A tone that makes no attempt to mask that this is common knowledge to him, simple as that. It's clear now that these are clues he's been giving me. And since the untimely death of my normalcy has been officially declared it's time to begin the autopsy and determine the fatal cause.

"I want to ask you something, Roman. A few things actually," I whisper when the teacher's back is to us. "Let's start with what you just said to me outside."

Roman leans toward me, a serious look about him. He raises his hand toward his mouth. He looks me dead in the eyes and places one finger over his lips as he slowly, quietly, shushes me. I stare at him a moment, wondering if he's serious. He cannot be serious. For six months he basically badgers me for questions and I finally ask one only to get shushed … no way.

"Are you kidding?" I ask, knowing he's kidding.

"Sshhh," he repeats gently and motions to Ms. Speakman. So … not kidding.

"Really?" I whisper-shout at him as my blood boils so fast and so hot it startles me. Unlike with Shamus, it's apparently very easy for me to feel mad at Roman—almost too easy, I

think as I turn away from him in a huff of white-hot irritation, which he seems to, annoyingly, find humorous. He's staring ahead but I see the corners of his closed mouth are turned up slightly, which only riles me further.

"What happened to mister *ask me anything,*" I whisper-yell again, in the meanest sarcastic tone that has ever escaped my lips, without even turning to face him. "You should have mentioned you were mister ask me anything *outside of class.*" This last comment flies out of my mouth a bit too sharp, loud enough to get Ms. Speakman's attention and earn me a warning glare. Great, more trouble. At this rate I may end up in jail before the first day of school ends.

I guess for now I'm left to wonder, for fifty minutes, to fume at Roman and wonder. Beyond wondering *how* he knows, I wonder *how much* he knows about my relationship with water. Like his relationship with Phoenix, it's a very complicated one. It always has been. It was complicated before I got to Rugby—a big part of what drove me to the geographic center of a nine million square mile continent after all—but since arriving here, this strained relationship has gotten down right baffling.

When I wake up every morning, frustrated and actually surprised by having had the same dream, yet again, and every night since we arrived here, Cian repeats some lyrical version of the following: *Why are you surprised when the thing you run from as hard as you can only gets faster and better at chasing you?*

And it's true. He's right. Highly, annoyingly, right.

But I am surprised, somehow, like clockwork, every morning, because during the waking hours I shudder at the thought of being adrift in open water. It's my deepest fear. Or something beyond fear, a concrete and absolute aversion etched in my cells that can hijack my brain into an instant and consuming frenzy. But somehow, in this record loop of a dream it's a much different story—I actually love it, being adrift, an abyss below me, cradled in the endless unknown, only the horizon to tell me that I'm on top of the water and not under it. The sway of the current, the freedom of my arms and legs and toes and fingers as they tread through the cool water, the way the immense waves lift and lower me at their will, the salt, I love all of it. And it makes me bat-shit crazy.

"Imagine having a phobia of spiders," I once tried to explain to Cian, "and dreaming every night about millions of them crawling all over you. And somehow in the dream you love it! You can't get enough!" To which he said, "I can see how that would be maddening. Tell me, are you all alone in the dream?"

That was the last time I mentioned the dream to Cian.

I'm not alone in the dream. I've never wanted to tell him that. The only conclusion I've come to is that I'm enjoying the person who's with me so much, even though it's someone I don't know, that I embrace being in the middle of nowhere, lost in the Red Sea, drifting hundreds of miles from land, nothing and no one else but the two of us in sight. This person's presence makes a fantasy out of my worst nightmare.

For some reason, if Roman were the one in my dream, I could find his comment less unsettling. Of course, it would still be eerie, wondering if he knows what I dream about, but I did start having the dream the night we met so at least as it pertains to my own mind, I'd maybe understand where it was coming from. But Roman isn't the one in the water with me. Of that I'm certain. And yet how does he seem to know about this water drama that has plagued me my entire life? No, I've never almost drowned and no one I know was on a vessel that capsized in the middle of the ocean and never found, presumed dead leaving me to wonder in agony. All I can say is that from my earliest memories of life, every cell in my being has compelled me away from water. Teaching me to swim—and I *can* swim—was a practice in otherworldly patience and cemented my unshakable trust in my grandfather.

I was small, maybe six. We lived in Italy, a couple hours from Rome along the Amalfi Coast in a tiny town nestled next to a small, fairly unknown beach called Varo Ferola. The swath of white pebble sand tucked between two huge rock outcroppings is maybe the clearest memory of my life. To the right side were two natural, graceful rock arches and there were mornings when the tide was low enough to make them look like the arches towered up to the clouds. The exposure was such that our private patch of beach got sun all morning until early afternoon. For one of those sunny morning hours, every single day, we walked together to the water's edge. Not holding hands but always completely parallel. For months we just let the cool liquid barely graze the very tips of our toes. Without discussion he knew just walking toward the water for me was the equivalent of cliff diving for anyone else so that's what we did, we walked toward the water, just a millimeter farther everyday until I was as at ease up to my neck as I was up to my ankles.

I'm wondering what that was like for my grandfather as I really look around the classroom for the first time. Roman was right. Including me, we are four in this class. I'm sitting in the front row, off to the side closest the windows and farthest from the door. In the desk right next to me, you guessed it, Roman. Phoenix is still in the farthest back row, odd considering all the middle chairs are empty. And there is another boy. Like Roman and me he's also sitting in the front row, but in the very middle desk. The first thing I notice about him is his intensely dark hair, jet-black and thick. I can tell, even though he's sitting, that he's a bit smaller than Roman. His height, his arms, the circumference of his chest, everything is a bit smaller. He's dressed differently, too. While Roman's clothes go almost unnoticed, a monochromatic blend of blues, pale sky T-shirt, medium denim jeans, a well worn navy zip hoodie … the other boy's clothes are mesmerizing. His style isn't like anyone around here. He's wearing very baggy cargo shorts, ripped and tattered in certain places, even though it's just barely forty degrees outside, a short-sleeve Nirvana concert T-shirt from the nineties that's worn thin from the length of its existence, and *flip-flops.* Flip flops that have seen better days. No jacket or sweatshirt. By and large the common dress here is rustic, practical, functional: flannel shirts, puffer jackets, rubber muck or snow boots ... He looks like he was airlifted in from Venice Beach.

Also—and this I find most spellbinding of all—he is the only one who seems to really be concentrating on the teacher's lecture, Roman is doodling some kind of picture on a scrap of paper and Phoenix appears to be counting the ceiling tiles, but from what I can see of his profile, his glacier-blue eyes are focused like lasers on Ms. Speakman, as if they are the only two people in the room. About once every two or three minutes he asks a question. I guess there is no need to raise your hand when a class consists of four people because he just interrupts her quite boldly and fires off his inquiry of the moment. He talks with intense energy and the content of what he asks seems to fully catch her off guard each time and she keeps replying by first saying in earnest, "That's a good question." He beams brightly for a split second each time she says this but I'm fully certain that's not why he continues to ask questions. Every time he starts another question there's patent genuineness in what he's asking. As if he's already forgotten how the last question impressed her and is a hundred percent wrapped up in acquiring this new bit of information.

As for me, like someone realizing they'd been caught in a inescapable riptide ten minutes after the fact, I start to become aware that this boy's body language has been pulling me in further with every passing minute—the way he tilts his head just so, looking pensive as he listens, the way he squints his eyes, nods and grins slightly as he learns. I find everything about him fascinating, or whatever quality is a million light-years beyond fascinating. At this point, even if I wanted to look away, I physically couldn't drag my eyes off of him. The longer I stare, unblinking, I swear I can almost see him vibrating and pulsing with life on whatever the exact frequency is that I'm tuned to. I swear I can feel his brain firing every time a synapse connects or a neuron transmits energy. I can feel the rhythmic vibration of his fingers tapping his pencil on the desk creating some kind of energetic waves in my body even though I'm probably fifteen feet away. He's a thousand-watt light bulb, humming with electricity and brilliance and I'm transfixed, drawn in like a moth, consumed.

Ms. Speakman must have noticed this because all of *her* questions are directed at me. Though I manage to answer them correctly, more than once she struggles to pull my attention away from studying him and always has to repeat the question for me. Near the end of class I realize that I don't think I took my eyes off him the entire period. A fact that couldn't have gone unnoticed by Roman or Phoenix for that matter. Coming to this conclusion my cheeks flush with a wave of embarrassment. I shift my eyes toward Roman, without moving my head, to see if he's been watching me but find him staring, in the opposite direction, out the window and I breathe a sigh or relief when the bell rings and Ms. Speakman informs us that we're having a quiz tomorrow, on the second day of school, which will cover the first two units, a little bit of which we touched on this morning, and she dashes out of the room as quickly as she came in. A whirlwind, and I decide to ask Roman if she's always like this. Or if maybe this has something to do with all the teachers gathered in the hall and the bell to start class never ringing.

But as I stand up I discover that sometime in the ten seconds it takes me to pack my bag, Phoenix and Roman have disappeared. I'm alone and face to face with this dark-haired boy, this buzzing, humming firefly of a person. My first look at him, straight on, brings me into a state of shock and I realize why the view of his profile was trapping my eyes like a magnet. He so closely resembles the boy from my dream, the boy in the middle of the Red Sea with me night after night after night, that everything in my body, save for my logical brain, is telling me it's him. It's him. He's standing just inches from me, I can breathe in his scent. I don't know if it's coming from his clothes, from his skin, or his breath but it's soft, easy and pure like an angel wrapped in a warm sun-soaked white linen shirt on a powdery sand beach in the Caribbean. My heart stops.

"Hi," he declares, the little familiar word somehow sounding brand new, like it was said in a language I've never heard before. I just smile at him, paralyzed. He doesn't say his name and neither had the teacher. But it's Jude, I know it's Jude. At least Jude is his name in my dream. Night after night I watch myself swimming beside him, always parallel, and when the waves, as big as high-rise buildings, pass between us they're no match for whatever force is activated, drawing us back together, when I call out to him, Jude. Jude, always on my lips as I wake. *Jude,* I think, whispering it inside my brain.

"I'm Jude. I'm new," he tells me.

"New?" I ask blankly, no idea what he means.

"*Yeah,* new ... here. New to this school," he clarifies, his face not hiding that he's surprised he needed to.

It must be universally understood, I gather, that when kids say "new" it automatically means being new to a school. An awkward side effect of my hermit lifestyle is rearing its ugly head.

"Oh, right. I'm new too, to this school"—or any school, I think but don't say. "I've lived here for six months." My voice sounds odd, nervous, and I realize I'm actually trembling.

"Where'd you come from?" he asks, and I almost feel like he's asking what planet. I could say Russia. That's where I was "living" last, for a four-week stint anyway, but it's not exactly where I come from. His question doesn't have an answer, it has a story. So I punt.

"Ah … where'd *you* come from?"

He doesn't just say "Alaska." He could have. That's an interesting enough answer as it is. But like a magnetic force of nature, pulling me and everything else into him, he offers the most spellbinding description I've ever heard, leading me to conclude that Alaska is in fact the best place on earth. His rapid-fire words sweep me away to the northernmost tip of the continent, to the extreme geography and beauty of the arctic tundra, to indigenous Inuit, ten-foot snow drifts, death-defying avalanches, fierce and loyal sled dogs, and the kinetically invigorating spell of eighty straight days of uninterrupted daylight, and though I've never been more enraptured it's still hard for me to listen over the rapid pounding of my heart at the sight of him in front of me.

I have to find a way to get hold of myself. If I just leave now and never come back, if I turn away and start running and never stop and never think of this again for the rest of my life, I could probably put Jude in some innocuous category in my mind— Interesting But Meaningless Coincidence Boy.

But nothing in my body or brain wants to be anywhere else but right here. Instead, my feet seem to melt into the floor as I stare up at him. He's taller than me by a bit, but not uncomfortably so. His skin is a clear and rare kind of creamy pale that I imagine is some sort of prize you get for being from

Alaska. Along with his bottomless arctic-blue eyes that sparkle behind eyelashes that are as dark as a night without stars and his lips that are a smooth soft pink, every feature is exactly, jarringly, identical to the boy's in my dream.

I've been to Alaska, once, when I was five, I think of telling him but before I can get the words out—

"Study with me after school," he says with all the confidence in the world, out of absolutely nowhere, but making it somehow sound like the best, most reasonable idea ever and seeming just the way he does in my dream—energetic, spontaneous, mesmerizing, and addicting. "If you want to. That's really the question. You're the smartest one in the class and I'm so lost. I'm afraid she has me pegged already as the bad student, you know, like the low man on the flagpole, you know what I'm saying?"

I bite my lower lip and squint a little, trying to fight back a smirk.

"It's not 'flagpole,' is it?" he surmises from my look.

"No, I just, it could be I guess but I think you mean 'low man on the *totem* pole' … which you definitely are not going to be. And … *I want to*, I mean, I'd be happy to. Help you … you know … study … together …"

Jeez, when did I forget how to string a sentence together?

"Your house, five o'clock," he suggests and confirms all at once.

CHAPTER 5

I guess I ended up telling him my address and staggered back out into the hallway because that's where I find myself. As my feet move me forward I look around and come to the conclusion that Jude must have evaporated back into the dream he came from because I don't see him anywhere. In fact there's no one at all in sight and I wonder how long we were standing there talking.

I walk a little farther down the hall and the inescapable feeling that Jude is real, that he is undoubtedly the boy I've been dreaming about, and that that actually just happened starts to sink in and my heart leaps out of my body. A massive smile that I would be powerless to contain even if I wanted to consumes my face. I just met a real life *boy of my dreams*, who's kind of … intoxicating, who I actually get to see again, today, and everyday! This revelation courses through me like a high-voltage current and everything inside me bursts to life. In this same moment I realize that I actually have no idea where I am, that I'm wandering aimlessly, and my state of spontaneous euphoria instantly collapses.

I don't have the slightest idea how to get to my next class, and it hits me, I don't even know what my next class is! Roman is nowhere to be seen. While he's been escorting me everywhere, I haven't been paying attention to, well, anything. As I turn this thought over in my mind I'm more than a little surprised at myself. I'm shocked. I'm shocked at how easily I seem to allow myself to slide into acting so comfortable with Roman, not noticing or caring if I'm dependent on him—even to a fault. For the first time I take a second to realize that with Roman, it feels, has always felt, only natural to let him take care of me. And right now this feeling has gotten me completely lost.

I open my backpack and find my schedule. A quick glance at the map and I instantly get my bearings and start on the shortest route to my next class. It's still a bit of a hike though, and I start to sense that lateness is a running theme in my day.

As I walk I don't even notice my mind wandering and thoughts turning to Jude until I'm picturing the two of us sitting on the white couch in the living room of my house and imagining him reaching his hand toward mine. I shake the distracting thought from my head, make my way through a corridor and find my classroom tucked at the end of the hallway. I'm late again by the time I finally arrive, but just like with the last class my lateness doesn't seem to matter. I follow a steady stream of students still filing quite casually into the class and settle into an empty desk in the middle of the room toward the back, no one so much as looking in my direction. I would have never guessed that by second period of my first day of school feeling utterly unseen would be a welcome situation, but it is. I'll take invisibility over absolute loathing any day. Strong reactions are something I'm beginning to get used to, I realize, recounting all the intense exchanges I've had today, from some of the other students to Mr. Envoy to Phoenix to Jude, when suddenly, like a rogue wave, my brain is submerged in an inescapable swell made entirely of thoughts of Jude; his angelic face, his thick ink-black hair, the alluring way he smells, every last and trivial detail of our conversation, the sound of his voice, the words he said. I picture us in my house, again, on my couch, and this time he's kissing me. I'm being consumed by the softness of his lips against mine when I finally catch myself.

"Stop it!" I mean to think but end up mumbling quite audibly, causing the girl a few rows ahead to spin around and remind me with a single stinging glance what an appalling individual I am.

"Sorry," I whisper to her before she whirls back around in disgust. Sorry for what, I don't know. Sorry for being me, I guess, feeling a bit depressed at how Actual High School is stacking up to Expectation High School, which is miserably.

I sink down into the plastic seat that's visibly too big for me to begin with. The attached desk, that's already awkwardly too high, now parallel with my neck, if I slid any farther I probably couldn't see over it! I feel like a foolish little lost toddler sitting in a grown-up chair pretending to play school. My best bet is to focus on staying invisible. Trying not to insight a riot with my tiny but apparently very aggravating presence.

Within a few more minutes the class is nearly full and even though it's already several minutes into the allotted class time the teacher seems utterly unconcerned. He's talking with a small group of kids at his modest metal desk, which he leans on, arms folded in front of him, one leg crossed in front of the other. Every now and again, he sweeps his mellow brown eyes across the room, seeming to survey the faces of his students. Each time he does this, he lands on me for a longer beat than everyone else, probably wondering to himself how a kindergartener got in here, but always keeping his neatly trimmed bearded face remarkably expressionless.

Roman is the very last student to enter—strange considering the incredible head start he got from Ms. Speakman's room. I wonder where he's been as he breezes through the door, both of his hands gently grasping the straps of his backpack at his shoulders. He finds my eyes instantly, as if there aren't thirty other people in the room. He gives me a big gentle smile, and just as he does, my shoulders lower away from my ears. I hadn't noticed I was so tense. What's stranger is that my body seemed to relax, quite on its own, the second I saw Roman.

"Let's get started," the teacher says, clapping his hands together once and one by one the kids that are gathered around him peel off and meander to their seats. A girl with glasses and a sun-bleached brown ponytail walks down the center aisle toward the back of the room. I straighten up as she nears my desk. She looks right at me and I think the worst. Her eyes squint a little and I ready myself for anything, anything but the warm casual smile that takes over her face.

"I'm Draya," she whispers, her squinty smile suspiciously genuine-looking.

"Ah … ah, *hi*," I stutter as she's nearly past me, on a time delay from the shock of being spoken to and I conclude I am, officially, just lame.

Roman takes the closest open seat to me a few rows back but quickly swaps seats with the guy sitting directly behind me. It's clear that everyone in this school is eager to please Roman. Facing forward I try to focus my attention on the teacher, but feeling Roman's presence behind me is proving to be a hefty distraction.

"Hey," he whispers so close to my shoulder I feel his breath on my neck.

I half-turn and whisper back, "Hi, again." I consider

shushing him or making some snippy comment about not talking to me during class, but nothing inside me wants to do that. I really *do* want to talk to Roman. I want to ask him about his comments in the hallway before math, about why he ran out of class so fast, and a million other things. I don't even know where to start.

"So … Jude's different, huh," he remarks before I have a chance, his choice of words making my heart leap up into my throat for some reason.

I have no idea how to answer. I'm actually terrified to answer at all.

"Different from who?" I say. A question I immediately regret.

"Me," he says casually, and for some reason making my stomach sink like it's a ten-ton granite boulder that just fell off a mountain into a lake.

The simple word, "me," hangs in the air, seeming to echo and growing thicker with every second that ticks by. I try to find a way to tread through it. It's not easy. How do I answer? How does he mean that? Is he looking to find out how I feel about him? *About Jude?* By all reasonable accounts I shouldn't feel any particular way about either of them, *not really.* Though to be fair, I don't think I could say that. Roman definitely feels a certain way to me. He feels secure. It feels immeasurably … *right,* for lack of a better word, just to be near him. It's just comfortable. His presence sooths and calms me. On the other hand there's Jude, this mysterious dream boy who I feel frighteningly obsessed with, who I can't keep out of my mind.

I should have absolutely no trouble categorizing them as different from one another. They're as different as night is from day. Roman is in control, though there is a breezy air about him, an attractively relaxed nature that exudes a deep confidence. His words feel almost calculated at times, while Jude appears to function on whim alone, or maybe gut instinct, with no filter, no pretense, and no inhibitions whatsoever. Calling them different would not be earth shattering but I freeze. In the silent minutes that follow, the idea that a reply to Roman's remark is required on my part fades farther and farther from my mind. I eventually turn my full attention to the teacher.

He starts off by telling us about an earthquake that was just detected by the brand new warning system on the ocean floor off the coast of Africa.

"A potential nightmare scenario. They're evacuating the entire eastern seaboard as a precautionary measure, and keeping a vigilant watch for signs of a tsunami. I thought you all should be aware," he tells us, his words sober, even grave.

He then switches gears, lightens his tone and tells us about himself. He goes on for a good bit of time about how he went from growing up an impoverished farm boy in rural Louisiana who only spoke Acadian, an obscure French dialect, until the age of 16, to being a Jesuit priest in El Salvador and earning the rare distinction "professed of the Four Vows," to traveling to Tibet and becoming a Buddhist monk, where he lived in complete silence for over a year, to later becoming a Nobel Prize–winning research biologist and finally reaching the pinnacle of his esteemed career and landing a coveted position as an eleventh-grade high school teacher in northern North Dakota, where he has no family and as he put it, "basically no friends." He classified his odd trajectory as "a pretty typical sequence of events." Also calling it, "just your average life path," without a hint of the sarcasm that a person with any sort of grasp on reality might inject.

In fact, Dr. DeCuir—"Gaebe," as he prefers we call him—is grossly, conspicuously, and frankly, suspiciously overqualified. Even for teaching Honors Philosophy. Even to the most overachieving high school students.

In his smooth Cajun drawl that I already love the sound of, he says, "Philosophy, from a common sort of pedestrian perspective, is often defined as 'the sum of an individual's beliefs'—beliefs which, as a system, inform and influence the individual's actions and so his life and so forth. But philosophy, as a science, is the *study* and *examination* of belief. Period. Philosophy, as a science, is what *we* are interested in. Are you with me? See the difference?"

He takes a beat to look over our faces. Every one of us must look terminally confused by the subtle distinction because he continues to think for another moment then informs us that he'd like to lead a discussion on science and ethics as it pertains to religion.

He starts by telling us about a recent scientific discovery.

"From mapping the human genome to carbon dating the soul," he says, holding up a copy of a medical journal bearing those exact words on the cover. He reads an excerpt from Dr. Karl Alastair, the foremost genome biologist in the world, who claims that he and his Iceland based research team "are mere days from isolating an illusive and mysterious cylinder-shaped structure encoded deep within the makeup of every human that he believes to be 'the map of the soul.'

"Alastair calls the genetic marker 'Animus,' which in Latin translates to 'that which animates,' or 'the breath, soul, consciousness.' His claim is that this Animus has a pattern of circles that's comparable to tree rings, that allows us to actually count the number of lifetimes lived."

Gaebe places the journal on his desk gently, almost sacredly.

He looks out at us, staring thoughtfully into each face. "This structure, that was long thought of as 'junk DNA,' non-coding genetic material with no discernible function, may now, quite possibly, be hailed as the holy grail of human existence."

The class becomes utterly noiseless. Still as statues. Paralyzed from the sheer impact of his words. He allows our silence to remain undisturbed, like he's waiting for our first impressions to fully crystalize.

"What would you say if scientists could find, and many say *have already found* a way to count the number of lives a soul has lived?" he asks.

After a collective beat several kids pipe up at once in an inaudible and impassioned jumble of differing opinions. One boy's voice rises above the rest.

"How would we even know, you know, that it's accurate? I mean, who's to say they are right? How would they even prove it?"

"Right," Gaebe encourages. "Show of hands, who here remembers their past lives and could count them to verify this claim?" He asks, raising his hand jokingly. Everyone looks around the room. There are no hands raised, until Roman raises his, a coy half-smile spread across his sun-kissed face. Everyone laughs in a sort of unanimous roar of adoration. All hail the King of Initium Valley High School.

"I have my ideas on how they'll go about proving this but we'll have to wait and see the proof, won't we," Gaebe says, and a few heads nod in agreement.

"It doesn't matter, I don't believe in reincarnation," one girl asserts, loud enough to take the attention of the class. "It's against my religion. So I feel like, I mean, this whole thing, it wouldn't even apply to me. Right?"

"Well, now wait a minute, Alex, let's look at this. Alex's

first point, it's against her religion. Good point, understandable, and very familiar territory for science to be treading in … And yet does it matter? If one's beliefs, religious or otherwise, don't align with what may be proven as scientific fact?" Gaebe waits patiently for more thoughts to emerge in us, but a distinct leeriness now blankets the room. "Does it matter?" he repeats.

After a quiet minute, Gaebe looks at Roman. "Your thoughts, Roman?" he asks, and for a brief moment, before Roman opens his mouth to answer, I watch their eyes appear to share some kind of hidden mutual understanding, a telepathic exchange that seems to go entirely unnoticed by everyone else in the room.

"No. It doesn't matter," Roman declares with a tone of final authority, like he's reading the words straight from the Constitution.

"Of course it matters!" Alex rebuts with gusto. "We have a little something called freedom of religion in this country. You can't just prove reincarnation is real … and then what? What, everyone is forced to change their religion or something? I'm telling you this would not apply to me, or my family."

Roman smiles gently at Alex, a compassionate smile that's so genuine it catches me off guard. Not the kind of look I would image a teenager even capable of.

"Biologically, Alex, what applies to one of us, applies to all of us. As far as your beliefs, people didn't believe in gravity," Roman says, all the eyes of the class turning toward him, magnetized by his conviction. "Doesn't mean it wasn't real. Gravity exists. It was always there. Humans suddenly knowing about it, humans becoming aware of it, discovering it, *believing* in it, that isn't what makes gravity real. I mean if gravity wasn't a part of your belief system a hundred years ago, if talk of the Earth being round and revolving around the sun in a solar system of other planets was blasphemy, was unholy, once it was proven, once it become indisputable, you found a way to work it into the fabric of the things that you believed. Right?"

Alex nods in a small but perceptible understanding. Roman continues.

"So a hundred years from now they might look back and not be able to imagine how we lived without believing in reincarnation. They might look at us like we look at the people who thought the Earth was flat."

I glance over at Alex, whose eyes have now softened and reflect her swift journey from resistance, right past acceptance, and straight to distress.

"That scares me," she admits, her once brazen voice now vulnerable, almost terrified, her gaze helplessly locked on Roman. "Just because science can do something ... this, kind of thing maybe they're not supposed to."

"What if they already have?" says the girl who said hi to

me earlier, distinct excitement in her voice. "I think it would be incredible. I'd love to know."

"Draya, on the other hand, would love to know," Gaebe remarks of the girl who, along with most of the class, I turn around to study. Her face is heart-shaped and her big innocent kitten eyes tell me she's unapologetic of her stance.

After a long lull in the discussion, Gaebe slowly walks down the center aisle.

"There are certainly things that science shouldn't do just because it can," he starts. "That list is long and well documented, but, and this is what I want you to ponder, is there knowledge that we aren't supposed to gain?"

He pauses for effect just as he happens to stop right next to my desk. His frame is lankier up close, thinner than I first noticed, and just under the cuff of his rolled-up sleeve I see part of a tattoo but can't decode the shape. His tranquil brown eyes, which look bigger than before compared to the gauntness I now see in his face, rest on me for a quiet beat. Then, while keeping himself stationed just beside my desk, he looks out at the class.

"Are there truths we should not be in pursuit of? Things we're not meant to know, or better off not knowing? Can certain knowledge be bad? What would the discovery of Animus really do? Could it hurt people? Or is everything inherently neutral until we choose how to put it to use? Can acquiring knowledge really affect us negatively? Or is it being discovered because it's supposed to?"

No one answers.

"Is Animus the apple from the tree of knowledge? And if it is ... is humanity supposed cast it out ... or eat it?" he asks, looking right down at me.

"I, I don't, I don't know ..." I stutter, but with the eyes of the class on me I feel the need to give an answer. "I mean, maybe ... *maybe* we are supposed to eat the apple," I say, feeling uncertain of the words as they leave my lips but allowing Gaebe's avid nodding to spur me on. "Maybe knowledge can never hurt us."

"Maybe ... But are you ready for what it will reveal?" he asks while looking into my eyes, like he's wondering about *just me*, if I'm ready. My eyes searching Gaebe's it hits me, *sorrow is knowledge,* and I instantly regret the answer I just gave him as my very favorite Lord Byron words suddenly spring to mind: *Sorrow is knowledge. Those that know the most must mourn the deepest. The tree of knowledge is not the tree of life ...*

When a ringing sound fills the room it takes a second to register. It's the bell. As everyone around me packs up and leaves for their next class, Roman taps me on the shoulder.

"Huh?" I startle, in a daze.

"Come on. Let's go," he says, almost shocking me back to life with his good looks and that unbelievable smile.

"Go ahead without me," I tell him, despite feeling his gravitational pull. With obvious reservation in his eyes he gets up and walks out of the room.

Once I'm packed up, I walk over to where Gaebe is erasing the whiteboard.

"Can I ask you something?"

"Of course," he says as he continues erasing without turning around.

"Why were you … I felt like you were referring to me, you know, specifically."

"That's funny. I wonder why you felt that way. Not to be rude, but I don't even know you," he says, turning around and reaching his hand out to shake mine and fully reveal the tattoo on his forearm. Like he's purposefully showing it to me.

"Eve," I say as I extend my hand and move my gaze from the black CMXCIX emblazed on his skin up to his thin smiling face.

"*Eve*," he repeats back, a certain intrigue in his voice, a little like Roman did when I first told him my name. "I'm honored to know you," he says in a pointed way before going back to his board and I get the nagging feeling, as I head for the door, that there's a reason he's honored to know me, a reason why he was clearly asking if *I'm* ready for what Animus will reveal, and that the number nine hundred and ninety-nine, the CMXCIX, might have something to do with all of it.

CHAPTER 6

After Philosophy, school zipped to an end in a flash. I decided to put Gaebe and his unusual tattoo and all my strange feelings about our exchange out of my mind and to take on the rest of the day alone, telling Roman, when he was waiting outside Gaebe's room for me, thanks for his help but that I needed to learn the schedule and the campus on my own. I even choose to sit by myself at lunch, getting a jumpstart on the piles of homework I had already accumulated, though I felt Roman watching me the entire time, wanting to come over to where I parked myself, at the vacant table closest to the exit. But he stayed away because I had asked him to.

Walking outside into the parking lot by myself I feel clearheaded and independent. Looking around I notice two things—crystal-blue skies without a rain cloud in sight and that every single person in the whole wide world has a car.

Okay, maybe that's a little dramatic, I tell myself. Maybe it only feels that way knowing that I don't have one, but after another second I quickly conclude that everyone but me actually *does* have a car as well as loads of friends and apparent plans. I'm also pretty sure I hate them for it as my brain swirls with a cutting jealously I can't deny, watching them make their joyous escapes.

I decide to try to let it go and visualize the route that will get me home the quickest—out Boulder Drive, down Huddleston, and toward Main. I note the time, 3:35, and estimate it will take me roughly 45 minutes to walk the 3.2 miles home.

I'm almost off campus, nearing the last row of parked cars, when I see Roman. I'd lost track of him after last period when I ventured back to Mrs. Silver's homeroom to gather what I needed to take home. Neither he (nor Phoenix, thankfully) were anywhere in sight.

Right now, he's about 20 yards away, leaning against a small white car getting an irate earful from a tall blond girl I've never seen before. In fact, anyone within fifty feet is getting an earful of her impassioned manifesto. I glance around—a few students are milling their way to their cars but no one pays much attention or seems to care. As her shrills and screams fill the air I distinctly hear the word "love" flung at him, multiple times—four times, to be exact, and counting.

But for his part, and I think this is what's throwing me off, he appears quite calm, too calm, not careless exactly but resigned, like this is merely a training drill for an actual catastrophe but not the real thing. She looks like a hurricane he had forecast and is simply waiting patiently for it to pass. From this, I conclude it must be a regular thing and keep walking. I even mumble "Not my business" to myself for good measure.

What is my problem anyway? Roman is allowed to have things in his life that don't involve me, for goodness sakes! Though I must admit, I'm actually kind of *bothered* by how that feels. If the word "bothered" is equivalent to being devoured by a shark, swallowed half-intact yet fully alive and finally perishing in a cesspool of boiling stomach acid and steaming fish guts. Then yes, I admit, it's bothering me.

I'll just block it out, I decide. And blocking it out really does work!

For nine whole seconds. The problem is, after ten seconds I give up because it feels like it *is* my business. Again, when did I get so nosey, I wonder, and decide I must convince myself, *it is not my business*, when an odd conclusion overtakes me like a sudden and swift wrestling move and pins me to the mat.

"It *is* my business," I correct myself, not quiet sure where the words are coming from but instantly granting myself permission to accept the reality that, for reasons yet to be determined, Roman is definitely my business.

Why would Roman be in the kind of relationship where

this type of fight is common enough that it doesn't even faze him? How could such a smart guy be so dumb in love? Who is this girl, I wonder as I pass by. Roman's eyes catch mine and I realize I'm glaring at her, but I don't look away. I can't.

I can say with near certainty, that although Roman is as incredible to look at as any boy I've seen in my life, that he's wildly kind and oddly attentive, I have no right or reason to feel what I feel right now. At the sight of her so clearly invested in something with him, something emotional, and something deep. I have absolutely no right to feel like I'm going to throw up. To feel like my stomach has itself spun up into a knot of sadness and dread churning on itself as it's hurled off a cliff.

There is absolutely no justification whatsoever for what I'm about to do. *Damn it*, I think, as I can't help myself from turning around and walking, ever so inappropriately, up to their obviously private conversation.

"Hey Eve," just rolls off Roman's tongue like he's not in the middle of a stressful situation while the girl looks like she might breathe fire at the sight of me.

"Is everything okay?" I barely get the words out of my mouth when I feel something like a gust of wind move through me. It takes a second to realize that she pushed me. Hard. I stumble backward several steps, partly out of shock, and partly, it seems, to intentionally give myself time to react.

"Get lost," she threatens. Her body language and her face are ripe with an unhinged rage, but all I see in her eyes is fear, the same fear I saw this morning in Mr. Envoy.

"No," I hear myself say, my single word reply appearing to bring absolute terror upon her that leeches further into her psyche the longer I stare and visibly amplifies when I take an apparently premeditated step back toward her.

She positions herself in front of Roman, and I'm instantly overcome with the need to get her away from him, but why? Why do I want to protect him? What on earth makes me so sure that I can protect him? Who says he even needs or wants it? Why do I care? I have no right to care. The absolute honest truth is, unless I'm with Roman, I'm not thinking about him. I certainly hadn't even given a thought to whether he might have a girlfriend. I also hadn't taken the time to consider whether he might be the kind of guy who would either date a girl who was unstable or do something to make a reasonable girl come totally unglued.

But everything inside me somehow knows that he's not that guy. Everything inside me somehow knows exactly the kind of guy that Roman is. He is good.

"I'm not leaving," I say slowly with the kind of authority that I hadn't entirely planned on which sometimes escapes from my mouth. The odd thing is, after a few suspenseful seconds, she turns and walks away and I almost don't believe it, even as I watch her go across the parking lot without ever once looking back.

"Thanks," Roman starts reluctantly, "that was going to go

on for a while." He rubs the back of his neck and looks at me as if he's embarrassed, which I find kind of odd considering he obviously has beautiful girls throwing themselves at him. Not something most guys would shy away from admitting. I watch as he tries to find the words to explain. "She's … that was, ah …"

"Really, you don't need to … I don't … I don't know what came over me," I find myself saying when I realize I actually do want to know who that was—and even more than that, I want to know what just happened. "Okay, you know what, seriously, what was that about? Is it me or are the kids here … not … normal?"

"They're normal. It's you," he says as if he's telling me the grass is green. The same way he told me that I don't get to be an island any more. In a way that's too matter of fact to not find totally unsettling, then he motions to his truck. I'm more than a little taken aback by his answer but it's either let him drive me home and find out what exactly is wrong with me or walk home alone and wonder.

His truck is absolutely huge. As I look up at the gleaming silver handle I wonder how I'm supposed to climb into this thing when the door swings open and a step comes floating out from somewhere underneath, like a spaceship. I look at Roman, who's holding the door open and grinning at me with what I can only describe as a look of contentment. I notice the outline of his chest under his shirt. I had certainly noticed this before, it's hard not to, but for some reason this time my stomach jumps into my chest and my heart races. He must have noticed, and maybe it freaked him out because his face kind of loses that ease. I climb up and he swings the door shut behind me. I sit staring ahead, not breathing as I wait for him to walk around to the driver's side. I clutch my backpack on my lap and for at least the second time today I find myself wondering why on earth I'm doing all this. When did going to high school ever make a teenager happier? Why did subjecting myself to jealously, hormones, and homework sound like a good idea again? But as Roman steps up into the car and stretches his seatbelt across himself, he gives me that gentle breezy smile that I'm coming to really like and I feel every inch of my body melt into a state of absolute peace.

I have been trying for months to understand why I felt distinctly better after meeting Roman than I did before he sat himself down at my booth. Why I was calmer, happier, more at ease. This was probably natural, I guessed, for someone new in town. I could say I had a friend in Rugby, a familiar face I might see around from time to time. The only problem with that was, from the first moment, Roman never felt like a friend. He felt like something else. I search my mind for the word. *Anchor*. He felt like an anchor, almost instantly. An odd way to feel about your waiter. Another gaping hole in what I was telling myself to make this feeling seem normal was that I could make a crystal-clear distinction between how I felt in general, for the whole of my life, and how I felt the moment he came into it. I felt relief. An unexplainable and unmistakable sense of relief.

It's quiet for several minutes as we wait at the red light to get off campus. I'm not trying to come up with something to say. I'm not worried about whether he is. I just stare out my window taking in Initium Valley as it spreads out in front of us, a massive prairie stretching almost as far as my eyes can see. In the faint distance to the east, Butte Saint Paul rises majestically into view; to the west Wolf Butte ascends its jagged rocks to roughly the same height. I've come to cherish the feeling of being tucked safely between these two massive flat-topped rock mountains. I have come to depend on seeing the big puffy clouds that seem to grow upward as they roll swiftly along the vast space from one horizon to the other. At this late afternoon hour, the rugged foothills in the distance are made coral and amber by the setting sun, and the fiery orange hue of the unending autumn sky imparts a pinkish blaze onto the tall golden wheat grasses that stretch from the road to the foothills. I can almost feel the soft blades graze the palms of my hands.

"You love it here, don't you," Roman states as the light turns green and I don't feel the need to answer right away, or even look in his direction, though I know that his eyes are on me as much as the road.

My gaze stays on the scenery out my window as I tell him,

"I've moved my entire life—'wandered,' I guess you'd say. 'Moving' implies some kind of settlement, which never really occurred to us or never exceeded a few months at most." I pause but he knows I'm not done: "I love it here … more than any place on earth." Finally, I look at him. "Don't tell anybody at school, okay?" I give him a warning smile though I'm actually pretty serious. He laughs at me in a way that makes me feel, though I lack a reasonable explanation, adored and cherished. I know I can't be these things to him. The girl in the parking lot maybe, but not me.

"The girl back there. What was that about?" I ask.

"Well, she doesn't like you. That's what that was about."

"That had to do with me? I mean, before I walked up?"

"Yeah. She was upset that I spent so much time with you today."

"Oh. Why? Is she your girlfriend?" The next logical question kind of escapes without warning, and once it's out, seems to make us both visibly uncomfortable.

"Yes, she is," he says with a sort of manufactured courage.

So, Roman has a girlfriend. A *beautiful* girlfriend. I guess it would be odd if he didn't—he could certainly date any girl he wanted. I wonder why he never mentioned her? Why I never saw her with him?

"How long has she been … have you guys been, you know, together," I ask and find myself anticipating the answer like I would anticipate a punch in the face.

"A little over a year," he says, and my stomach plummets through the earth.

"Wow, that's a long time," I marvel, certain the words "never had a boyfriend" have spontaneously appeared on my forehead.

"Not really," he says, and I can't decide whether he's downplaying their relationship or the 365 days contained in an entire year.

"What's her name?" I ask, trying to sound like it doesn't bother me, in the devouring shark sense of the word "bother."

"You know, when I told you that you could ask me anything I meant it but, these weren't really the kinds of questions I had in mind ..."

"I'm just getting warmed up," I tell him.

"Ruby, her name is Ruby." An awkward silence creeps in. A silence filled with us both surely thinking of all the questions I should be asking.

"Well, she seems *great*," I say instead. He furrows his brow, confused, then he lets out a laugh in spite of himself, his chin lifting, head tilting back and eyes wrinkling at the corners.

"No, I, I meant that," I try, wondering at exactly what point in the day it was that I became such an incredibly bad person.

"No you didn't," he tells me, still smiling. He's right.

"No, I didn't," I admit and can't hold back a guilty laugh.

"She's fine, actually. She had a bad day, that's all. People love to gossip, and her friends, if you can call them that, I guess they saw us walking together."

The idea that this girl Ruby, who is probably the most stunning girl I've ever seen up close, who Roman likes enough to date for a year, whom he probably loves, would be threatened by me, that she would be even remotely concerned about losing Roman ... to me! It just doesn't make sense.

"Okay, since you seem to be a little shy about asking me some *real* questions," he teases, "unless of course it's during class—"

"Ha-ha."

"I'll start," he continues.

"Okay, fine." I ready myself.

"How did you end up—" he blurts out rapidly, then suddenly stops. Like he doesn't know whether he is supposed to be the one asking questions of me or something.

"Roman," I say, knowing the time has come to level with each other. "Ask me." I reassure him. "I'll tell you. I'll tell you anything," I admit, realizing it's true.

We look at each other like we're at the top of the highest bridge on earth, a vast and swaying suspension, miles above the tallest mountaintops, above every bird and cloud, and we're about to jump.

"How on earth did you end up here, in Rugby? How did you know?" he asks, turning his intense gaze toward me, his green eyes burning with thirst for my answer and seeming to scan my face for clues revealed in my reaction to his words.

Like always, with Roman, my face gives me away. He can see that I'm not thinking, "How did I know *what*?"

I'm thinking, "Three … two … one … *jump!*"

CHAPTER 7

"I didn't know …" I tell him, only to realize that's completely inaccurate, that this isn't going to be easy to describe.

"I mean … I didn't know where I was heading … specifically. I just knew the way … where I was supposed to go. I knew the way *perfectly* … if that makes any sense at all," I fumble out, like I'm trying to describe the taste of air or water.

But Roman nods his head.

"I understand," he says, and it's my turn to talk again. But knowing that not a soul on earth has ever heard what I'm about to tell Roman gives me pause. This moment feels undeniably sacred. Roman can feel it too. I watch as he tightens his grip on the steering wheel, almost bracing himself.

"I got to choose," comes out slowly. Having never left my

lips before, the words seem to want to creep slowly toward the light, tentatively at first, but Roman's face falls into a warm and encouraging little smile, just the hint of his white teeth behind his soft lips, his green eyes glowing, seeming to light the way, and I feel safe.

"We had never, I mean, me and Shamus, my brother, we'd just traveled with my grandfather, as long as I could remember. It was never a matter of 'Where are we going next?' or 'Why are we leaving?' By the time I was about eight, I understood who my grandfather was."

I look at Roman and know what's coming before the words leave his lips.

"Who is he?" he asks, the words rushing out at me like they've been pent up inside him for six months. Three tiny words that create the question I have dreaded my whole life.

I inhale and without thinking, I jump into free-fall.

"He is a unique being. He … intercedes, when the chaos of this world knocks things off course. He knows things, about the universe, that humanity has always been largely unclear about." I pause to collect my scattered thoughts; it's like catching butterflies in a net. "There is fate. It's a powerful force, inescapable really. One can transcend their fate, to sort of break the system by becoming fully aware of fate itself, but it's so rare because it's so difficult, it almost never happens. Fate almost always gets its way, playing out in perfect synchronicity. In the end, things ultimately always make sense. But then there are these other times. Events sort of build toward an impending interruption of fate that can't be allowed, a derailment so big that it would set the collective fate of our humanity too far off course. Cian describes it as a kind of continuous drum roll that sends out something like a vibration he can somehow hear. He taught me that in quiet stillness he hears it and knows exactly where we need to go next, and when to be there. And sure enough, a life that is in some way critical to the history or survival of humanity gets cut short. And Cian is right there, at the exact moment and he ..."

I just stop. What am I doing? Roman looks at me, his eyes squinting slightly in confusion, his lips softly closed in a reverent silence. He has been soaking up my every word but I'm suddenly struck with the fear that I'm destroying the one actual relationship I have. Roman glances over his shoulder and begins to pull the truck onto the dusty and gravely side of the road, kicking up a cloud of white powder, showering the undercarriage with pebbles. When we are parked he shuts off the engine and turns his whole body to face me, his chest completely square to mine.

"Please, keep going," he begs me without shame, like I'm standing before him in a scorching desert and pouring him a tall glass of cold water. I decide to close my eyes and keep falling. Something inside knows he'll catch me.

"He wakes the dead, Roman," I say, eyes scrunched tightly

shut, zero breath moving into or out of my lungs. After the quiet seconds that follow I open my eyes to find Roman looking unaltered by my words.

"Okay," he says. "Go on."

After a moment I continue, slowly at first. "So … it was never up to us, where we would go." Roman nods. "Not in a bad way. We never expected it to be. Then one day, last February, we were in Moscow and Cian just looks at me, in this … new way, and says, 'Eve, where would you like to live?' I was surprised, but in a strange way also not surprised. Like I knew this was coming or something, and I was ready. But Shamus … it was not easy for Shamus. He was very angry." I pause, lost in the wrath-fueled journey Shamus experienced during the week we traveled from Moscow to Rugby. The wrath-fueled journey that he is still very much embarked upon today.

"I remember wondering why on earth he even came with us. He liked Russia. There was this woman there named Kristina that he was spending a lot of time with. I thought he might even love her, or whatever emotion closest to love Shamus is capable of. He could have stayed there. I prayed that he would. He's thirty-five years old after all and there was certainly no gun to his head, not by me or by Cian. And leaving, to follow me, the little sister he hates, in whatever direction I wanted to go, toward a place of my choosing, seemed to be his perfect poison. It nearly killed him. Twice that I knew about, he drank himself into a death-defying blackout, or 'walking coma' as Cian had called it, staggering around recklessly, an empty vessel of destruction. The first time we found him stumbling along train tracks just moments before the impact of an oncoming bullet train and the second time we got word from a docking skipper that a man with a death wish had taken someone's rowboat and was headed out to sea, dodging icebergs and an aggressive pod of killer whales. I got up the next morning, figuring he was dead, only to see him showered and ready, waiting to begin another day of his ultimate torture. When he wasn't drunk and belligerent he was sober and belligerent but he was always right there, every morning, boarding the next plane or train with us even though there would be suffering in every step for him, misery in every mile. Witnessing him mentally resist while physically submitting himself, to a fate of my choosing, filled me with a sort of eerie peace. Not that his suffering brought me happiness. But that I could give myself what I needed, even if it appeared to make someone else deeply unhappy."

There is a very long moment of silence. Roman is just looking at me, like he's allowing my words to soak into him and waiting quietly to see whether I'm finished. I'm not done. Not really. There is still so much I want to tell him, but I want to check in with how he feels about the things I've shared so far, so I stop.

After another few moments of quiet Roman says without

any reservation, like it's another bit of something he's been holding back that he finally lets out: "We thought we were going to have to come find you," as if this should make some kind of sense to me.

It doesn't, of course.

"I don't know what you're talking about, Roman."

"Phoenix and I. We just couldn't believe it when you showed up. Here, of all the places. Me especially. When I saw you that night ..." He stares off beyond me, like he's reimagining that strange snowy night. "It sounds crazy, but I already knew you were out there before I even went through the door, and when I saw you sitting in that booth, every cell in my body exploded into life. I just knew."

"You knew what?" I demand, confused and frustrated, trying to get a handle on how this conversation shoehorned into another completely separate but somehow equally bizarre realm as grandfathers who can wake the dead and unexplained senses of direction when Roman suddenly realizes how beyond lost I'm feeling. His eyes melt with what looks like all the sympathy in the entire universe.

"That it was *you* ... that of course you found us. Of course you would," he affirms, shaking his head and brushing my hair behind my ear, a tender display of affection that I should probably find alarming both because he has a girlfriend and because the moment feels simultaneously natural and romantic. *Should* being the operate word here.

"Found you? I don't understand. We had never met before."

"No?" he asks with the strangest mix of shyness and confidence I have ever heard.

"Roman, what are you talking about? No. We had never met."

"Eve, I'm telling you, we had met before that night," he says, as sincere as if his hand were on a stack of Bibles.

"Where?" I ask, quickly accelerating from confusion to aggravation. "We had never met before that night, Roman." Of that I was absolutely sure. "Trust me, I would remember meeting you," I boldly venture so far as to say, not realizing how exposed the statement would leave me feeling or anticipating the barrage of deep and disorienting emotions that would body-slam me as I saw that Roman, though momentarily looking away, definitely enjoyed hearing that.

After a few heavy seconds tick by, he squares his eyes back on mine.

"We had already met for the first time, on two hundred and ninety-eight separate occasions to be exact. And the answer to where these meetings took place is … everywhere, virtually. Everywhere you can imagine."

He pauses, seeming to wait for my response, but I don't have one. His strange words have turned my mind into a blank canvas, a barren desert void of words, thoughts, even the emotions I was feeling seconds ago.

"Did you feel something … odd … when you met me?" he asks, sounding faintly fearful. Looking like he's afraid I might say no, that I might tell him that I felt nothing. That maybe, just maybe, he is mistaken. That somehow, I'm the wrong girl.

But I *did* feel something, I admit to myself, and all at once the breath rushes out of my hollow numb body as the same cosmic electricity that I experienced that night rushes back in.

"Yeah," I tell him, breathless, like I'd just sprinted a hundred miles in thirty seconds. "I felt something."

"What did you feel?" he asks, still sounding nervous that my answer may not be what he thinks it will be.

I've wanted to ask Roman this very question for months, with no real way to ask it. The hundred times he'd randomly told me that I could ask him anything, the bizarre moment of our meeting always sprang into my mind. I have wanted to quiz him about why it felt the way that it did. Why meeting him felt like having déjà vu in the middle of the clouds during an electrical storm. Like being swaddled in the softest silk while launched at the speed of light into space on an ancient asteroid. For months I have wondered why and wondered if it felt the same for him—and now is my chance! What is wrong with me that I can't get the words out?

"Fear," he says, locking his emerald eyes onto mine. "Let go of the fear, Eve."

I take a breath and let go.

"Lifetimes," I admit out loud and to myself for the first time. "I felt like, the moment I saw you, that I had known you … for lifetimes." I watch as the corners of his mouth draw upward. His evergreen eyes glisten brighter than ever before. Maybe it's the shimmering light from the setting sun but I'm certain they actually sparkle, like all the stars in the cosmos were hidden in them and just revealed to me.

"You have," he says plainly, and his words are like an unseen force that lifts a boulder off my shoulders that I didn't know was there, shooting it like a rocket out of the atmosphere. I take in a sharp breath and feel almost dizzy, like there are acres of brand-new space inside my body that weren't there before and are not yet oxygenated.

"I have? I mean … *we* have … known each other … before?"

"Yeah. We've known each other alright," he says, a subtle blush casting over his cheeks. He grabs the back of his neck again, the way he did in the parking lot as Ruby walked away. "We have been together—our *souls* have been together. We were soul mates, we loved each other, Eve, for almost three hundred lifetimes."

My palms instantly sweat and the rapid pounding of my heart against my chest grows louder as it quickens. The icy tingle of rushing adrenaline sends an arctic blasts down my arms, like a surge of helium through my veins, making them feel weightless and frozen and numb. *My body is speaking to me.* It remembers him. My body, my every cell, completely believes him. But my mind sits squarely on the stubborn mountain of unconvinced. I scan his face like I'm some kind of human lie detector

"How do you know this?" I ask distrustfully, like I may actually be trapped in this truck with a perfect stranger.

"I was born, for some reason, or reasons I don't fully understand yet, with all the knowledge of all of my past lives … and the past lives of other people too."

"I don't understand." I'm running what he's saying through my mind over and over, but it's just not computing. "This is too much …"

"There's more, Eve. I have to tell you something else." He kind of panics, seeing that I'm shutting down.

"Roman, I don't …"

"Eve," he says, but I'm shaking my head, blocking him out. It's too much to process. I'm not sure I even believe him, and I don't want to hear whatever he's about to say. He reaches over and takes each side of my face in his warm soft hands. "Eve," he says, trying to call me out of the dizzying hurricane of my mind.

"No!" I yell at him, yanking his hands away by the wrists.

"You *need* to know something!" he shouts, grabbing my face again, this time to study me, both his eyes shifting from one of mine to the other and back several times rapidly. "You really don't know what you are, do you?" he concludes, but leaving room for what sounds like a doubt he can't shake. Some nagging shred of a thought left in him that I *must* know what I am.

"What, Roman! What am I?" I say sharply, clearly not wanting to know. In no way do I want *him,* of all people, to be the one to tell me what I've always suspected, what Shamus has already made perfectly clear. That there is something wrong with me. Very wrong. Abnormally, defectively, incurably wrong.

With everything inside me terrified of what he might say, and trying to delay the inevitable, I do the only reasonable thing. I attack.

"What about you, huh? Let's talk about you first. So *you're* telling me we've lived two hundred and … and … what was it …"

"Ninety-eight," he says calmly.

"Two hundred and ninety-eight lives … Together! Like, *together together*. That you know all of this and *everything* about all of these lifetimes … so you can literally remember us, being together … that you have been my *soul mate*, my *love of lifetimes* really … really? Roman, you're either a pathological liar or an absolute freak!"

I regret the last sentence as soon as it leaves my lips. It's quiet for a few seconds.

"Are you done?" he asks in a way that's far kinder then the choice of words would imply, but I don't answer. Instead I look away, out my window, trying to escape from all of this. The sun is just finishing its majestic dip below the westernmost crest of Wolf Butte and the sky has turned a stark violet. If I wasn't sure if I needed to apologize to Roman, the sky is telling me, in no uncertain terms, that I do. Purple means to repent. Cian taught me the importance of observing the smallest details of life and it absolutely never fails. Hidden in plain sight, the earth and the universe are giving us symbols and signs, always pointing the way. A hummingbird here, a golden beetle there, a purple sky, all helping us stay on a path or helping us find the one we've lost.

"I'm sorry," I say without looking at him, and without thinking I ask the strange little question that comes into my mind.

"Who are you?" I whisper.

He waits for me to turn back toward him but I don't. I can't. I can't seem to drag my eyes away from the unearthly beauty of this sunset. Like it's the last one I'll ever see in the same way. Like his answer will change me forever.

"My name is Alexander … at least, it used to be. Alexander Davidson, the famed little boy who, at age three, solved a murder that happened in his previous life, including the body and the evidence … the gun. Later determined to be the murder weapon of the body discovered, my body, before this one. In my last life, my name was Samuel, and I was shot three times in the back and then buried in an abandoned boat yard.

Buried before I had stopped breathing, and died alone and afraid. I was just twenty-three years old. The year was 1971 … Once I died I followed the man who killed me. I saw where he hid the gun."

As I turn back to look at him he's lifting up his shirt to his chest and leans forward showing me three strange marks sprayed across the middle of his back.

"I was born with these. Pretty odd birthmarks, wouldn't you say."

"They don't look like birthmarks," I say.

"No."

"They look like scars," I admit, reaching out instinctively to touch them.

"From the moment I could talk I kept telling my mom that's where I was shot," he says with a little half smile. "I kept telling her where the gun was hidden, and where I was buried … my body, when I was Samuel. My mom must have thought she was having a nervous breakdown."

I run my fingers slowly along his broad back. It's as warm as the most comfortable blanket and smoother than I could have imagined. I finally reach the three scars … *birthmarks.* A lighter tan than the rest of his olive skin, and raised just slightly. With their round shape and splayed edges, they feel just like I'd imagine bullet wounds would feel after they had healed for a very long time. The last thing I notice is the strangest of all. The marks are distinctly cooler than the rest of his warm body and back, at least ten degrees cooler if I were to guess. As I move my hand from the scar to an unmarked spot and back and forth a couple more times he looks me in the eyes and nods. Yes, I'm feeling what I think I'm feeling.

"When the marks on my back matched the bullet wounds on the body, *identically*, the body whose murder I pieced together in remarkable detail for investigators before I could even read, my mom finally believed me. Everyone believed. And the man who murdered me was convicted." He takes a slow, deep breath. Maybe it's the sound of his breathing that catches my attention, but something does. As he takes another smaller breath I flatten my palm just above his waist on his right side, spreading my fingers wide below his shoulder blade. I study the way his ribs expand and torso rises and falls gently as the flow of his breath moves in and out of his body. I feel like time is frozen somewhere in the stillness of my hand so I don't dare move. I wait for another breath.

He turns his gaze to me and searches my eyes. "What are you doing," he asks in a low whisper, but I don't answer, because I don't know, not really. All I know is that the longer my hand stays the more I become aware that his breathing is what's holding his soul inside his body, it's the only thing holding *his soul* in *this body*. And like some invisible energetic fingerprint that's one of a kind, I recognize the unique sound and feel, the familiar rhythm and flow of his soul's breath and suddenly my heart and mind fully understand what my body knew the moment Roman said it.

You do know this soul, Eve. He's the one you've loved, more than any other. And knowing that he was filled with terror and violently ripped from the world, the breath of his soul leaving his petrified body in hopeless gasps, a bottomless grief tears a hole through the center of my being that's so big and so wide I want to walk through it, right off the edge of the earth, and never look back. So I do, no other option even exists. I let it swallow me, this massive black hole, this omnipresent, invasive sorrow, and I'm drowning in a void without gravity, without oxygen, then I'm washed away to a place I instantly recognize, a place I've been, a place that resides somewhere within me where suffering and surrender and peace form one fabric woven into a familiar blanket. It's a blanket of eyes that goes on forever, stretches through all galaxies and also lines the inside of my soul. I have felt all this before, not in this lifetime, but it's in me just the same, it's in my DNA and I understand that this is why I felt so compelled to protect him. Because I know how it feels to lose him.

He has been my love of lifetimes, and my broken heart is the proof.

I only notice there are tears streaming down my face when he starts wiping them off my cheeks. He watches them well up in my eyes until they spill over my lashes, one after another, streaking down my face, then he wipes each one away before it reaches my chin until the tears stop coming.

"We moved a year after the trial," he continues, his gentle voice reflecting a deep understanding of how fragile I feel at this moment. "We moved halfway around the world and I became Roman Davidson. So, that's who I am," he finishes just as the grief begins to lift and almost as quickly as it came on, fully subsides.

"An even better question is, who are *you*," he says.

And like an unwanted old friend, my fear rushes back in. But this time, just like the grief, I close my eyes and let the miserable, terrifying, uncomfortable thing that I hate come inside and grab me. And even as it starts choking me, sitting on my lungs, squeezing my throat, making my heart race, I don't push it away or cover it up or throw it on anyone else. This time, for the first time, I go into my body, rooting it out, every last shred of the familiar gnawing, nagging anxiety, going toward it, not away from it like I've always done. Instead of the usual manic tailspin of denial, the frenzy of resistance that devours me when all the utter unpleasantness of fear is trying to descend upon me, I don't resist it. And accepting elevates me somehow, shifts me to a new place where I begin to watch it, to observe it. Where I'm kind of floating above the fear instead of drowning in it.

"I'm Eve," comes softly out of my lips as they rise into a resigned smile. "Just a normal girl," I say, knowing it's the last time that I'll say that, knowing it isn't true. Knowing he's about to tell me exactly who I really am.

CHAPTER 8

He takes my left hand, holds it in both of his, and returns my little smile.

"Just Eve, huh? And yet you wonder why people have such a strong reaction to you. Why you scare them, effortlessly, why they either like you or hate you right away. Why you basically broke the placement test, and why I'm not surprised when you tell me your grandfather can wake the dead. You wonder all these things and frankly, it surprises me you don't understand it all ..."

"Why?" I question, diving into the deepest depths of his eyes with mine.

"Because, Eve, you're the oldest soul on earth."

"I'm what?" I demand, confused by the words themselves.

"The oldest soul on earth ... by a lot."

"What? No. I can't be anything like that ..."

"Well, you are. You've been in all of my lifetimes, every single one of them. All two hundred and ninety-nine of them, present included. But I haven't been in all of yours. Not by a long shot."

"So what are you saying?"

"I'm saying reincarnation is real. And you've lived more lifetimes than anyone on earth, now or ever. Mostly short lifetimes, one right after another, continuously reincarnated. The oldest soul there is. Every single person you meet, virtually every soul on this planet, Eve, you have a history with, some better than others. It isn't a history they're actually conscious of, but they're reacting to you based on latent feelings—who you were to them, what you did, how you made them feel, every person on earth feels something about you. Deep inside, everyone remembers you."

"Why don't I feel that for them?"

"That part of you is completely switched off as far as I can tell. When it comes to people, to others souls, you're like a blank slate. It's usually that way for everyone, but for some reason, this time Phoenix and I came in knowing what we know and everyone else has some residual feelings about *you*, but you don't seem to have any of it. My guess is it would be too overwhelming. I don't know how you'd even function with just a sense of the memories of all those lifetimes, all that history, plagues, war, famine, death, all those experiences. Having the knowledge of your encounters with the seven and a half billion different souls in this world … I don't know how you'd even walk down the street, you'd probably go insane." He pauses a second, seeming to wrestle with himself about wanting to say something or not. Then, "For some reason, things are different this time. A *lot* of things are different this time," he tells me softly and I wonder if he's talking about us. That this time, for the first time in one of his lifetimes, we won't be together. "I'm sure there's a reason you don't know how you feel about anyone and a reason you do know other things, like the answer to every test you take or question you're asked. It seems you remember all of that."

"I do," I admit.

"Because you've learned it all before, so many times, some of it you even wrote or discovered or created in other lifetimes. The older the soul gets, recalling the information it once learned becomes more and more like breathing … doesn't it?"

I nod.

"And in this lifetime, with how old your soul is now, everything you've learned is completely available to you. How else would you have aced your placement test so easily? And you're a Lord Byron fan, aren't you? And you meddle in string theory?"

"I am. And I do. But I never told you that."

"That's because you were Ada Lovelace."

"Who?"

"She was you, for 36 years in the 19th century: daughter

of the great Lord Byron, the Duchess of Lovelace, a staggeringly brilliant mind, a groundbreaking mathematician, fatally beautiful"—his breath leaves him like he's picturing her … *me.*

"As Ada, you wrote the first algorithm, you know," he tells me, looking proud.

"I did?"

"You did. The whole modern technology revolution … it kind of started with you. You were the first programmer, wrote the first code in 1842. A force of nature, radically ahead of your time."

"Were you there?" I ask, knowing he wasn't in all of my lifetimes.

"Yes," he says and I know that means we were together.

"Who were you?"

"I was your husband. William King, the first Earl of Lovelace. We had three children." He looks at me funny, like he's looking at Ada, and I sense hurt and dysfunction in his eyes.

"We weren't happy, were we …" I guess.

"No. Not really."

"Why not?" I ask, but he doesn't answer right away.

"You had a gambling problem, and you hid it from me," he says finally. Like William is getting the long lost chance to confront Ada. "It was your thing for numbers, I knew, but with that hobby, in those days, came a consortium of male *associates…*" He tells me, like the wound is still fresh. "I was never sure if you were actually unfaithful," he says, almost wishing I could tell him one way or another but knowing I can't. "And I was a workaholic," he admits, "and a real narcissist." It's obvious he remembers all of it, clearly, and feels it too. I look down, not sure what to do with this strangely misplaced feeling of guilt swirling around inside me.

"Don't worry," he tells me as consolation, "I remarried after you died."

"You did what?" I say with a surprised little laugh.

"It wasn't love. 'The heart will break, but broken live on.'"

"That's one of my favorites."

"I know. It always was. You were infatuated with his work. He left your mom when you were a baby and never returned. Then he died when you were just eight. Your last wish was to be buried next to him. And so you were."

What he's telling me feels like news and not news all at once. Like he is reminding me of something I forgot rather than telling me something I never knew. And like some missing piece to a puzzle, I think maybe I needed *him* to tell me, not because I couldn't have ever figured it out on my own but because of who he is to me, who he's been, how deeply my trust in him must go. And while it's bizarre and far-fetched, if it's true, and nothing in his clear and unblinking eyes suggests that he's lying, if I am the oldest soul on earth, it could explain so many things. Like why Cian, an infinitely wise person, more in tune with the universe than I can even comprehend, treats me the way he does, like my words and instincts have some inherent importance, some innate justification, simply because they're coming from me. And why Shamus's hateful feelings, like so many of the kids at school, seem pre-coded in his DNA, and have always reeked of a hidden fear I never understood, all the elements of fear I'd imagine him having if he sensed, or maybe even knew, that I was something more than the idiotic and meaningless pest he proclaims me to be. If we have a history that only he knows.

"The oldest soul … on earth. I am the oldest soul on earth?" I ask him just to have a reason to say it out loud, to try to see if I can process the idea. If it fits.

"You are."

"How do you know this?"

"I just do," he admits. "Like how you described your grandfather, being tuned to a certain vibration other people couldn't hear, that continuous drum beat, and just knowing what he needs to know, to do what he needs to do … for why he's here."

"It's like that for you?"

"It's very similar to that. For me, and for Phoenix too. It's some kind of telepathic knowing. We were both born like this, knowing certain things, coming to fully understand new things when we need to, all the same things actually. Also the knowledge of our own past lives and all the people around us."

“And other people, who weren’t always around you?”

“Like you, yeah. I’ve known about you my whole life. I thought about you constantly. I even talked about you all the time, when I was little, before I discovered how odd that made me sound. I knew I was supposed to find you. And I’ve always known about Shamus.”

“My brother? Why? Is he an old soul like me?” I ask, suddenly struck with fear, not wanting to be anything that Shamus is.

“No, he’s not, he’s a very new soul compared to you. A lot like me in fact,” he says, startling me. His having anything in common with Shamus is a surprise.

“It’s getting late,” he says, then reaches down and turns the keys, and the truck roars to life. He glances over his shoulder and pulls out onto the road.

“How many lifetimes has he lived? Shamus.”

“This is his two hundredth.”

“What does it all mean? Is there a reason you know about Shamus? Why were you born this way? And why Phoenix?” And then, “*How many lifetimes have I lived?*”

With the last question, suddenly, my mind darts back to Gaebe, to the discovery of Animus and to our strange conversation and I wonder, *does Gaebe somehow already know this about me? If Animus becomes real and if we have to be tested … everyone will know. And what will happen then?*

“I don’t know the answers to those questions, not yet

anyway. I'm on sort of a need-to-know basis with the universe." He smiles at me, but seeing my distraught face, adds, "I don't know how many lifetimes you've had. Honestly, I have no idea."

"I don't understand any of it. I have so many questions. *What about Animus?*"

"Just try to relax," he says, but my mind is spinning, I want to keep talking to find out more, but before I know it, we're already parked in front of my house. And Jude, the boy of my dreams, is sitting on my front steps, at 4:59 P.M.

"He's punctual," I remark, trying to diffuse the awkwardness I instantly feel being here with Roman, Roman who I apparently have loved, fully and completely, for lifetimes, as another boy, one I'm reminded at the sight of that I'm eager to spend time with, sits on my steps, waiting for me.

"He's a lot of things," Roman adds. But it isn't jealousy I'm picking up in his voice. I almost think it's ... encouragement. "Jude is great. He's an incredible guy," he tells me, emphasizing the word *incredible* in an obvious way. Yup, I realize, it's definitely encouragement, and I get the distinct feeling that in this lifetime, Roman and I are not supposed to fall in love.

But the sight of Jude waiting on my steps is overwhelming. I couldn't be more content here in this truck with Roman, I want to stay here forever, feeling like I'm safe, like I have someone who's looking out for me ... almost feeling like, maybe, *I'm actually already loved by someone* ... and wondering if I already love him, while at the same time every cell in my body is brimming with anticipation to spend more time with Jude. To hear his voice, to see what unexpected things he's going to say and do. I even know, as I sit here with Roman, that I want Jude to kiss me. I *really* want him to kiss me and I don't even know what to do with that feeling. And if I believe what Roman just told me, if I believe that he and I have been soul mates for hundreds of lifetime, it makes sense why being with him feels the way that it does, feels so comfortable, so good, and so right, which makes my eagerness, my excitement about Jude, at just the sight of him, all the more conflicting.

Just then, I notice the empty driveway and remember that Cian and Shamus are gone and I have no way of knowing when they'll be back or even where they went, and my stomach flip-flops. I'm excited to be alone with Jude and I'm happy he won't be subjected to meeting Shamus. Jude who's so zealous and brilliant, who I get the sense that doesn't know how to be any other way. And Shamus can only be Shamus, merciless, malicious and cruel. With Roman, Shamus has no real power, it's obvious, nothing he can do or say can really affect Roman, and somehow Shamus knows it. But with Jude, I fear things would be different.

"I'll see you tomorrow," Roman says as he forces a smile and a little wave to send me off, to go spend time with Jude, and I can see that this is hard for him. The same way seeing him with Ruby was for me.

As I reach for the handle to open the door I stop. *How am I supposed to get to school tomorrow?* I think of asking Roman to come pick me up, knowing that he would but also knowing it would incite more rumors and drama and more angry tirades from Ruby. I don't want to be the cause of that for Roman.

"What is it?" he asks.

"Nothing, thanks for the ride," I say, somehow prompting Roman to notice the empty driveway.

"Do you need me to pick you up tomorrow?"

"Nope," I tell him. Then the words "I'm getting a car today" come flying out of my mouth as I open the door and step out. I return his smile before I swing the door shut and wonder how on earth I think I'm going to manage to do that.

But walking toward Jude, his electric blue eyes on me, I'm suddenly not worried about it. His infectious lighthearted smile bathes me with a dose of levity. I don't worry about a ride to school, buying a car, how many lives I've lived, or anything else. I even forget that Roman is still pulling out of my driveway until I hear the loud roar of his engine as he drives off down the street, then have to remind myself that it's obvious Roman and I aren't supposed to be together to stave off the sudden wave of guilt that comes over me. Why would he have a girlfriend and be telling me what a great guy Jude is if he and I were going to be together? Why would I be so excited to spend time with Jude if I was supposed to be with Roman? When he said *a lot of things are different this time,* I thought maybe he was talking about us, but now as I look at Jude, I'm completely certain that he was.

CHAPTER 9

Once Jude and I are inside I stop worrying about Roman and start worrying about being home alone with Jude as I'm overrun with the same uncontrollable thoughts that were sneaking into my mind at school. Also unnerving me, I'm not sure what people usually do when they go into someone's house for the first time. I've never had anyone over. And I'm not sure that what Jude is doing is normal. I'm not sure if it's Jude or if it's my house, but he's wandering around my living room looking at everything. Studying *everything*. It seems odd to show yourself around the way he is, without saying a word, walking from one thing to the next picking them up to examine them. He holds something up and looks at me questioningly.

"It's a shrunken head … from Africa." I tell him, and realizing this might not be a normal object in a normal person's house answers my question. It's not Jude that's odd.

"I've never seen one of these. Is it real?" he asks, intense and fascinated, and something comes over me.

"Are you holding it?" I find myself teasing him, feeling strangely spontaneous and noticeably more playful than I ever remember feeling before. I even detect a bit of recklessness coming on.

"No, not like ..." he starts, as an amazing sort of bashful smile seeps through his serious expression. "Not like is it imaginary. I mean, is it real? A real head?" he clarifies, his pensive look coming back.

"I know. I was kidding ... It's real," I tell him, a bit reluctantly. Who has real shrunken heads in their house?

It's the same thing with ancient Egyptian vases, a spearhead from Ethiopia.

"Oh that one's very old," I stammer as he picks up a spearhead, the one that's literally prehistoric. "Like, museums don't know we have it," I tell him, "meaning they should probably have it." He gets the hint and puts it down gently just as the phone rings. I already know who it is—Ansel North, the only person who ever calls and always calls the day Cian and Shamus leave. I have to answer or he'll just keep calling again and again until I do. I drag myself away from Jude and into the kitchen where the one phone in our house rests on the counter.

"Hi, Ansel," I say, more quietly than usual, not wanting to

have to explain who Ansel is to Jude; telling Jude about Ansel would lead to having to tell him about Cian and telling one person a day about Cian is definitely my limit.

"How are you, Eve?" Ansel asks from the other end of the phone, the same question he always asks.

"I'm fine," I say, rushing the words a bit and giving myself away.

"Are you busy with something … or is someone there with you?" Ansel is a kind of a verbal detective, able to perceive and interpret the slightest variance in my voice. If I wanted to hide something from him I'm not sure I'd ever be able to.

"No, I just … have someone here from school. To study," I say, hoping he won't ask for a name and find out that I'm home alone with a boy I just met. A boy I barely know who is in the living room handling all of Cian's priceless artifacts as I stand here in the kitchen imagining what it would feel like to kiss him.

"School! That's right, how was your first day of school?"

"It was …" I start, deciding how much to tell him. "It was different than I thought it would be."

"How were the kids? Were they nice?"

"Ah, well, I'm not winning any popularity contests."

"Give it time," he advises before taking an uncharacteristic pause. Cian's oldest and dearest friend Ansel and the word "quiet" never occur together. After an unusual and extended beat of silence: "Have you seen the news today?" And even though I get the distinct impression that Ansel isn't simply making small talk I couldn't imagine how anything on the news could be more compelling than my pressing desire to get off the phone and go back to the glacier-eyed boy in my living room.

"I don't ... we don't really watch the news," I say, something Ansel already knows. *It's bad for the soul, bad for the energy, bad for the planet,* Cian always says, a fact that Ansel knows well. "Why?" I ask hastily, as a plan for how to buy a car is beginning to take shape in my mind.

"It seems like you're busy," Ansel says, obviously a little surprised by how immature and impatient I sound. "It can wait. How about I call you later. Will sometime tonight work?" he asks, and I tell him to give me a call about nine. "Be safe," he says in a warning tone and I feel like informing him that actually Cian told me to be reckless but decide against it before hanging up and heading out of the kitchen.

I find Jude where I left him, engrossed in the hundreds of mysterious objects that adorn the shelves and walls in the living room.

"Do you have any money?" I ask him out of nowhere.

"About a thousand dollars—it's in my savings account," he tells me freely as he reaches for Cian's favorite prehistoric Phoenician stone carving.

"Can I borrow it for a few minutes?" I ask, a question just odd enough to steal his attention from the 5,000-year-old little man-shaped statuette.

"Sure," he agrees freely without seeming to need to ask what for.

"Great. I only have like fifty bucks in my account, we'll use yours, it'll be faster." Then I ask if he has online access to his account, if he knows the username and password as I motion him to follow me and lead the way toward my bedroom. He trails behind a bit, as everything we pass seems to beckon for his attention, and he informs me rather indifferently that he doesn't know the username or password of his bank account because his mom is incredibly overbearing and insanely overprotective.

"She has some real trust issues," he tells me casually as he pauses to look at a framed picture of a fourteen-year-old me riding an elephant in Nepal. "Is this you?" he asks with a charming little half-smile, a funny question considering I don't feel like I look much different today then I did the day the picture was taken. It's obviously me. He knows it's me but he studies it for some reason, then he says in the most honest and truthful way, like the picture is being consecrated by his words, "You look young here. I mean pretty, how you do now, just a lot younger. And you're much more beautiful now," he states, like it's a fact and I wonder what exactly I'm going to do with this captivating boy that I'm falling madly in love with as I grab his arm and attempt to keep him moving.

"Why does your family travel so much?" he asks earnestly,

the way he asked questions about calculus, but it's a red-flag question and I don't want to answer. I don't want to tell Jude about Cian or any of the strange things Roman and I just talked about. So I drag him past the picture into my room.

"We just like to travel," I finally answer as I sit at my computer. And it's enough as he's immediately spellbound watching me quickly hack into his bank account.

"Wow," he says, as I effortlessly navigate around the firewall.

"I hope your mom isn't home monitoring it," I say as I transfer the money.

"She probably is," he smiles and shrugs.

Now, as we sit in front of Lou Briggs of Lou's Used Cars less than an hour later, Jude is a living ball of kinetic energy. A restless mix of eager and exhilarated.

Lou rubs his bloodshot eyes. It looks like he's had a long, rough day.

"I like you," he admits to me, awkwardly, a fact I recognized the moment we walked in but am still surprised to hear come out of the mouth of a car salesman. "I'd love to sell you this car," he says of the white four-wheel drive jeep I picked out. "Believe me, it'd be a bright spot in what's been a hell of a day," he says, his eyes reddening. "But I can't sell you a car, I can't let you drive off the parking lot," he informs me, reluctantly pushing the check I just wrote him for seventeen thousand dollars back across his Formica desk to where Jude and I sit stupefied on the other side. That I don't have a driver's license wasn't even an afterthought. Our first hiccup since the second I sat down at my computer and within a few minutes began turning Jude's nearly one thousand dollars into twenty thousand.

"Have you ever done this before?" Jude had asked me, his eyes fixed on the screen, his intrigued voice sounding monotone, even hypnotized, as he watched the rounds of poker go by one after another and our balance steadily rise.

"No," I said. *At least, not in this lifetime*, I thought after a few very successful hands, knowing the rules of every game and how to win. Thanks to Ada Lovelace.

I made what I figured was enough money to buy a car in about twenty minutes, transferred the original amount back into Jude's bank account and the profits into mine, Jude's eyes still transfixed on the screen and shining with every possibility on earth at once from what we had just done.

Now, as we sit here in front of our first roadblock, I can tell that Jude doesn't want the adventure to end, and certainly not like this. He doesn't want to wait in line for the rollercoaster and not get to ride the ride. I can tell he's racking his brain.

"Wait, I have a driver's license," he says.

"Can we use his license?" I ask, sliding the check back

toward Lou, who looks down at the nearly twenty thousand dollars of bank-verified cash.

"You want to buy this car ... *in his name?*" Lou clarifies the bizarre situation as I shrug, what does it matter, and Jude fishes his wallet out of his back pocket and quickly produces a valid North Dakota state driver's license. We both hold our breath as Lou looks from the license to the two of us to the check and back to the license, everything inside him probably knowing better. "Alright," he concedes. "Whatever. I mean what the hell, right? The end is near," he adds, sounding strangely resigned as he walks into his office to make a copy of the license and for the first time I notice the large flat screen TV hanging from the ceiling on the opposite end of the showroom. It's tuned to the news and filled with images I can't process even as I watch. The scene keeps replaying from different angles but my brain can't make any sense out of it. I figure the problem is that the volume is turned off so I get up and walk toward to the screen and as I get closer realize, volume or no volume, I'm seeing exactly what I thought I was seeing, and that's the very reason I can't process it. Because it's a wall of water, a wave, if you can call it that, toppling skyscrapers, washing people off the roofs of the highest buildings in Manhattan, ripping the Statue of Liberty and the George Washington Bridge from their foundations, and my mind is slow to register the incredible images as reality.

The words *Tens of millions feared dead ...* catch my eyes as they scroll across the bottom of the screen. I start to process that the footage of the massive wave was filmed earlier as they cut to a reporter in a helicopter. The words *Live aerial view of NYC* appear just below him. The live shots of the receded water below reveal cataclysmic devastation. The metropolis of Manhattan reduced to a heap of rubble.

Lou walks up, picks up a nearby remote, and unmutes the sound. All we hear is the howling wind and rhythmic blades of the chopper and right away I can tell that the reporter is in shock. Not just *shocked* but actually *in shock.* His eyes are flat and dead, his breathing is rapid and shallow, and he keeps licking his lips and trying to swallow but his mouth is bone dry. He's staring mindlessly at the surreal devastation below and only becomes aware that they've cut back to a live shot of him when a finger from behind the camera points in his direction, indicating it's time for him to speak. He just blinks for a moment or two with a blank look on his face. His hollow black eyes staring vacantly into the lens. Then he finally starts coming to life. Slowly, like a windup toy.

"What we are learning is that a little over seven hours ago," he says, sounding detached and heavily medicated, "a magnitude 9.7 earthquake shook the ocean floor 100 miles off the coast of the Canary Islands. The earthquake sent a mega-tsunami barreling toward North America that reached a top speed of more than five hundred miles per hour when it hit the eastern seaboard less than thirty minutes ago at 7:09 P.M.

Eastern Standard Time, an unholy wall of water that rose to nearly three hundred feet above sea level. Some reports are saying that the wave reached twenty miles inland, some claiming as much as fifty miles, as it crushed everything in its path." Then he just stops. There's apparently nothing more to say.

The camera operator pans away from the desolate face of the reporter but all there is to see are a seemingly unending line of other helicopters and wreckage, meaningless debris, the chaotic remnants of civilization where Manhattan once was.

Lou, staring zombie like into the desperate and terrifying images, very slowly hands me a black car key, an unsealed envelope of folded up multicolored papers, and Jude's driver's license, one at a time, without ever looking away from the TV.

"Thank you," I offer, my voice somber, but he doesn't reply. He never takes his eyes off the screen. *He's in the screen*, I realize, *and I don't think he's ever coming out.*

How many more Lou's are there right now across the country, the continent, the globe, thinking this wave marks the beginning of the end? Who are trapped so deeply inside their screens right now?

I turn away from the images, key in hand, as if I could just leave them here in the showroom, with Lou. I head straight for the exit. Jude is already outside. He's sitting in the driver's seat of my new jeep. I guess it's technically *his* jeep, I remind myself, watching him as he stares up at the stars.

Who is he, I wonder, I know he isn't like anyone else I've ever met. He's too dynamic, too enthralling to be a regular seventeen-year-old boy. Is he like me and Roman and Phoenix—is there something different about Jude too? As I watch him intently studying the night sky, like he's discovering new constellations, I realize that meeting him was as strange of an experience as meeting Roman—full of electricity, just a different kind. And after everything Roman told me, and the way he talked about Jude … I look down at his driver's license in my hand, as if it will tell me something about Jude that I need to know. Like I could somehow see if he was an old soul, like me, or another soul mate maybe, just by looking at his driver's license.

Next to his picture the words "Judah James Wolfe" make me realize that I hadn't even known Jude's last name. And that I've only known him a few short hours. Not nearly enough time to have such an intense attraction. Sure, I've been dreaming about him for six months, but could that really be why I'm so drawn to him …

Then, as if it's darker and bolder and floating above everything else, his birthday seems to rise toward me off the small plastic card: December 21, 1999.

What is going on here?

What are you, Jude Wolfe?

CHAPTER 10

That Jude and I would be born on the same exact day, on opposite corners of the world, could certainly pass for a coincidence. The odds are not that bad.

Then again, it could be the second sign of the apocalypse.

Come on, Eve; does two people having the same birthday, and possibly a third, equal the apocalypse? No, of course not. But after everything I've learned today I know it means *something.* It has to. I also know I need to tread lightly here, I can't just walk up to Jude, guns blazing.

Surprise, turns out I'm the oldest soul on earth, and I just found out that you and I have the same birthday so I know you're keeping secrets from me. How old is your soul anyway? How many lifetimes have you loved me? C'mon, how many!

No, I've got to be discrete. Any other tactic and I'll sound like a psychopath.

I need another way in. *Think, Eve. Think.*

I look down at his license again.

"Here you go, Judah James," I say as I climb into the passenger's seat and hand him back his driver's license.

"It's my dad's name. *James.*" He tells me, followed by an awkward silent period. Not getting anywhere I decide I need to dial it up.

"So, you're an organ donor, huh?" I say, from what I read on his license—feeling distinctly psychopathic.

He tilts his head, as he looks in my eyes, confused.

"I won't need organs when I'm not on earth," he informs me so matter-of-factly that I feel an almost physical tug from my soul at the truth of what he's saying and the purity in his voice and how sharply it contrasts with every seventeen-year-old part of every cell in my body. He waits for me to speak. I must look like I plan to, but I'm disoriented by his charming face and relaxed body language and it takes a second to shake the stars out of my eyes.

"That's a good point," I finally say, gathering myself. "It's just surprising, I guess, a bit of a higher dose of mortality than I'd imagine from a teenager, who's supposed to feel immortal and invincible." I'm trying to investigate who he is, but trying to still sound casual in case our conversation doesn't go that way, and hearing myself fail miserably.

"Do you want to know something, Eve?" he asks, his voice energized like he's about to share a secret.

"Yeah," I say eagerly, in almost a whisper, wondering what kind of bizarre celestial thing he's going to tell me about whoever or whatever he is … why we have the same birthday, what past lifetimes we've had … a shared destiny maybe …

With a worried expression, he warns me, "It's a little funny."

"It's okay," I whisper, trying to brace myself for anything, transfixed by the flickering lights in his steel-blue eyes. "What is it?"

After a couple beats of intense eye contact, my anticipation building so high it's about to kill me, with almost no sound he mouths, "I don't know how to drive my own car." His eyes open wide, smiling, and instantly jar me out of the deepest depths of my mind as he points to the long gear shift on his right that rises between us out of the floor of the jeep.

With a single sentence he managed to usher me fully out of my head and into the present moment. The moment at hand, the one where we're supposed to be driving off the parking lot.

"'Your car,' huh …" I smile and give him a warning squint.

"Yeah … I mean we could check the paperwork, just to be sure." With eyes twinkling, he smiles back as I quickly slam the envelope of papers into the glove box and lock it. "But hey, it's cool with me if you want to drive it …" he offers, a fearless mix of sarcastic and flirtatious.

Excitement coursing through me, I tease him, flirting

back: "Because you don't know how ..."

"Do *you*?" he asks suddenly, like all at once he realizes I actually might not know how to drive it either. In truth, I've never driven a stick shift, or any car before for that matter, but as I look down at the three pedals near his feet ...

"Yeah, I know how."

Over the next few hours I discovered that Jude does, in fact, have a couple very rare, undeniably superhuman abilities.

At the beginning of the night I wasn't sure what to call the first one. Like the reverse effect of the vibrations that come to Cian or the telepathic knowledge that's delivered between Roman and Phoenix, Jude's unusual gift is something that emanates from him. Instead of receiving a signal he sends one out, like an ultrasonic pulse, which I witnessed animals and even the landscape around us respond to.

Like the gray wolf, which in North Dakota is endangered, a "ghost wolf" I've only heard about but never seen. I'm convinced that the wolf that ran along the road beside us for ten miles, all the way to the base of the butte before coming within ten feet of where we parked to gaze at Jude was chasing this frequency. Same with the bald eagle that soared overhead, that was never out of sight, that even landed in the middle of Jude's front yard when we pulled up to his house. The titanic bird of prey that seemed to dwarf everything around it with its omnipresence never took its majestic eyes off Jude, seeming to stare at some invisible aura around him.

By the end of the night I understood that it's actually just *love* that's pouring out from him, but his capacity to capture and feel and scatter it is on a different level. Love on this level is magical. This kind of love is where miracles come from, it encompasses all things, includes all things, it's sheer, and unadulterated by life as it radiates from him. And when I get a glimpse of the world through his eyes it infuses me, cracking open my heart, a heart that I didn't even know was so closed off to all the immeasurable bliss available in every moment, until I saw what a heart that's fully open looks like.

The second otherworldly quality he possesses is something I don't even recognize as human, something I know I've never felt. Not in this lifetime or any other. And it's that he exists divorced from any attachment to existence itself, with a freedom so unrestricted and unrestrained, a liberation so widespread it almost feels contagious and, at times, definitely feels dangerous. It's strange but the way that he's detached from this life is the most oddly life-affirming thing I've ever witnessed. The fearlessness that permeates him, as innate as my fingernails are to me, that's programmed into his every cell, informs him every moment the very secret of life itself, *that we actually don't have anything to lose, so we can just go ahead and live.*

I'd noticed this right away, when he invited himself to my house without reservation. Without worry that I might say no.

And when he offered me all of his money so freely, without any conditions or fear of loss. But I only truly began to understand the depths of this second strange gift after we climbed to a cliff near the top of Butte Saint Paul, higher than I ever imagined myself climbing, with just another kid my age, especially at night without a plan or a rope or even the right shoes.

We sat under an eternal black canvas dotted with billions of piercing white stars. The ethereal blanket of the night sky of the northern hemisphere looked even more unearthly from the stunning height to which we had climbed. I was finally done looking up when I looked down, over the edge. He saw me noticing the far drop. As I tried to process the staggering height mixed with the jagged boulders below, I felt his eyes on me.

"That's so scary," I remarked of the terrifying view before scooting further back away from the edge where we'd been sitting next to each other.

"Why?" he asked, puzzled. A rather bizarre question. *Why?*

"Why? Because you could fall. Easily. And you would die."

He looked back at me as I told him what was certainly not news, and at that moment, in his moonlit face, unhidden, I could see that he wanted to kiss me. He stared right at my mouth, then into my eyes, and then back down at my mouth, biting his own bottom lip gently as his breathing slowed, got a little heavier. Almost as soon as I accepted that he wanted to, he was leaning back, and he was kissing me. Fearless. Just like that. My first kiss. One tiny, sweet, soft, cosmic kiss, one that felt like I'd imagine falling from a star onto a cloud then into a love song might feel, that revved my heart to full throttle and lit the center of my belly on fire. When the little kiss was finished, he sat back and smiled at me. Probably because he knew I wasn't ready for it to end.

Then he swept himself up to standing in one agile motion and took a few steps toward the edge. Not tentatively, not with shuffling feet scooting slowly, not like anyone else would approach the gravelly, unsecure, edge of a treacherous cliff, over which your painful demise awaits ... no, his steps were bold, unafraid, as if he were walking from one room to the next in his own house. He crossed his arms as he peered over the side in the same way—to the death that stared him in the face he appeared to simply stare back, indifferent.

"If you're trying to make me nervous, it's working," I said, hoping that would prompt him to act more carefully. But he just stared down. "Are you picking the exact rock you want your skull to hit first on the way down?" The aggravation brought by fear was obvious in my voice. He turned around and smiled, which was worse, because now his back was facing the abyss, his heels hanging partway over. If I had been standing where he was, the way he was standing, I would have fallen. Without a doubt. Anyone would have fallen.

"Come away from there! Seriously. You could lose your life!"

Even though I was begging him he didn't move, but he also didn't look like he was toying with me, or trying to get a rise out of me, or flirt, or show off ... no, more than anything he looked like he was sad for me. That he felt sorry for me because I didn't know something. Something he couldn't imagine what it would be like to live and simultaneously not know.

"You can't lose your life, silly," he said to me in a way that was both simple and sympathetic, in a way that made me wonder if he was from another planet. And no one taught him the rules of earth. How gravity always wins.

"Uh, I beg to differ. Losing your life is a distinct possibility, particularly for you, particularly at this moment," I said, but as I looked as his feet, precariously placed as ever, I began to get the sense that the earth and the gravel were holding him securely in place. That the landscape felt the same aura that the eagle and the wolf perceived, that Jude was capable of miraculous love, and because fear didn't live anywhere inside him, the universe and gravity, even the shifty little pebbles under his feet were in some kind of flow with him, some cooperation with him, and with his destiny. And he didn't appear destined to die tonight.

"Can you lose something you don't have?" he asked. "I mean, logically?"

"No." *Obviously.*

"You can't lose something you don't have. And you don't

have a life ..." he told me, turning back to face the abyss. "You *are* life," he said, projecting his words out into the universe. Like he was having a conversation with me and with the infinity of the cosmos at the same time. "Once you understand that, then you know ... it's okay to really live, even if sometimes it looks reckless. It's okay to be a little reckless."

I could just barely comprehend what he was saying, the idea that "you can't lose your life, because you don't *have* a life, because you *are* life,"—my understanding was like what you can see of an iceberg above the waterline. Most of it, a whole giant upside-down underwater mountain, was still obscured. Though to be fair, I might have grasped his profound statement a little better if I wasn't so distracted by the "it's okay to be a little reckless" part. Because of the "recklessness" that Cian was talking about, and preoccupied further by what the chances might be that the only two things that Cian said to me this morning before school were both repeated back to me later, word for word.

I'm "not an island any more," courtesy of Roman. How could I be when I'm the oldest soul on earth with a pre-wired connection to every other human in the world? After I left my house this morning, the island sank. Whether it sank at school or in Roman's car or on the cliff with Jude doesn't matter, but the tiny isolated blissful thing that I was, is no longer. Now I feel like the moon, making waves wherever I go, just by being me.

And thanks to Jude, I'm also "a little reckless." Or maybe a *lot* reckless. Which according to Cian and Jude is just fine and dandy. But I still know, and am still troubled by, how the chances of Cian's words coming to life are just like the chances of my birthday being the same as Jude's—either a strange but insignificant coincidence or one with an infinitely ominous meaning. And island or moon, careful or reckless, I'm not sure that I'm ready to find out.

PART TWO

FROM THE EVENTS TO THE UNTHINKABLE

CHAPTER 11

Jude's mom wasn't thrilled when we pulled into her driveway after midnight.

Bathed in mud, the jeep didn't look like a freshly purchased pre-owned vehicle to her fuming eyes, and she wasn't believing a word that Jude was saying about where we'd been, what we'd been doing, and how the tires had gotten stuck in the soft earth for at least twenty minutes, all of it the truth. Still, she wasn't happy, but her anger, I could see, was a much bigger problem for her than it was for Jude. His solemn face and steady respectful eyes told me he knew all about the wrath he'd get. And it didn't bother him.

"She's probably going to lose it," he tried to prepare me as we neared his house.

He knew what he was signing on for the moment we embarked on our unknown adventure, and he never once mentioned, even as the hours rolled by, that he should get home. He didn't care, I realized, as I heard her screaming behind the closed door.

Turns out, I'm quite skilled at driving a manual transmission, and off-roading, and navigating hilly terrains in the dark. Not as good, apparently, at staying focused on the details of the landscape while Jude blasts music at full volume and hangs out of the unzipped top of the jeep howling at the moon, hollering things like "I love my new car!" at the top of his lungs and "I'm so happy Eve bought it for me!" That's when I laugh until my sides cramp, cheeks ache, and drool leaks out of the corner of my smiling face from the whipping wind.

That's when I drive right into ditches.

I did show Jude how to drive "his own car," in a sprawling open prairie where I figured he couldn't hit anything. I explained how to use the clutch, how to alternate it with the gas, and how and when to shift the gears. He listened as I spoke, the way he always seems to, with every cell in his entire being. Then he tried it. He stalled … just once. After that, miraculously, he had it. Never stalling again.

Now as I pull up to my house, it's almost one in the morning and I feel completely reckless. Wonderfully reckless. I'm high from the day. Still amazed that I actually go to school, still reeling from the things Roman told me, still vibrating with life from being with Jude. I close the door of my jeep and walk toward the house almost embarrassingly amazed at myself, feeling like I've got the world on a string. Like I can pretty much do anything. Not to mention the liberation of being left home alone. Knowing I can actually do anything I want. I can come and go as I please. *Maybe I'll even invite Jude over again tomorrow*, I'm contemplating as I approach the porch, hear the phone ringing through the front door, and suddenly realize, *I forgot about Ansel!* I've never missed a call from Ansel.

Over the last five years, since I was twelve and Cian felt he didn't need to bring me everywhere he went any more, that I was capable enough to care for myself, Ansel has called, always on the first night and again once they returned, and every time I have answered. Always sitting by the phone waiting for it to ring. I wonder if he's worried sick as I rifle through every stupid useless compartment in my backpack. Has he been calling since nine? Has he been calling me for four hours straight! The phone keeps ringing and ringing and ringing, and it's starting to drive me insane as I search through my bag in the total darkness. *Maybe it's not being able to see anything that's driving me mad*, I think, which causes me to notice the porch light is out. Which is strange. I'd changed the bulb myself, no more than a week ago. I even think I remember flipping the switch inside so it would be on when I got home.

Then I notice the flower pot, the one we hide the spare key

under, is slightly off from where it usually sits and I start to flush with panic. I look over my shoulder while still fishing through my bag, finally feeling the key at the bottom and pulling it out with my trembling hand, and fumbling to get it into the lock for what feels like eternity. When the key slides into place and I finally turn the deadbolt and open the door, more darkness greets me.

Had I really turned out every single light in the house when Jude and I left? Would I have done that knowing it resembles midnight by just six o'clock this time of year?

I know I wouldn't have. I know I *didn't.*

I turn to my left and look at the wall next to the inside of the front door, at the switch for the porch light, and see that it's flipped on, just how I thought I left it. My heart feels like it's trying to reboot. I reach up and twist the bulb to the right and have to stifle a scream that wants to escape when the porch light flickers on.

Someone unscrewed the bulb.

I look from the doorway of the dark house to the front yard and street. I don't know whether to go in and bolt the door to protect myself from what's outside or run outside to escape whatever may be inside. I decide to lock out whatever's out, though I have no evidence that it's safer inside. But at least I can answer the phone. I can stop it from ringing. I can assure Ansel that I'm fine, though I'm far from fine.

I turn on every light in the house that I pass as I make my

way to the ringing phone in the kitchen. I'm almost through the living room and have turned on enough wattage to see our house from space when something on the floor catches the corner of my eye.

It's Cian's favorite Phoenician carving. One of the few things Jude *didn't* pick up, at least so far as I noticed. It's lying face down on the carpet, a good ten feet from where it would be if it fell off its shelf. If Jude had picked it up when I was out of the room, and if he'd have *accidently* dropped it, he would have had to also *accidently* kick it a good three yards for it to be where it is now. But I tell myself to try to remain calm, to try to control my heart rate, to somehow will it to stay under whatever range brings on instant cardiac arrest, somewhere near the uncharted new paces it's currently exploring.

I pull myself into the kitchen, forcing the forensic investigator I didn't know lived inside me to leave the mystery of the carving behind, just like I did with the porch light and the flower pot and all the lights I know I didn't leave off. The phone must be answered. My hand is visibly shaking as I reach for it, and I know my voice isn't going to sound much better. Knowing Ansel and how he can read my voice like a blind person reading braille, he'll have a SWAT team here in under a minute. Which might not be a bad thing.

I pick it up but say nothing. I suddenly think, that with everything going on, that maybe Ansel isn't the one on the other end. That maybe whoever is calling is responsible for the lights and the flowerpot and the carving.

"Eve?" It's Ansel.

"Yeah," I say relieved and breathless.

Ansel makes a big sighing noise, like he's been waiting to breathe for the past four hours. As he takes another few breaths in and out I can almost hear all his worst fears being quelled.

"I suppose where you've been," he says once he's finally breathing almost normally, "is really none of my business. You're not a child any more," he says with resolve but still waits, giving me a moment, I assume, to tell him just where it is that I've been, what I was doing until one in the morning and with whom. But like a stubborn child, I say nothing. I feel bad that he's been calling, that he was worried, but he's right. I'm old enough to decide where to go, whom to go with, and when to come home. But something in the very edge of my silence threatens to disrupt the close relationship that Ansel and I have shared my entire life. The once-solid dynamic of protector and protected blurring in the lull. I can almost hear the insecurity in his silence. It's apparent. I'm now keeping secrets from him.

"Shamus isn't with Cian," he says finally, almost smug about it—*Okay, Miss Independent, here you go, deal with that!*

As he might have intended, his words are like a lethal dose of Novocain, they numb me to within an inch of my life. A high-powered narcotic, from my once-fiercest advocate, delivered straight through the phone without mercy.

"Where is he?" I ask, transforming back into Ansel's damsel, a helpless child.

"Cian is in the Northeast, where the flooding is," he says, knowing full well that Cian isn't the one I was talking about. Cian rushes to terrible places all the time to do good things. Shamus, I fear, would rush to good places to do terrible things. "We don't know where Shamus is."

"What do you mean?" I ask with the familiar feeling of not wanting to hear the answer.

"He disappeared just after they got underway this morning, before the earthquake, before they were even out of North Dakota. Cian had to continue on without him. Of course. But he wanted you to 'keep an eye out for your brother.' That's what he said to tell you."

To keep an eye out? Is he kidding? Cian knows full well that Shamus would take my eyes out, both of them, if he had the chance?

Now that he does *have the chance!*

And it hits me, like the bullet train that narrowly missed Shamus in Russia, how truly terrified I am of my own brother, my own flesh and blood, and I'm overcome. Like I hadn't allowed myself to accept how much the brother, who lives under the same roof as I do, scares the very life out of me. And I realize that the one thing that terrorizes me more than his very presence is not knowing where he is.

I tell Ansel that I'll keep an eye out for Shamus. He even makes me promise, to actually swear, to let him know if Shamus returns home. I do, but I keep my estimation to myself, that if Shamus comes home while Cian is away, I wouldn't have to tell Ansel, because Ansel watches the news, and he will certainly hear about the defenseless young girl murdered at the hand of her own brother. For the sake of continuity and in keeping with the end of days theme, they'll bring in an expert, a professor of familial criminology and sacred symbols, who'll reference the Bible. Genesis 4:8, of course. Audiences will be riveted. Ratings will surge.

After I hang up the phone, I peek around the corner into the living room and stare at Cian's statue, the ancient relic lying facedown on the carpet. If it levitates off the ground and flies on its own across the room, I'll be relieved. Less afraid of some paranormal phenomenon than the alternative, that my brother is the cause of where the carving now rests.

With all the courage inside me I walk toward the carving and put it back on its shelf. I grab the TV remote by the couch and hit power. I need to find out exactly what's going on. I want to understand more about the tsunami, and what people think it means. Shockingly, the footage I left in Lou's showroom is not what fills the screen when it comes to life.

Every inch of the screen from top to bottom and from one corner to the other is filled with, of all things, the moon. Our moon, I can tell by the pattern of its craters, but burning a bright crimson color that's as vivid as it is startling. The words *From Mega-Tsunami to Blood Moon, what does it mean* across the bottom of the screen. The eerie moon appears to be shaking slightly as the camera tries to frame this tight of a shot on such a distant object, which only gives the ominous feeling that the moon itself is wobbling and bleeding, about to fall out of the sky. I hear the anxious voice of a female news anchor apologize for the shaking image. She keeps reassuring her viewers that it's the camera. That the moon is not actually trembling. An odd thing to have to tell them, but an apparent necessity after the day Earth and its inhabitants have endured. As I stare at the image my eyes begin to burn. The cable box informs me that it's quarter to two in the morning on what's probably been the most thoroughly exhausting day of my life.

Ten minutes later I'm in my room staring at my bed, blurry-eyed. I sit down on top of the comforter and lay back stiffly, still in my sneakers and clutching an enormous kitchen knife in my sweaty fist at my side. I try to sleep. But with all the lights on and with my eyes wide as saucers, it's not easy. Add the images of both the blood moon and the tsunami ceaselessly flashing in my brain and I figure it will be impossible. Plus the ranting of a religious scholar, whose name I didn't catch, that were dubbed over the image of the moon, keep careening like a runaway train through my mind. He talked frantically about signs of the end of days, about the great flood and the moon turning red, both foretold in countless sacred texts.

"Humanity needs to prepare itself. There will be four beings, from the four corners of the earth," he predicted in his terrifying rant, his monologue of death and doom, at which point the news anchor began to weep on-air as they continued the broadcast. "Calamity, catastrophe, ancient plagues, clouds of insects, beasts breathing fire, if it all begins to happen we will know that we are out of time. There will be nothing to do at that point. But before that, perhaps an answer will make itself known to us. Some kind of an answer, something that we can do, that we are supposed to do, will perhaps emerge. At that time we should cling to it for our survival, move heaven and earth, to try to reverse what appears to have been set into motion."

Before I know it I'm dreaming. I'm aware that it's a dream but still swept up by it. The first thing I notice is that I'm not in water. Then I notice something else. My name is not Eve.

My name is Vibia.

I'm twenty-two years old. I feel my hand being held by a smaller hand. I look down and see the round cherubic face of a child. She's my child, my daughter.

Her name is Lucia.

Her hair is long, wavy and blond, right now in a braid that's tied in a crown around her head. Her eyes are distinctive—a radiantly pale wintergreen—and she's four years old today. I remember doing her hair. The smell of her silky tresses that always reminds me of sunshine and fresh lilies.

We just left our house and are walking down a cobblestone path toward a busy marketplace in the distance to buy flowers and food for her birthday celebration. I become aware that Roman is here. He's at the little house we just left. The one with the pretty garden I love. He's working. He's a writer and a politician. I can picture him: tall and pale with green eyes and dark, almost black, hair.

His name is Quintus.

I smile down at Lucia, thinking of Roman, that this is our baby, our angelic green-eyed daughter whom we both love immeasurably, but she's not looking at me, she's looking over her shoulder, her face worried. I follow her small, outstretched arm with my eyes to where her tiny finger is pointing.

In the near distance behind us blackish grey clouds plume for miles into the sky and almost seem to be building toward us. There was a loud boom, I didn't hear it but I know it happened. I remember the boom. I remember I felt it. Feather-light ash rains down, covering our arms and hair, our faces and clothes. I watch it cover Lucia's braided hair. It covers everything in sight. Then the sun vanishes, entirely hidden by the tower of grey smoke, and the white stone walls of our neighbor's homes almost disappear as if it were the middle of the night, not close to noon.

We turn and face the darkness that seems to begin rolling toward us like a tide. Inside me, I know death is coming. It's coming for me and for Lucia. Death is but a mile away, and it's racing toward us. I grab her soft hand and we run toward it, back to our house, toward Quintus. Running into the sure face of death, to Lucia's father. Everything inside me as frantic to protect this little girl, as I am desperate to reach Quintus, but her little legs can't run fast enough.

I scoop Lucia into my arms, sprint to our front step and pound wildly on the wooden door until before my eyes it turns to fire and disintegrates beneath my fist. Quintus's face stares back at me from inside the house as the sound of an approaching freight train barrels toward us. Lucia and I both grab onto him just as the super-heated grey wave of ash envelopes the three of us in our embrace.

I sit up so fast I literally see stars, little white flashes of dizziness that burn my eyes from the inside out, and something burns in my lungs. It's a lack of oxygen.

It takes a few seconds to notice I'm back in my room, that what just happened was a dream because I'm still sweating, choking, suffocating, and gasping for air, feeling like I died and am coming back to life.

When something very strange happens.

As I grasp the reality that once my name was Vibia, that I actually died at Pompeii, that I loved Roman who was

Quintus and we had a beautiful daughter, I find myself staring wide-eyed into the face of a person standing over me ...

The person who's been watching me sleep.

CHAPTER 12

At first I didn't recognize the long slender face above me. The sallow sunken cheeks and pale blue eyes, the ones that apparently stared down at me as I slept, and probably gave a glance or two to the butcher knife in my hand.

"Kristina," I say as if I'm telling her her own name as I discretely scoot closer toward the safety of the wall behind me. Kristina, whom I last saw crying onto Shamus's shoulder in the Sheremetyevo Airport as we departed from Moscow. Kristina, who I learn within minutes has never been out of Russia, speaks perfect English, and desperately loves my brother, despite reason and logic, the cup of tea in her delicate hands, apparently for me, the frumpy black-and-red plaid button-down shirt, barely covering the alabaster skin of her skeletal frame. The only button-down shirt he owns. The one I've seen him wear just a handful of times. The one he was wearing the day we left Moscow.

"It's six forty five," she tells me, her accent heavy, but her voice soft, kind. "I know you go to school; I thought I should wake you." Knowing Shamus as I do, her helpfulness only makes her seem more suspicious. But by her keen eyes I can tell she doesn't dislike me, in fact she just might follow me off a cliff if I ask her to. I know this instantly. And admittedly, I'm happy about it, and happy she would have woken me. With the impending apocalypse I forgot to set my alarm clock and being late again wouldn't help my quest to avoid Mr. Envoy at all costs. Yet I decide against thanking her, because the eruption of Mount Vesuvius and my subsequent death by incineration was what actually woke me, and because she obviously broke into my house, and she loves my sibling rival, my enemy. So I just shift my eyes from where her tiny bare feet are standing to my bedroom door, awkwardly a few times, until she turns and walks out.

As I drive to school I reevaluate a few of the choices I've made so far this morning. First, not finding the nerve to confront Kristina about her unlawful entry I'm feeling like a coward, wondering what I'm afraid of. And not eating breakfast as a protest against her cooking it for me may have also been a mistake considering the pain in my hollow churning stomach and how incredibly delicious the thin golden pancakes she called blini smelled. Another potential lapse in judgment—allowing her to stay at my house while

I'm at school all day—isn't sitting well. What do I really know about Kristina? Why would I trust her? But most of all, my decision not to call Ansel is buzzing around like a fly in my mind. I thought about calling him. Really. I even stared at the phone in the kitchen as Kristina took a shower, *in my bathroom without even asking*, knowing I could have called him without her hearing. I wonder why I didn't. Maybe I didn't call him because he told me to. Because I'm too busy building my case for independence on the flimsy technicality that he said to keep an eye out for *Shamus*, not Kristina. Maybe, over night, I've turned from the oldest soul on earth into a cranky infant or a stubborn toddler, or, perhaps, a normal, defiant teenager. And there's something alarmingly odd about being normal.

But despite my morning full of questionable choices, I have to admit that parking my own car in the parking lot of a high school that I attend feels like a victory. A victory, that as I approach the sidewalk in front of the school and spot Jude walking toward me, turns into a triumph. His energetic stride and intrepid eyes contrast sharply to the rest of the students and staff, who trod through the front doors, an ashen-faced sea of the numb and traumatized.

Instead of going to first period we are herded to the gymnasium, where I find myself sitting on the hard wooden bleachers between Roman and Jude, between ease and exhilaration. Between home and adventure. Roman, who somehow found me among the hundreds of faces washing through the halls and seems to be battling an intense fear of not being by my side, and Jude, who is sitting there being Jude, without filter or fear.

"I got in so much trouble last night … definitely worth it," he tells me without any sense of discretion, which apparently causes Roman to need more oxygen and take an incredibly deep inhale as he turns away to look someplace else. I can only imagine what he's assuming that means while Jude starts getting that same "I want to kiss you, I want to kiss you right now" look on his *incredibly* alluring face. And I wonder, as I close my eyes and welcome Jude's soft lips onto mine, once I return from touring the far reaches of the galaxy, if the feeling that I'm cheating on Roman is sitting like a rock in my gut just because he's right next to me. Logically of course, I know I'm not cheating. I'm not with Roman. My brain knows that. But my heart and my body are flipping out. Like two escaped mental patients unhinged and on the loose. They want everything they see. They want to be near Roman, he's their meds, he feels so good, so right, they get the sense he's always been there for them and that they might even actually be addicted to him; then again, they've been off their meds for a long time, so who can really be sure. Then they get totally upended at the very sight of Jude. *They lose their shit.* Because he captivates them, they desire him, my crazy heart and my confused body.

I wonder if Roman has feelings like this? Does he feel like he's losing it? If I'm this torn and confused and don't even know the things he knows about us, he must be about to snap. It must be even harder for him than it is for me. I wonder how he really feels about Ruby? If he's as conflicted as I am, *or more*, how can he even sit there while Jude kisses me? While I let him? While I clearly want him to? When I couldn't even control myself when I saw Ruby with Roman. What if she kissed *him*? If I had to watch her do that? What would I do?

Wanting to get a look at Roman, to see if he seems okay, I turn away from Jude like I'm looking behind me, over my shoulder for some reason. I spot Phoenix about ten rows behind us, surveying everyone below. And since we are arranged according to year from ninth grade through twelfth, Ruby and what looks like her band of devoted tenth-grade misfits are several section over and quite a few rows back, but their glaring hatred at seeing Roman, once again attached to my side, reaches me without a problem. As I turn back to face Roman, he smiles at me. Not too stiffly, or through grinding teeth. He just smiles at me when our eyes meet. Like it's the most natural thing in the world.

"He's great, right?" he seems to push himself to say, referring to Jude, but I don't answer. It's like I'm physically unable to. I can't even smile back, because hearing him almost force himself to say that breaks off an entire piece of my heart for no reason. I start to feel so nauseous I might actually throw up. Like I just cheated on my soul mate while he had to sit there and watch. Is he making himself appear fine with it? To be *happy* about it. And if he is ... why? Is it because Jude is now my new soul mate? And Roman somehow knows that? I start to sweat, as my heart works to pump more blood through my body then could ever be required for sitting on a bench doing nothing.

Between all the feelings in my ever-swelling collection of emotions, guilt is winning out, *by a lot.* If I'm the sun and Roman and Jude are planets circling me, right now all the rest of outer space is a noiseless empty vacuum of guilt. What's even worse is feeling so much remorse when no one is asking you to, when it isn't expected of you but everything inside is telling you it should be. And even more disorienting to know Roman is right here with me, and being so glad that he is, while I'm falling in love with Jude, and enjoying every minute of it.

So I decide to completely ignore them both, because if I don't my head is sure to fly off my body, leaving a giant hole for my heart to escape and run for its life.

I just need to face forward. To try not to think, and especially, not to feel. To zone out. I stare ahead and see what must be every teacher and administrator in the entire staff sitting in folding chairs on a makeshift stage in the middle of the basketball court. They're facing the student body and the hundreds of parents and other adults from the community who showed up. Who look like they don't know where else to go or what to do. I see the pregnant woman from Higgins Market, who always eyes me as I shop; her arms are clutched around her belly and her tears never stop streaking down her face.

First, we listen to a debriefing by Mr. Envoy, a fact-based and noticeably emotionless recap of the events of the last twenty-four hours, the details of what caused the tsunami, how it decimated 2,900 miles of coast from the northern tip of Canada's Prince Edward Island to Key West and as much as fifty miles inland in places, about the staggering number of total known dead, despite the hours of evacuation time—14,400,000—and the even more staggering number of those unaccounted for—more than 112,000,000 either dead or missing and presumed dead, which I work out in my head as about thirty-six percent of the U.S. population. He skips the subsequent rising of the blood moon altogether. Knowing Mr. Envoy, he refuses to assign meaning to something he can't quantify.

Once he's brought us up to speed on all the things we already know, Principal Billings stands up. Resoluteness emanating from every inch of her buttoned-up strikingly moon crimson–colored pantsuit and fancy twisted updo. Utter capability evident in every thoughtful step she marches toward the glow of what seems like an unnecessary, almost inappropriate and very suddenly blazing spotlight at center court. In her most somber and subdued Texas twang and over the ceaseless sounds of sniffling and muffled crying, she reports that likely everyone among us lost relatives and loved ones in yesterday's tsunami. Our fellow students, our teachers and staff lost cousins, aunts and uncles, lots of grandparents, and many friends. A few of the staff lost sons or daughters away at colleges along the East Coast. And some students lost brothers and sisters. "And Draya Stone lost her mom and dad," she says, her voice dignified, remarkably composed.

Lucy and William Stone, Mrs. Billings shares, were on vacation in Cape Cod, celebrating their twentieth wedding anniversary. I look around for Draya but when I don't see her in the bleachers I figure she isn't here, and for good reason.

But then, standing near the exit in front of the brown double doors, I see her. Huddled under the protective arm of an older woman, her grandmother perhaps. The bright eyes and breezy, fearless expression Draya wore just yesterday gone, snuffed out. Like the woman comforting her she looks traumatized, like everyone else.

Traumatized by the tsunami, and haunted by the blood moon.

"And I don't think this is over," our principal feels it necessary to speculate. A statement I find so hasty, and so reckless, my mind starts searching for a motive. A possible reason why she's saying this? *What's in it for her?* "I fear it's only just beginning. We know that's what the blood moon is telling us."

The declaration of her outrageous opinion as unequivocal fact narrows her into my sights. In my mind, we're suddenly the only two people here.

I watch her carefully. Teetering in her stilettos, her carefully coiffed hair frozen in place, as she talks like a war general of "fighting back against the rising tide." The way her large diamond earrings twinkle in her personal spotlight as her smoothly delivered words tear holes through people's minds … and it pulls me to a place where I get very aware of myself in a strange unfiltered way. Where everything is clear. What are thoughts and what are feelings sift neatly into separate categories. Where fears that are my own are easily deciphered from the fears of others.

I want to stand up and say, "Excuse me, Mrs. Billings, but I don't feel traumatized. I don't feel paralyzed … I'm not haunted by the wave or the certain appearance of the moon that followed. And you don't know what, *if anything*, the crimson moon tells us. Your speculation, at a time like this, is bordering on criminal."

Maybe it's me. Maybe no one else is seeing what I'm seeing—the high crime of spreading a fear of ridiculous proportions. Turning a wave of water into eminent global destruction.

Calm down Eve, you're just numb. Tell yourself you're like everyone else.

But I know I'm not. Maybe it's the old soul, or Jude's

influence, or Cian's. Maybe it's because I don't know anyone who died but I don't feel the strong urge gripping everyone else, to push back against "The Events," as Mrs. Billings has dubbed them, and encouraged us to do. I don't see the point in renaming it either, in trying to change it from a tsunami and an unusual lunar phenomenon into a crusade, into "The ominous tragedies that sparked the fight to prevent unknown celestial revenge from initiating human extinction," as she put it.

What? Really Mrs. Billings? How did we get all the way over here?

And suddenly, like a curtain in front of me has been lifted, I see the faces of the terrorized and grief-struck … like time is slowing down to show me something. I'm not *in* the room. I *am* the room. I'm everyone in the room and all the energy in the room and distinctly myself at the same time. I see all things with absolute clarity.

Words begin flowing through me, telling me that it's their rejection of what *is* and insistence on what *should be* instead that's causing most of the suffering … it's their interpretations, even more than "The Events" themselves, that are igniting their nightmare fantasies.

Yes, people died. That has happened. The color of the moon as it pertains to the wave is irrelevant. It's true, those who died will be missed, and not seeing them any more will be difficult at first. But like any time souls leave earth, those

still here must walk through the tunnel of acceptance or their grief will never subside, dissipate back to peace. It's either peace or fear. Whichever is fed will win.

I know these things better than my own name. They sit in the deepest depths of my being. These truths reside in the same mysterious place I visited in my grief, over Roman's death as Samuel, where the truth that suffering and surrender and peace form one fabric. This place, where all truth lives, is inside my very soul.

I look around again and feel like I'm the only living person in a room full of ghosts. But then I notice Roman, eyes squinting, forehead furrowed, thoughtful and concerned, stress radiating from him, and just as quickly as the odd curtain rose around me it slams down, taking the realizations that were so obvious a moment ago and flinging them back out into oblivion at the other end of the universe from where I sit.

An anxious knot emerges in my stomach when I turn to see Phoenix standing against the back wall at the top of the bleachers, vigilant, alert, and battle-ready. But when I glance at Jude, the calm look on his face, how he gives me the most serene little smile, I spin out into a galactic state of unknowing, lost in a black hole of confusion.

But I still know one thing in this moment, surrounded by the huddled, helpless masses. I know this is *not the end of the world.* Unless people get so carried away by their fears and

decide that it is ... then it will be.

I keep what would be my incredibly unpopular opinion to myself when the chance to express our feelings, articulate our worst fears, and feel the support of our community is offered. It spirals quickly into an exceptionally bizarre kind of pep rally as one by one, kids and their parents approach the microphone. It becomes a fake-it-till-you-make-it courage fest to push back, to flush out whatever is causing these warning signs, to be a part of the solution, to show grace on the outside when what you feel is hysteria, to act steadfast when everything inside you wants to collapse into the chaos.

I try to tune out the attempts of one person after the next to sound brave through their out-and-out panic. It's hard to listen to bravery when it's just being faked, when it borders on delusion, when it isn't even being held together with toothpicks, for goodness sakes. I'm finding it hard to summon any motivation to applaud their simulated courage, more self-congratulatory than authentic, self-awarded badges of honor to quell fears they are buying into or allowing their own minds to manufacture and spread like the plague. Fake bravery isn't bravery. It's just another layer of illusion I'm watching come to life.

And it's remarkable, really, how quickly and easily the bravery *fairy tale* is constructed, right on top of the end-of-days *storyline*.

I can't watch any more. At the same time, Roman's arm

catches my attention, out of the corner of my eye. He doesn't know what to do with it, whether he should leave it down, fingers tapping nervously on the bench or cross it into the crook of the elbow of his other arm as it props his chin as he listens. An inch away from mine, his arm is longer and leaner, so much like the arms I remember wrapping around me in my dream last night, almost identical really, but for his paler skin when he was Quintus.

I want to tell him that I dreamed about Lucia last night. I want to talk to him about what happened to us in that lifetime. I want to marvel with him, that we died there, yet here we sit. And where is Lucia? Is she here? Do we know her?

But instead I ask him the most important question, the one question that has been burning my heart more than anything.

"Roman," I whisper.

"Yeah? What's up?" he whispers back, his voice as kind as ever, and I marvel at how unconditional I feel to him, how eternally accepted.

"What day were you born on?" I ask quietly, without turning my head, not wanting Jude to hear what I'm asking. "You never told me," I remind him. He nods again. I guess he knows he never told me. Which makes me a little concerned that there's a pretty good reason why.

"The 21st," he says without looking at me, without needing to witness how sheet-white I turn as the all blood drains out of my face.

"December 21st, 1999," he elaborates, as if he needs to clarify for some reason. He didn't need to. I know now that this is all connected. And I get the sinking feeling I'm at the center of all of it.

When the long strange assembly is finally over, one that ended with a tone-deaf a cappella rendition of "God Bless America" led by high soprano Mrs. Billings stumbling over all the wrong words too loudly into the microphone and most of us spending the entire length of the song trying to figure out whether we should be holding hands, some people walk out of the gymnasium like they're newly engineered robotic optimists, stiffly masquerading as inspired, rejuvenated, roused, ready to face … the end of the world … head on, I suppose, or stop it, though no one could say quite how. Some people walk out only because crawling out would hurt their knees, scarring them further. So they trudge woefully, their powerlessness on full display, their ashen faces more morose than ever, and their silent weeping growing harder to contain.

But of the thousand or so people gathered, I bet not a single one walked out the same way I did. Feeling guilty about "The Events." Feeling somehow responsible.

Suspecting I'm to blame. *Helpless as to why.*

CHAPTER 13

Since I may be the unknowing architect of the apocalypse I figure it's not that grave a sin for me to waste a few gallons of water.

And the sound of rushing liquid, when both the hot and cold sides of the faucet are wide open, gushing into the porcelain sink and the gurgling echo of the tiny drain operating at full capacity may actually be working to calm me down a little. To soothe me into a more clearheaded place. So I let it run.

As I stand in the girl's bathroom and stare into the mirror as it steams over my reflection, trying to convince myself that I have nothing to do with any of the events going on in the world is actually quite a bit harder than it sounds. It's proving to be impossible. But despite the repeated failed attempts, I continue telling myself that just because I'm the oldest soul in the world and Jude, Roman, and I were born on three different ends of the earth on the same day, a day that so happens to be the same day that the Maya calendar ended on in 2012, *thanks Google*, in a year that happened to be the end of a millennium of a modern age marked by turmoil, bloodshed and strife, that just because my grandfather can wake the dead and my undeniably evil brother went missing as the events occurred, that doesn't mean I have anything to do with any of it.

I exhale loudly and feel like it's settled. I'm innocent. Harmless as a kitten.

But the banging sound of the swinging bathroom door as the metal handle slams the wall behind it is only slightly less jarring than the telling latch click of the heavy deadbolt flipping over to the lock position and a distinct reminder that not everyone is convinced that I'm so innocent. Not everyone thinks I'm harmless. Some people fear me. And generally, human nature does a fine job of compelling people to destroy what scares them. Fight or flight. When "flight" isn't a possibility and something is threatening their way of existence, "fight" comes in ready to do whatever it takes to clear the path.

Thankfully for me, this girl's restroom has been designed with a long and utterly useless entry hallway, it's only discernable function is to provide a blind corner really, before the room opens to the main area of sinks and stalls where I'm standing, using my last moments of life wisely to speculate about the details of my impending murder.

Yesterday I'd have said that Ruby Shaw has the face of an angel. A Victoria's Secret's Angel. Despite our less than ideal first encounter and the scowl of disdain she wore, her otherworldly attractiveness was as obvious as her obsession with Roman. But now, as I cower in the corner, surrounded by her goons, I'm not so sure.

"I think the only way she'll leave Roman alone is if we kill her," one of her minions suggests as her fist connects with my stomach sending the air rushing out of my body and sort of scrambling the signal in my already cloudy brain.

"You seem to be confused," Ruby says with an exaggerated tilt of her head. "Do you think Roman would date you? Is that what you think?" She asks me moving closer to crowd me into the corner. Her face an inch from mine, I can see that Ruby is not as beautiful as I had thought she was. Frankly, she's quite hideous I think just as her bony knee comes barreling into my stomach. Once I'm down and she starts whaling on me, I realize it's her words that make her seem somehow suddenly unattractive. It's the unending string of vulgarity erupting from her mouth, the profanities and shocking slurs expressing her highly inaccurate estimation of my sexual experience level. I would try to convince her of my novice status, I might tell her "I've had two kisses in my entire life," if it weren't for her punches mostly landing in the general area of my mouth. I had no idea you could stuff so many different adjectives for promiscuous, all into a single sentence, and really pull it off. But as her surprisingly hammer-like fist connects with my apparently papier-mâché cheekbone she accomplishes it without a problem. Yeah, this is definitely not her first rodeo. I'm so busy losing consciousness, that I barely notice when Phoenix shows up, though she's like a towering giant from the view I have with the side of my head smashed on the tile floor. Even with one eye possibly permanently fused shut, I'm still surprised I didn't see her earlier, when the gang of eight deceivingly talented street fighters disguised as harmless-looking teenage girls first appeared around the corner. But I figure, as the taste of blood rushes into my mouth, that maybe she was hiding in the hallway. Because she's the main event, here to finish me off. I have to wonder if that's really necessary though as the crunch of my arm breaking beneath Ruby's stomping foot brings on a rush of what I can only guess is my body's way of preparing to die, this numbing, humming vibration that reverberates through me and banishes all the searing pain from my entire body.

I figure, that if I could ask Phoenix, if my jaw was in working order, and if she actually liked me, that she would tell me what this wave of relaxation was all about. She'd remember from her past lives, and reassure me that the blissful trip I'm departing on, how I feel like I'm floating farther and farther outside of my pain-ravaged body, is just the release of some psychedelic death hormone. My brain's last gift to my crumpled useless body, intended to ease my transition from vivacious living girl into lifeless corpse. I realize that I'll never get the chance to even ask her when the last thing I see is her rushing toward me just as everything goes black.

It's the unmistakable sound of the ocean, that distinctive docile roar, the noise somehow contained within every conch shell on earth, that first let's me know that I really am dead. I suppose I've even gotten to go to heaven when I hear the rhythmic lapping of small waves coming ashore one after another and the joyous high-pitched squawks of seagulls in the distance and realize that I'm not even worried about being at the beach. A place I hated when I was alive (which for some reason I never did figure out why), that always equaled death to me. But that doesn't matter now. Now I am dead. Nothing matters. And this might be my heaven. Seems God has quite the sense of humor.

When I feel a gentle, salty breeze and the warm sun on my face my happiness at being in heaven, suddenly turns to self-contempt … of *course* I went to heaven! Because I was an exemplary person! I was a model sister, under less than ideal circumstances, and as a granddaughter—well, I'd classify myself somewhere between a blessing of unending abundance and a treasure to behold. And side note, it's quite clear now, because I'm in heaven and probably God's favorite angel to be honest, that I had nothing to do with the deaths of well over a hundred million people just as I left the planet! Bam!! Put that in your pipe and smoke it, Ruby Shaw!

Alright Eve, rein it in. Your self-pitying rant is not very heavenly. Take a deep breath. There, that's better.

Though it was brief, I had a pretty good life. At least I got to finally go to school, and to live in the same place for a while. I even kissed a boy, twice. Or got kissed by a boy … what does it matter at this point?

"What boy? Was it Jude? Or *Roman*?" Phoenix's curious voice leaks into heaven to ask me … which I find strange. Then I wonder if breathing is normal when you're dead? I don't think it is. I distinctly remember breathing a second ago. I'm breathing right now so maybe … *I'm not dead.*

"You're not dead, you idiot," I hear Phoenix snap.

And if I'm not dead I'm not in heaven, so the ocean near me must be real!

I open my eyes as wide as they'll go. See the piercing blue sky above from where I'm laying on my back. I look as far left and as far right as my eyeballs will allow. When I move my fingers at my sides and feel fine powdery sand, I sit up in a breathless huff but I don't get dizzy and my arm is noticeably not broken. Neither is my unharmed, pain-free face. There is in fact a very large ocean in front of me, which I'll deal with right after I figure out how the golden dunes, *Cian's golden dunes*, are everywhere else around me. I stand up, easily, like I haven't just been beaten to within an inch of my life. I spot Phoenix. She's a good twenty yards away, sitting in the sand at the edge of the water and staring out at the horizon like she's trying to solve a riddle. What is she doing here? How did I get here? Why does she have to be so close to the water? I'm trying to force my ocean hating feet to take a step toward her when she asks me a question.

"Do you feel better?" Almost like she actually cares, which strikes me as strange. Even stranger is that she asked me without words. From all the way across the beach, and she never turned around or actually spoke.

She then proceeds to tell me, in the same speechless but fully effective way, *Eve, you are a huge pain in my ass. You know that? You need to figure out how to keep a low profile, do you understand? Quit drawing so much attention to yourself, stop trying to steal the boyfriend of a girl whose hit list you already topped!'*

Alright, that's it, let's get one thing straight, I yell back at her in my mind, surprised how easy it is to communicate this way, how it's light years more efficient than using your voice and words. *I'm not trying to date Roman. I know he has a girlfriend. I really like Jude! It's just that Roman and I ... we're kind of ... bonded.*

Trust me, I know all about you and Roman. Frankly, I know way too much.

Sorry, but it's a little awkward for me too. Seeing as how both you and him know way more about us than I do. And I'm not trying to steal Roman away from Ruby ... I don't think. He just doesn't seem to be able to leave my side.

But you do love him, right? Don't you. She sort of accuses me, to my shock.

I don't reply. I have no idea what loving a boy even feels like.

But then I picture my open hand resting on Roman's back and feel a jolt of contentment-induced euphoria. I see myself grabbing onto him in my dream, *or my memory*, in Pompeii, and feel the simultaneous terror of losing him again, and the rush of absolute love. Everything I felt dying in his arms.

That's a yes; she confirms and finally turns to face me with contempt.

Okay, I don't know if I'd say I love *him. Not in this lifetime yet anyway. I mean, I don't want anything bad to happen to him ... and being with him feels, you know, perfect and everything and I'm sorry but admit it, Ruby is an abysmal next choice!*

Phoenix raises her eyebrows at me.

Whatever! It doesn't matter anyway. He loves Ruby now.

You're right. He does, she responds, her words pushing all the air out of my body. *And I'd appreciate it if you could keep reminding yourself of that, please.* She starts coming toward me without really walking—it's more like the space between us contracts.

Thanks, I will, I tell her. *Just so long as you're okay with me vomiting profusely at random?*

She shakes her head at me, terminally annoyed. Right in my face now. Only her face is higher, because she's at least a good foot taller, and I find it more than a little depressing that here, even in this strange and magical place, where broken arms spontaneously heal and people communicate without talking, I'm still a hopeless shrimp.

Phoenix has a question pinging in her mind like the ricochets of a stray bullet fired into a tank. That I know just by looking at her. An important question. A question she'd rather, apparently, chop off her own arm than ask me.

Did you kiss Roman? she finally demands. *Tell me you did not kiss Roman,* she almost pleads, with the slightest hint of irrepressible fear, a feeling the great and mighty Phoenix appears powerless to conceal. But I never kissed Roman, so her question only makes me picture Jude, and instantly feel the thrill of his presence. Then I picture our kiss. I watch it again like I'm watching a movie. Our perfect, sweet, intoxicating kiss ... the one I had no idea he was about to give me. The one I never wanted to end.

Before I attempt to tell her, Phoenix smiles widely, abundantly satisfied. Frankly, she looks relieved. As if everything is resolved. All is right with the world. I'm allowed to kiss Jude, apparently according to Phoenix. Roman, not so much. Not that I mind kissing Jude, trust me, it's like taking a free ride to the gates of heaven. And Jude's the one I think about constantly. But her having a preference, that's what I don't understand.

Suddenly we're just heading down the beach. The thoughts I was just having have fled my mind. I don't have the slightest idea where we're going but for some reason that's irrelevant. And I'm not sure if the knowledge is coming from her or some place else but as we travel over miles of desert sand I come to fully comprehend that this place, the place I always thought of as the golden dunes, where Cian has brought me so many times, is called Eremis (Air-ah-miss). It's an over world to Earth. Not a world unto itself but a realm that exists like a sheet of carbon copy or tracing paper over Earth, where all non-human forms of living creatures reside that are visible to us under normal circumstances. That a very thin veil separates Earth and Eremis. A bird flies through the sky in Eremis and we see that same bird at the same time fly through the sky on Earth. And that what's done on Earth is reflected in Eremis and whatever is done in Eremis is reflected on Earth. That all humans can easily get here. They just don't know it. Not yet.

I'm being taught that if I could see farther there would be more desert and more dunes, and no matter how far I travel the landscape will keep going, that Eremis is actually unending, when Phoenix comes to a stop and I do too at the same time without any effort or warning. There's something in the sand a few feet from us; it's hard to make out what it is, but it definitely doesn't belong. It's a weapon of some kind, and Phoenix is looking it over in her hands. Like we've been examining it for a while I understand that it's made of materials that aren't from Eremis and almost looks like some type of spearfishing gun, without the spear. In the sand where it was lying, a few footprints suddenly become visible. Then a whole trail of footprints light a path that we follow. The distance we cover appears to be thousands of miles but in a matter of seconds we travel to where the footprints end. The water's edge now at least a few hundred yards from where our bare feet stand in the familiar amber powder. Though there's a great deal of desert between the water and us, it's not hard to notice that the entire ocean as far as I can see is a startling red. Crimson. I notice a river of blood flowing all the way to the ocean out of the body of a massive whale-like creature that's lying dead in the sand, just a few yards from where we stand, whose giant carcass rises some fifty feet above our heads, like a building on its side, some kind of metal rod punctured through the thick wall of rubbery skin covering its monstrous grey body. A perfectly placed kill shot, right to the brain.

I stare up into the lifeless open eye of the dead creature, an eye that's as large as a basketball. It's completely blacked out, like the flat dead eyes of the reporter in the helicopter after the tsunami. But, as I stare into it, the dullness starts to melt away, revealing a brilliant reflective light that shines right at me from deep within the dark sphere, inside the lingering soul of the slain beast.

He tells me he was the last living *Livyatan Melvillei*: a carnivorous whale that ate other whales, and any sharks that had either taken to killing when it was unnecessary or had eaten the flesh of a human. Mel, he tells me his name was, has been around since the time of the Megaladons, the post–dinosaur age sharks that were so mammoth they could kill two great whites with a single bite. And ever since, this important animal has been keeping evil at bay within nature and keeping the strongest in the seas from completely rearranging the order of the animal kingdom; the last predator of predators.

Shamus did this, I realize and relay to Phoenix simultaneously. She nods her head; she knows. She must also be able to see what I see. Shamus, swimming through the water here in Eremis, taking aim at the sacred whale and firing that alien weapon we found, striking Mel between the eyes from a thousand miles away. She must also see Mel's stunned body sinking like a rocket to the ocean floor, crashing with an almost supernatural force, like a detonating atom bomb, just the kind of impact that might cause an 9.7 earthquake on the ocean floor, then being displaced by the resulting explosion of the sea, an internal tsunami that expelled him from the water like vomit, washing him to this his final guarding post. His last watchtower.

I look to Phoenix, this horrifying realization swelling

inside me, and follow her gaze as it goes from the eye of the whale to the sky above us where a countless number of oversized vultures are circling, like a slow-motion tornado, just overhead.

There must be a thousand of them, I estimate, both sets of our eyes to the sky.

Two thousand, minimum. Phoenix seems sure, her voice as grave as the sight of their visibly giant claws. Talons they'll use to hold their heavy bodies in place as they devour Mel. Making the circle of life feel especially vicious today. Even *unholy.*

We continue to gaze upon the monstrous raptors, entranced by how their circling formation morphs into what looks like a choreographed exercise when one after another, they swoop intimidatingly toward us, warning us to vacate from the feast or become part of it. As they more openly and boldly threaten us, Phoenix asks a question that's as ominous as the crosshairs of Mother Nature trained upon us:

You know when my birthday is, she says, like a statement, as the vultures make their final preparations to descend upon the body of this once-sacred animal, this vast, edible aircraft carrier. The animal we can't seem to drag ourselves away from, one sure to feed all the vultures in the world for countless generations to come. Maybe even into eternity.

I lower my gaze to look at her, and am about to say without words that I do not know when her birthday is but I know when it isn't. That I'm certain it can't possibly be December 21, that it can be any day other than that, especially if she was born in 1999, when I see that behind her are no longer the endless dunes but a flat wall covered in white medium-sized tiles.

We're standing in the girl's bathroom. It's the same way I leave Eremis with Cian. All at once and feeling like everything I just experienced might not have been real. Yet I have no injuries to my face from being punched and my arm isn't broken. Ruby and her cohorts are nowhere to be seen, but when I look into the corner, where I cowered as they pummeled me, there's a large pool of thick maroon liquid on the tile and more spattered on the walls. My blood, I assume. And from the dark dried look of it, it's been there a while.

"My birthday?" Phoenix repeats her question, using words this time.

"I don't know," I say—because I don't, and because I'm terrified that I do.

She appears annoyed at having to actually spell it out for me. The frustratingly rudimental details of the space-time continuum and the over world realm of all living creatures that we just visited together and what cosmic link our star-crossed souls have with all of it. By her grimace of irritation, this is boring baby stuff. That the actual adventure and the real mystery haven't even begun yet. And it won't begin until I finally get up to speed.

"I'll give you a little hint … it's the same as yours," she sighs like it should be obvious, like I should have already known, like she's having to teach a Rhodes scholar how to read, and like she has better things to be doing than to be taking me to other dimensions and explaining the ineffable and inconceivable all day long for crying out loud. "Only, and this is where you need to pay attention, this is where things get really interesting, I was born on a whole different continent, in a far corner of the world, in the highlands of Peru … is any of this making any sense to you yet?" she asks rather rudely.

"Yeah, I get it, alright!" I yell. "It isn't hard to figure out." *It's just impossible to comprehend, that's all.* That she's the fourth one of us, born on the same day in what geographically amounts to the fourth remote corner of the world from New Zealand, Mali, and the northernmost tip of Alaska, and I realize at that very moment that while things are odd on Eremis, bizarre, at least they're simple, straightforward. That life itself is infinitely weirder and vastly more complicated here on Earth. I'm either getting answers I don't want or questions that scare me. And all the unwanted answers I do get only lead to an unending cycle of more questions, every one of them more frightening than the last. Like the question burning in my heart more than any other right now.

"So what if I *had* kissed Roman?"

What would happen then?

CHAPTER 14

I don't mind Phoenix's manic hovering, *not really.* I don't even mind her scaring off the few people I may have had a slight chance of befriending, like Draya, or the girl who smiled at me after assembly and quietly introduced herself as Iris. Phoenix is just doing what she somehow knows she's supposed to do, and I have a strange feeling that I need to honor that ... plus there's no physical way I could possibly stop her if I wanted to. And now that I've learned Roman, Jude, *and* Phoenix all have the same birthday as me, that we're probably the four beings of death, doom, and destruction from the four corners of the earth, sent to annihilate the human race, and I'm the kingpin of it all, *the unholy grail* ... well, let's just say I think of her more as a bodyguard than a friend.

The thing you want in a bodyguard, or personal physical

protection engineer, is someone who is no-nonsense. Someone who's direct, who never beats around the bush. Someone with no need for things like kindness or subtlety.

"To be clear, we're not friends," Phoenix explained for example, as she escorted me from the bathroom to the cafeteria. It was obvious she had no plans to answer my question about Roman. I think she may have been punishing me for even asking. And maybe my later attempts at small talk, to suggest we share some feelings about some things we'd just experienced—my near-death, teleportation, giant dead whale and whatnot—were unnecessary. And maybe, like plenty of other people, she just isn't my friend. And although it left something to be desired in the tact department, I guess it was good to find out precisely where I stand. And since she wasn't busy being friendly she could focus on letting people know with her eyes and by the way she walked that she could rip their head clean off their shoulders without even thinking twice or coming to a full stop in the hallway. And wouldn't you know it, not a single soul even glanced in my general direction. Not one hateful sneer. Not one stink eye. And that's a plus.

But since we're clearly not friends, I can't help asking, "So what are we then?"

And I learn that Phoenix and I have what she calls "a working relationship." I'm attacked, she rescues me. I stumble, she catches me. I mention Roman again, she smacks me. "That's how it works." Seems simple enough.

Now she's stationed like a guard in front of my lunch table, the one tucked away at the back of the cafeteria, the one closest to the exit, the one I may have unknowingly commandeered from a handful of freshman boys now sitting on the floor. And yes, having a bodyguard in high school is unconventional. It's dreadfully awkward-looking and a little embarrassing. Nothing about it is remotely normal, which I really dislike. But I did just get jumped I have to remind myself every now and again. It's easy to forget when you just go to another realm and your body heals itself instantly. Phoenix's obvious objective is to intimidate my aggressors and keep me safe so I can fulfill my destiny. And judging by her aggressive glaring at Roman halfway across the cafeteria, he and I being crowned prom king and queen doesn't appear to be part of the prophecy.

Roman looks miserable at what I can only assume to be the table for the fabulous, good looking, and popular, for the souls so self-involved they can pummel me into a bloody heap and then actually not notice when I'm sitting nearby, magically unharmed. And I have to wonder what Roman would do if he knew that a good twenty percent of the people around him had committed an attempted murder in the ladies room earlier this morning. On his soul mate! Or ex–soul mate, I guess. Would he get up? Go sit someplace else?

As I watch him now, his gentle way, that kind smile, I

know that he would.

The funny thing about Roman is, I won't think about him much, but then when he's near me, in the same room, when our identical eyes can actually meet, something in the depth of me, where my dormant feelings for him must reside, is activated, stirred from apparent hibernation.

I have to peer around Phoenix to steal a glance of him and only get the chance every now and again. Once, I saw Ruby pouting her lips at him and batting her lashes in a puppy dog face to which he smiled at her then discreetly turned to see whether I was watching. He rolled his eyes when they met mine, when he realized I saw their gross poo-bear moment, and I gave him a "you made your own bed, buster" kind of look. Another time I looked over and he was looking at me. Staring, unblinking. Ruby was talking to another boy at the table—Sam I think, who's in Philosophy with me. The one who asked how they'd prove how many lives a soul has lived. She was laughing wildly at something Sam was saying, tossing her hair, flirting shamelessly, but Roman never flinched. As long as she was preoccupied, it seemed, all he cared about was staring back at me. And I felt there was something he was trying to tell me something through the invisible superhighway from his eyes to mine.

"Eyes forward," Phoenix demands, snapping her fingers in front of my face when, of course, she catches me and Roman fixated on each other. But just as I'm looking away I see Ruby squinting in my direction in disbelief. In horror. She cocks her head and furrows her brow, craning her neck to try to get a better view of me around Phoenix's imposing stance. Ruby's sheet-white face reveals terror and a wires-crossed kind of confusion from the message her eyes are sending to her brain, the message that I'm somehow impossibly uninjured. I smile smugly and give a little wave, delighting in her distress, just as Jude scoots into the seat closest to me, a shiny apple in his hand. If I had to draw a picture of the apple of the tree of knowledge, I'd model it after this one.

"Hey, you," he says, taking a juicy crunching bite of the flawless green fruit.

"Hi," I say, searching deep into his smiling cobalt eyes as he chews. If there's someone I'm *supposed to be with*, I certainly won't mind if it's him. If he's my new soul mate, I can more than live with that. I just want to know for sure.

"What?" he asks with a smile as I study him.

"Nothing," I say, marveling at how it only takes a couple seconds in his presence for me to forget there are any other people on the planet, much less in this very room with us. Isn't that what a soul mate is, I wonder.

That's when the news of the unimaginable starts coming in. It begins as a trickle. The first rumblings of what would horrify the world more than anything yet. First a solitary girl running by us in tears.

"What did she say?" Jude asks Phoenix.

"It sounded like … lost a baby—her aunt did, I mean. Her aunt Celine … miscarried, I guess?" I'm coming to understand that Phoenix's senses are heightened, like a hunter, at all times. That's how she was able to accurately decipher the jumble of high-pitched sob filled words as the girl sprinted by us in a blur toward the arms of a friend.

People's phones begin to ring, more and more people begin to weep and cry. At least three people just pass out cold on the linoleum.

By the end of the day it's a rushing broom, sweeping every last shred of rationality out of the whole of humankind as it's confirmed that, as the blood moon returned to the sky at midday, every pregnant woman on the planet either miscarried or delivered. Every infant stillborn.

"The Unthinkable," combined with the runaway train that "The Events" had so quickly become, makes one thing abundantly clear by dusk of the second day of school. The end is upon us. Or so most people are certain. The return of the crimson moon seeming to seal the deal, signing humanity's death warrant, injecting nearly all of humanity with a high-octane serum of mass hysteria and unhinged pandemonium.

Like everyone else in Rugby, I'm locked in my house watching the news. Committed to watching the TV until it goes out. Surprised there are still broadcasts, power, and a signal with what's happening around the world. Every city, every town is in chaos. The words "martial law" are a punch line by 10 P.M. This is the end, the part where people do whatever they want—shoot them, they don't care, no one cares about anything. There is no means or method to control people who think they have nothing to lose. Our economy swan dives into free fall. Our government abandons ship, our elected leaders scatter, they disperse, like roaches when the lights come on: Washington is reduced to one guy, a senator from Oklahoma, a young handsome man standing on the steps of Capitol Hill, staring at the columned beast of a building before him and the massive looming white dome above it. Like he's seeing the frailty of civilization, the flimsy projection of strength and order; he stares unblinking, then raises the Glock in his right hand and blows his brains out. Even if he knew he was on live TV, I don't think he cared. The president? Our commander-in-chief? Yeah, no one knows where he's at ... probably mainlining whiskey in a bunker under a mountain somewhere. There was no plan for this. There never could've been. You don't prepare for the end. You prepare possible ways to keep doing everything you've always done, but you don't prepare, you can't prepare, for the absolute end of that.

There are riots everywhere, of course, looting and arson, plundering, pillaging, and raping, but the news stops covering all of that to focus on the speculation—the attempts to explain "The Unthinkable" that begin to flood in from around the globe.

Some say it's, "aliens just getting a jump start on the eradication of our race for when Earth becomes their new home in the next day or two." A few experts believe it's "Mother Nature doing what needed to be done, a one-time, sweeping population control measure, completely out of our hands." Still others say it was "a rare fetal pandemic." One expert theorizes it was "some kind of elaborate terrorism, an undetectable electronic pulse, which caused the spontaneous end of every pregnancy on earth." Which quickly spirals into the same mysterious electronic pulse theory with a different perpetrator, "a mad scientist whose developed the ultimate biological weapon for a rogue nation," after which global finger-pointing ensues. Accusations go from Russia, China, and Iran to Germany, Israel, and the United States in a matter or hours. There are fistfights at the UN. Diplomacy, as we know it, has ended.

And of course, there are the religious scholars. Like Professor Marcus Joplin, whose voice I recognize as ranting during the coverage of the first blood moon, who struggles to stretch the possible interpretations of ancient prophecies of religious texts in an effort to tie "The Unthinkable" back to his whole God-is-so-mad-at-us-he's-ending-the-world theory. My personal takeaway from him is that the book of Revelations technically says nothing about anything that could remotely be confused with "The Unthinkable." He mentions that in one breath and then dismisses it in the next, so he can continue to argue his same point.

Then another man says something that catches my attention. His name is Swami Nanak, a guru from India with a thick grey beard, long strands of brown wooden beads around his neck and a serene expression that looks like a smile even at rest, just like Jude's does. "The ultimate truth," he says, "is that humankind needs to work out its karma," and I almost feel like, *wait, I knew that.* Maybe they're just replaying something I already heard, I think, when the more he goes on, the more familiar it sounds. "It's time to see if we are more evil than good or if we are more good than evil. The score is being kept, as it has always been, only now perhaps no new souls will come for this fight, no babies will be born or even conceived until our karma is worked out here on earth, once and for all. Everything that is, is as it should be." His translucent green eyes are like Cian's and his words are a lightning bolt that strikes the top of my head. *That's it! That's what's going on.* Every inch of my body from my neck down to my ankles floods with chills, then all my flesh is covered with goose bumps.

That's the truth. And that's why I'm here. For the battle of good and evil. I've done this before ... in another lifetime. Now, it's my soul's job to ...

"That's horseshit." Kristina doesn't mind telling me what she thinks of the swami's theory and chasing my sudden stream of consciousness out the window.

Kristina, who was disappointed not to find Shamus here

when she traveled thousands of miles to visit with the awesome news that she's staying forever. Kristina, who I'm starting to suspect, has no where else to go and I wonder if is this how it ends, feeling suddenly alone, abandoned by Cian, locked in my house, with Shamus's misdelivered mail order bride, as humanity decides to burn down the world?

Really? This is how it ends? Yeah … really. Maybe it is.

And I start to get very scared. My chest feels tight; my throat too tight to breath, and air doesn't seem to be able to reach the bottom of my lungs any more.

But by several days later, in Rugby at least, things have stayed rather quiet, or so it seems. I'm busy being shocked and feeling slighted, that my second day of school, ever, was also my last. School was cancelled "indefinitely." While I'm busy pouting other people are being more productive, gathering to pray and helping one another stay positive. Maybe they were onto something with all that fake bravery—it seems the tide of hysteria, at least in our little corner of the world, has turned. I suspect it may have something to do with our resident pregnant woman, Valeria, and how she's still pregnant, her baby-to-be healthy and very much alive.

Our local news promised not to do a story on her, for fear of putting her and the baby and Rugby in the spotlight at a time like this, when the rest of the world has gone mad. She's just in the spotlight in Rugby. In fact, she's all people talk about.

It's now common knowledge here that the baby is just fine, Valeria is six months along, doesn't know whether it's a boy or a girl, doesn't want to find out, and doesn't want to think of a single name until the baby is born. She likes the romance of choosing a name after she meets the baby. Valeria's all into romantic things like that. Like when she persuaded her lawyer husband, Porter Danton, that they should leave their sophisticated life in San Francisco to raise bison on the prairies of North Dakota when neither of them had ever lived outside California or stepped foot on a farm. I imagine her sometimes, in her stainless steel and granite city loft, sitting on a white mohair sofa wearing designer yoga clothes, pouring over the cozy pictures in the L.L.Bean winter catalogue, dreaming of all things flannel and the pretty sweaters she'd wear, and I wonder at what point the isolation of the Plains states, the hundred-mile drive to any decent shopping and the endless steaming heaps of bison poop finally set in.

Even the biggest, coziest sweaters can't hide her overwhelmed look, the shocked, polite stiff smile always fixed on that tiny porcelain face. But she is really adorable in those sweaters, and now she's also kind of a shrine of peace and calm in Rugby, and we're all glad she's here. Her pregnant presence makes everyone feel like maybe things really aren't as bad as what's being reported. Maybe here, in the geographic center of North America, in our little slice of the Great Plains, we can be safe from the chaos unfolding in the cities. We're certainly safe from things like tsunamis here in the precise dead center of this vast continent. And we have "Val," as she goes by, so we know, or can ignorantly speculate, that there must be plenty of other pregnant women on the planet. At least a few anyway …

At least we hope.

CHAPTER 15

It's been one week since the tsunami as I sit on the couch in the middle of the day, watching TV, which Cian would not like much. But Cian's not here. I don't know when he'll be back, I don't think it'll be any time soon with all the death and destruction and I have a sudden need to know and understand as much as I can about everything happening in the world. I'm also kind of relaxing. Chilling. While someone else cooks meals around here for a change.

Kristina, who, like a spy, knew to kill the porch light so the neighbors wouldn't suspect she was breaking into the house, and who didn't have to look far to find the key so cleverly hidden under the pot next to the door. Kristina who had all the lights out, she eventually told me, so she could surprise Shamus in his bed, to my utter revolt, wearing her favorite shirt of his, beyond gross. Kristina, who doesn't like things she doesn't understand. Things she doesn't understand scare her. That was why she put Cian's Phoenician carving halfway across the room and facedown on the carpet—it was "looking at her," and she didn't want that "scary little thing" to be anywhere near the pretty three-thousand-year-old Egyptian ceramic bowl she loved. The one she thinks a stack of salty golden potato latkes looks so nice in.

And you know what? I agree … about the latkes, but I struggle to process how Kristina doesn't mind being alone with Shamus, evil incarnate, but is scared of a tiny statue. When she asked if she could stay until he gets home I told her that she could if she agreed to keep cooking and to stop asking me where Shamus was exactly and when he'd be back.

And the woman can cook. And as it turns out, I'm a much bigger fan of Russian cuisine than I realized while we were in Moscow. Kristina insists that's because we ate the "disgusting tourist food they serve at hotels," which I'm coming to understand is not even in the same universe as "real Russian food," as Kristina says. Like her mother makes. And having her here, cooking meals, taking care of most of the chores before I have a chance to notice they need done, the chores that have been mine since I was old enough to say the word "soap," I have to admit, is really nice. Apparently I've been in major need of some serious mothering. Cian doesn't talk about my mother and I don't ask. But I do know her name was Evelyn, that I was named after her. That's about all I know. I was almost never around other kids and it didn't occur to me that they all had a mom and a dad and not just a grandfather and a brother until I was old enough to also realize that it didn't matter much. Because I had Cian, so I never felt like I was missing anything.

But Kristina is full of questions that she can't believe I don't know any of the answers to. She can't imagine how I don't know anything about my birth mother and biological father and keeps asking me the same things in different ways, thinking that my memories are just repressed and if she finds a more clever way to ask she can somehow excavate the information from the lost recesses of my brain, some dusty file cabinet hidden in the back of my mind will magically open if she pries hard enough.

"She died during your birth, does that sound right?" is flung at me before I even wipe the sleep from my eyes or take a bite of my farmer's cheese blintz with homemade applesauce.

"I don't think so—I mean, I don't know," I say, and decide against telling her that nothing sounds familiar about even having a mom or dad. None of her guesses ever hits a nerve.

"It must have been a tragic accident. Tell me, is Cian your mother's father?" she asks for at least the third time, her brow furrowed as she investigates.

"I don't know. He never told me."

"And you never asked!" She looks at me like I'm an alien

in a human suit when I shake my head no, indifferent, then smear gobs of jam onto the crispy yet chewy bread things she just took from the oven.

"You're getting fat," she informs me like she's telling me I have brown hair and I just nod in agreement. I have gained a few pounds. I can tell by how tight my jeans have gotten around my backside and by the fact that I actually feel the need to wear a bra for the first time in my life. I look noticeably curvier. But she just cooks and cooks, three or four meals a day, and snacks, and everything she makes tastes *so good.* Most the time I'm not even hungry but end up eating it all anyway.

"Maybe I'm just filling out?" I say with my mouth full.

"That's just another way of saying you're getting fat."

"No, I think it's different," I say. "You know, when it's just certain areas ..."

"Nope. Sorry. You're wrong."

"Okay," I concede, knowing I'm still going to eat everything she cooks.

I like talking to Kristina. Yes, she's too direct, and overly honest like Phoenix, but not so uncaring and robotic, in more of a harshly opinionated way that I find oddly nurturing. Like someone who cares enough to tell you that you look horrible today, then cocks their head with genuine concern and asks what's wrong. Someone who complains on and on about vacuuming or doing the dishes but smacks your hand away whenever you attempt to help. Like she's always trying to tell me, "you know what, I hate your living guts but find you totally worth caring for."

Which, actually, feels really nice to know.

The thing I like best about Kristina is her advice. Though I obviously question her taste in men, somehow I like hearing what she has to say about love and relationships, and everything I tell her, it's like she's really been there and seems to know just how I feel. And since Roman and Jude have both stopped by—separately, thank god—several times over the last week it didn't take her long to begin to form her opinions about each of them and the whole situation.

"Is good what you're doing to them," she told me once when Jude left a few minutes before Roman's truck pulled up.

"What do you mean? What am I doing?"

"You're the queen, they have to fight for you. To the death."

"I'm not sure they're fighting for me, actually. Remember, I told you. Roman has a girlfriend. And I don't think anyone has to die for me."

"Oh *dushka*, you are so naïve." She calls me that a lot. *Sweet innocent girl.* I play dumb and she assumes I don't know what it means.

"What girlfriend?" She smiles wickedly. "She does not even exist to him." Kristina completely dismisses Ruby as nothing more than a ploy, an act, a ruse. "He just wants you to know that other woman desire him and to think you can't have him, you know, so that makes you want him even more. But he can't hide in his eyes how he feels. How he wants you. That he could never imagine his life without you. Lots of married Russian men have girlfriends for this very reason. You know, to keep the romance with their wives."

Of course some of her commentary, while fascinating, doesn't really apply to my situation, but other parts seem to back up things I had kind of suspected. Like Roman and Ruby's relationship, and how it doesn't seem to mean anything to him. *Not really.* And the way I've started to think about Roman more and wanted to spend more time with him ever since Phoenix told me that I wasn't allowed to, but of course, never told me why.

"Whichever one of those two boys steals your heart away, it will kill the other. Trust me." She says as she peers out the curtains at Roman walking up the driveway toward the door. When I don't say anything, because her words feel terrifyingly literal, she gives me a big hug.

"This is not your problem, *dushka*. The men must often die for their women, for the right woman, this is since the beginning of time."

"Okay. Can you make me that delicious potato pie thingy?"

"*Da*," she says. "And it's called *babka*. I'll make it for dinner. Invite Roman." She sets off for the kitchen after planting a little kiss on my forehead. Besides being an affection person, she's always trying to teach me things, little words here and there. I don't tell her that I can speak Russian better than she does.

"I like Roman for you," she tells me just after he leaves as we sit on the couch at midnight with cups of hot herbal tea and these little cookies I assume she makes with the help of fairies out of pixie dust, sugary air, and fluffy clouds. "He's so handsome. Is like a real grown man should be. Strong, quiet, and very sexy."

"You know Roman is seventeen years old, right?" I ask her, surprised.

"No!" she exclaims in disbelief. "I thought he was twenty-five, even maybe twenty-seven."

I get that Roman carries himself with more self assurance than any teenager I've ever seen and can't very well hide how intelligent and thoughtful and wise he is, but still, her estimation that he's closer to thirty than to my age is a little ridiculous.

"Okay, first of all, why would I hang out with a twenty-seven-year old man?"

"Why wouldn't you?" She's so baffled I don't even know where to begin.

"I just wouldn't," is all I tell her, realizing that she might be around twenty-five herself, that I don't know how old she is, that she might be a lot younger than my thirty-five-year old brother, and that I might insult her. "People here, especially teenagers, usually date someone around the same age."

"Oh, that's funny. Well anyway," she continues, "*Eve-y, solniska*," whenever she calls me *Eve-y sweetheart*, I know she's about to tell me something she feels like she has to tell me but what I might not want to hear. "Listen, I think Jude is a sweet boy, he's cute and I see how he makes you laugh, but to me, I don't know, he's very different, I don't know what it is, but I don't think he's for you. There is something there, yes, something maybe special I think, but what is it I'm not sure. For you I feel Roman is …" she pauses, trying to find the English counterpart of whatever word she wants to say. "Roman, for you is … *rodstvennuyu dushu*," she says finally, but never telling me what it means, because she doesn't know how to translate the Russian equivalent of "soul mate."

I don't think to play dumb. I'm too shocked, too busy wondering whether the fact that Roman and I are soul mates, or have been for hundreds of lifetimes, is actually that obvious? And for the moment I forget how perceptive Kristina seems to be about what's going through my head, how I'm some kind of open book to her, and my face instantly gives me away. My face tells her that I already understand exactly what she just said.

"You speak Russian," she realizes out loud, the same familiar dread in her voice and her eyes I tend to cause in people, hijacking all of her at once. And I watch, as her fear of things she doesn't understand devours her entire personality, and with it, her reflexive affinity for me.

CHAPTER 16

The way Kristina drops it so easily, like it never happened, is unsettling. Her obvious shock, how the terror and alarm I distinctly saw on her face just dissolved into a stiff smile as she quickly cleaned up the cookies, then made an excuse about being exhausted and went to bed. And what troubled me further was the feeling that the Kristina I'd gotten to know and really like would have interrogated me for hours from every possible angle with questions as to how I could know Russian when Shamus doesn't, where I learned it, from who and when, how this might tie back to who my parents could be and why on earth I hadn't mentioned it earlier. It was almost as if the Kristina who instantly liked me was being silenced by another Kristina, one who desperately feared me. And I know from the words that flowed through me in the gymnasium that fear can win. And it *will* win, if it's fed.

"Where's the inquisition!" I want to scream at her the next morning as she wordlessly cleans the kitchen from top to bottom.

"You don't need to do that," I tell her instead, as she fanatically washes the front of every cabinet door with a bucket of bleach and steaming water.

"It's fine. I don't mind," she chirps happily, sounding like a different person altogether. And for some reason, it scares me deeply. Watching her furious scrubbing is like watching someone cleaning up a crime scene. Frantically and methodically getting rid of any trace of evidence after a murder.

Or before one.

That's the reason I find myself knocking, and then pounding rapidly, on the enormous iron front door of Phoenix's house that, I'd say, classifies as a castle.

Kristina's turning tide of feelings toward me was disturbing and it didn't sooth my worried mind when after sterilizing everything in sight, she vanished into thin air. I couldn't find her anywhere, despite scouring every inch of the small house for over an hour, growing increasingly uneasy with each passing minute. There was only one thing more unsettling than the heart-pounding suspense of not knowing where she was and that was the festering idea that she was hidden, that she was there, lurking just out of sight, preparing to take me out. That, and the sudden sneak-attack thought that maybe she wasn't alone, that for all I knew Shamus was home … that he could have been there all week, chased me from the only real home I've had. So scared I never looked back.

"You have two boyfriends and you ran to me when you finally got suspicious of your strange uninvited houseguest who just happened to show up for the apocalypse?" Phoenix concludes after she opened the door to find my anxious face and giant duffle bag stuffed with all the clothes I could fit into it in under a minute, the bag that's about to topple me over. "At least you stayed long enough for her to fatten you up a little bit but you're still too weak," she observes of my slightly softer, somewhat curvaceous body while poking her finger deep into my puny bicep before grabbing the heavy bag off my shoulder and tossing it inside behind her, flinging it, like a pack of gum that slides a good thirty feet across the black and white checkered marble into the grandly appointed far reaches of the unending foyer.

"Ouch!" I exclaim, rubbing my feeble arm.

She glances behind me, surveying everything in all directions. From where her front door sits at the top of a steep hill she appears to look thoroughly over the vast property in matter of seconds, through all the levels of manicured gardens from the grand marble fountain down the long hill of stone steps and the half-mile driveway that winds down the grounds of the estate before pulling me inside and closing the massive door.

"You know what," I start as she begins walking away and I follow her, "why does everyone keep calling me fat? I'm blossoming okay, and I don't have two boyfriends, I don't even have one, technically. Okay, Jude and I may have kissed two or three or … fourteen times actually but we never said we were going out. It hasn't even come up so I'm not his girlfriend, *I don't think* and Roman and I are …"

She stops and stares back at me. I swallow hard as I think she literally looks like she's gotten stronger, even taller in the last week and I don't want to get smacked but I have a feeling lying to her isn't a good idea.

"I don't know what we are," I state truthfully, to which she doesn't appear to approve or disapprove of particularly. "And how do you know about my houseguest?"

"Do you think I would let you out of my sight, after having to save your life—once, that you knew about?"

"So … then, you're watching me I take it? You've been spying on me?" I ask. Sounding a little like the invasion of privacy bothers me. Which it does.

"I'm sorry, would you rather I just let your brother kill you in your sleep?"

I didn't nit-pick about privacy any more after Phoenix informed me that Shamus *had* been back, that he returned to the house, with Kristina, while I was out late with Jude on the night of the tsunami. That he was there, that they were both there in his room, when I got home. That the phone rang earlier but stopped and only started ringing again at 12:55, when I pulled up after dropping off Jude, and that Shamus left, in the middle of that night, while I slept.

So many questions darted through my mind at once. Did Ansel actually know Shamus was there? Why did Shamus leave? Where did he go? Why did Kristina stay?

"Why didn't he kill me in my sleep when he had the chance?" is the one question I ended up wondering frantically out loud.

"Because I wouldn't let him," she said, then told me how they faced off silently over my sleeping body, how she was standing in front of me when he walked in my room at 3 A.M. How he backed out, slowly, "evil seething from his dark eyes," and left on foot, to where his car was parked about a mile away and drove west. "He hasn't been back since. Not yet, anyway."

Within a few minutes of knocking on Phoenix's door I know two things I didn't know when I left the little house on East Gate Drive with the undeniable feeling that my departure was permanent. First, privacy is vastly overrated. And second, *I have to learn to fight,* which hits me like the same bucket of cold water in the face when I decided I had to go to school and when Shamus peeled out of sight and everything inside me knew I needed a car.

Naturally, I find myself in her basement, which is more reminiscent of a dungeon for how cavernous and primeval it feels, standing in nothing but the black sports bra and small spandex shorts she handed me.

I wait on some kind of platform, that feels spongy and springy under my bare feet, and look at the unending racks of strange weapons fixed to every wall, and what look like battle flags from ancient wars with crests of kingdoms past hanging from the thirty-foot ceiling overhead, as Phoenix and her entire family look me over like a specimen of beef. And not, apparently, a prime cut of it.

"Excuse me, is that an actual pirate flag?" I ask, overly polite, to mask the terror that surges through my cells at the sight of the massive black tattered skull and crossbones banner hanging prominently above the titan-sized limestone fireplace. "Sort of screams authentic to me. I mean, you know, of course not a big deal at all … if it is … pirates are people too!" It all makes sense now—Phoenix is actually a pirate, from a whole family of pirates, and I'm about to be plundered.

What I assume to be her parents for their striking resemblance are standing close to Phoenix. They study me, pointing and making quiet comments to one another in a technical way. Though no one answers my question, both the "mom" and "dad" give me a genuine smile, quelling some of my anxiety. Their eyes are distinctly gentler and kinder, wiser even, without the intensity of Phoenix's, but they have the same thick dark hair as her, and side-by-side, they look like three towering majestic trees plucked from the Amazon.

One of her younger sisters, I figure, walks over, grabs my hand, lifts my arm up, parallel to my shoulder and shakes it gently.

"Hi," she says, lowering that arm and grabbing the other. "I'm Sequoia."

"Hi, Sequoia. Question for you."

"We're not pirates," she says sweetly as she grabs my shoulders turning me a hundred and eighty degrees and then back around after about a ten-second beat.

"No I was wondering what this was? Sort of an assessment of muscle condition or like a public shaming?"

But I just get another kind smile as a response. "Have you ever exercised at all," Sequoia asks, not judgmental, but with a strange sort of removed objectivity. By her face, she appears to be no more than ten.

"Define exercise," I say, thinking of mentioning all the walking I've done since I learned how around age one but I decide that using my legs and body to get from one place to another won't actually count for anything by their definition.

"You know, agility, sprints, interval training, martial arts, sparring ..."

"No, none of that. Not ever ..." I inform her and she looks a little worried, which worries me. "I do walk really well," I tell her, and she smiles again.

Phoenix, I learn, has two younger sisters, Sequoia and Zeppelin. They're fraternal twins. Sequoia has short black hair cut straight across the bottom of her neck and Zeppelin's is long and dark tied into a huge topknot the way Phoenix wears hers. They both have Phoenix's distinctive caramel-colored eyes and her staggering height, already taller than me by several inches. Unlike their parents, Sequoia and Zeppelin are very "American" in how they dress and speak. They were born here when their mom and dad, Fiorella and Maricielo Torres, moved from Peru just over a decade ago, "Because the forest told us to," Fiorella explains when I ask how exactly they ended up moving to Rugby, North Dakota, from the other side of the planet. Not something you hear all the time.

"We always knew Phoenix was special," Maricielo elaborates. "When she was young many of the great shamans of the Amazon would come to see her; they called her "Little Ayahuasca," which means "vine of the soul," as she was born with an unbroken connection to what they call "Mother Ayahuasca," the one source. When Phoenix was six she told us that the trees and the forest had said we were to come here, and so we did."

"I got pregnant within a weeks time of arriving," Fiorella continues, "We'd been hoping for another baby since Phoenix was born. We got two." She beams at her twin girls. "We knew we were being given the sign that we were on the right path." Then she asks, "I'm curious, how did *you* end up here, Eve?"

That's kind of a long story to tell in my underwear.

"Can I have like a robe or something first?" I ask. "Like a T-shirt possibly ..."

"After you fight," Phoenix says. Zeppelin comes onto the mat and positions herself across from me. She bends her knees and positions her arms into a fighting stance. I stare across at the somewhat smaller version of Phoenix.

"I'm not just going to fight her," I declare. Not because I'm afraid, but because I'm not fighting anyone yet. I don't know how. No one has ever taught me.

"Don't worry, she knows what she's doing," Maricielo assures me.

"I have no doubt she knows how to fight," I say. That's obvious just by looking at her, though that's not my objection. "The problem is, *I* don't."

Apparently however, as she suddenly lunges at me I see her coming without a problem and have plenty of time to anticipate her jab, effortlessly blocking it with my forearm, and I realize that I *have* been taught to fight. Just not in this lifetime.

The wide smile on Maricielo's face appears to shock Phoenix as much as me. She watches her parents share a satisfied look.

"That doesn't prove anything," Phoenix announces,

unable to hide her worry that it does prove something.

But before I can wonder what that something might be, Sequoia is suddenly circling her long leg through the air on its way into a roundhouse kick to my face and I find myself grabbing her ankle like it's the easiest thing on earth, spinning it and flipping her to the ground like she's made of rags, without even thinking, just like when I drove for the first time or understood Kristina's Russian. The same barely conscious way I took the entrance test, operating on complete and total autopilot. As I unhand Sequoia's foot I see her stunned face and think, there it is again. That look. That fear. The wide-open, disbelieving eyes. The gaping mouth, all breathing halted. I'm coming to recognize this same familiar look, given to me with increasing frequency, hanging desperately on the faces of those who have no logical way to interoperate or explain what they just experienced.

Phoenix's eyes narrow. Rage radiates from her every molecule. Her fury is aimed at me, is the result of me, being me, doing what I do, which, apparently, is anything I want or need to do at any moment.

"She's truly incredible," Maricielo proclaims.

"Because she can fight better than a couple of ten-year-olds?" Phoenix spits as she lifts her shirt over her head and stomps over to me. My heart is in a sudden drag race, instantly screaming from a steady resting cadence to a breakneck sprint. Every inch of her is lean muscle, everything but her arms and legs covered with ancient writing, tattoos too intricate to decode in my fear-racked state. She's a gladiator and the living Dead Sea scrolls all at once and she wants to fight.

"In one life," she says, casually, taking her stance across from me, "I forced my own sister to chop off my head and bury it separate from my body, it was my dying wish, that it wouldn't be done by my legions of enemies. In yet another life, I remember summoning the bravery to remain silent … as I was burned at the stake," she finishes with the authority a person who can claim those words would use.

My mind is swirling. Terror is seeping in. I have barely enough time to square myself to her before I'm laying flat on my back, gasping for the air that was forced out when she swept my legs from under me in less time than it takes to blink.

"Explain that," Phoenix says to Maricielo, her breathing unchanged.

"Fear entered. She became afraid. The way she was in the bathroom. Too much time to anticipate and no idea yet what she is capable of."

Choking as my breath returns I sit up and raise my hand. Maricielo nods to me, like I'm free to speak whenever I'm able to do so, which takes another minute.

"Um, what am I capable of?" I ask, and his eyes sparkle at my question. The way Roman's did when I told him I felt I'd always known him. I stagger to my feet.

"Everything," he declares, causing Phoenix's obvious outrage to boil over. She takes another sudden swipe at my feet, but this time, I see her coming from a mile away, the same way I did with Zeppelin, and I jump to avoid her cutting my legs out from under me again.

From the air I look down as her leg sweeps by. The distance from where I seem to hang, floating, down to the mat appears to be a good ten feet, maybe more. This must be my imagination. Then I look down at my own body, and for a split second, I see myself wearing a bright yellow robe and carrying two swords, crossed valiantly in front of my chest. I'm perched high atop a ten-ton war-elephant. In front of me I see a smoldering foreign countryside lined with unending rows of fast-approaching warriors. Behind me, are a few thousand men; I'm the one leading the charge. Then suddenly I see Phoenix's long leg as it finishes its frustrated circle of death and returns to the other in crouching position beneath her. I hurl myself from atop the elephant and land on the back of an enemy fighter, slicing his throat in one swift motion. I watch blood rain upon the shocked faces of the men nearby. Then I land again, this time on the fighting platform, the two swords and yellow robe are gone and my feet hit the taut canvas with an incredible boom, my knees bent and left arm raised, ready to block the punch Phoenix throws, right fist coiled to deliver the one I throw that connects to her jaw and sends her flying off her feet. A surreal image, Phoenix crumpled against a wall several yards away.

"Lady Trieu," Maricielo puts his hands together and bows to me. "Said to be the Vietnamese Joan of Arc. You rebelled against the Chinese forces that sought to conquer your homeland in the third century. Phoenix tells me I was your older brother, and tried to dissuade you from revolt … and failed, of course." He smiles at me.

I watch as Phoenix gets to her feet. I'm not sure what fate said about this moment, but her burning eyes confirm one thing: this wasn't part of her plan.

Though she's reluctant to leave the fighting platform and at first puts up a childish fuss, Phoenix allows Maricielo to escort her to the far side of the cavernous room.

They stand under what look like relics of the holy wars of the twelfth century, and I realize they are: the battle-beaten sword, a silk banner with French writing, a dragon shield and shining armor, all relics from the Crusades. Maricielo talks privately to his daughter, his voice a distant murmured mix of Spanish words, some French, and an indigenous Peruvian language, one spoken long ago in the Amazon Basin.

I'm enraptured as I watch her lay bare her vulnerabilities, crying to him, evidence of their ironclad father-daughter bond in every word of their exchange.

"You understand Urarina?" Fiorella guesses, sounding unsurprised.

"I'm sorry she's so upset," I say. "I didn't mean to cause

this." My way of answering her question before returning my focus to Phoenix and Maricielo. It's more fascinating than I'd have imagined seeing Phoenix so fragile. Her bravado has been masking an Achilles heel I now see exposed, inexperience handling feelings, especially those of frustration.

"She's a new soul," I guess.

"Yes. And this is good for her, Eve. You are good for her. *Su sufrimiento es opcional*"—suffering is optional, her repetition of what Cian had so often said to me confirming that I'm in the right place.

"It's time for Phoenix to grow," Fiorella says, her tone almost joyous.

But my eyes are fixed on Phoenix, on her anguish as she roughly wipes the tears from her eyes with the back of her hand, tears she resents, insolent tears that infuriate her for how they insist on falling, even existing.

"I would think that you, of all people, would understand about the option to suffer life's challenges." She seems puzzled by my apparent lack of transcendence, confused by my obvious concern. Because she knows I'm the oldest soul on earth and thinks I should understand a transformation when I see it. Maybe one day I will, but right now I just wish I could take back how I upended Phoenix's world in an instant.

Fiorella's tilted head and deep gaze tell me she's waiting for me to explain why I don't seem to truly understand what I'm witnessing.

But watching Phoenix drown in a stew of her own helplessness, frustrated beyond words, all I can think about is Shamus, and the feeling I get when he seems preordained to usher obstacles into my world, that his life's purpose is, quite simply, to destroy mine. I want to explain to Fiorella that maybe not all suffering is created equal, that some excruciating things provide no option but suffer.

"You know," I say, "even when you've been taught this from the time you're little, as I've been, as Phoenix has, it's still so hard to remember, impossible really, when things seem designed so specifically to harm you, brought to you for the express purpose of causing you to suffer. I'm sorry, but true suffering never feels optional."

"Until you realize that all suffering, *especially true suffering*, is the whisper of the angels, the very hand of God, tapping you on the shoulder, trying to wake you."

"Wake you from what?" I say, my voice tempestuous.

"From your dream of yourself, Eve. Like Phoenix, the *warrior,* the *fiercest fighter there is* ... the *unbeatable.* Do you know, I have prayed for this moment to come? That as soon as possible she would suffer this enormous crushing blow."

"Why?" I'm as baffled, as maddened, as I am intrigued by this mother who clearly loves her daughter and isn't a masochist as far as I know, yet is deliriously pleased by her poor girl's bitter anguish. *Why?*

"So she may see that even if she's beaten, if she loses a

battle, that she does not vanish in a cloud of smoke. That if she's not the best, she does not cease to exist. That she may then begin to unlock herself from the prison she's been building for lifetimes."

Talking to Fiorella, I realize, is like having a conversation with the female counterpart of Cian, the only other person who continually tells me things I struggle to understand, one right after another.

"What prison?"

"The prison we create. We build it brick by brick out of all the things we cling to, hoping they will define who we are. Our *mind* creates an *identity,* 'Phoenix the ultimate warrior,' which is then defended by the *ego,* which says, 'Eve can't beat you, no one can beat you.' When your battle record is who you are, losing means losing yourself. You see? The mind, the identity, and the ego, they yearn to exist, they beg, they shame us, they trick and deceive, but lies do crumble. It's been said, Eve, that three things cannot long be hidden ..."

"The sun the moon and *the truth,*" I finish the quote; suddenly very happy I ended up here. Thinking that maybe my mother would be just like Fiorella.

Maricielo, compassion and pride for his daughter evident as ever, ushers Phoenix back toward the group. She's still visibly rattled, her whole world just flipped upside down, but now at least she looks focused and composed.

After we spar for more than an hour—me, and the girl who was actually the soul inside the body of Joan of Arc, among other famous warriors—the unanimous conclusion is that Phoenix and I are equally matched.

Incredibly. Painfully. Equally. Matched.

Every time I land a punch or pin her to the mat she lands one or slams me right back. I fly into a wall only to drive her into one the next minute.

But Phoenix is determined to prove she has the edge. So we fight until Maricielo turns out the lights. Then, because she insists, we go one more round, in the dark, our senses heightened. Finally Fiorella yells at us to stop: "Wash up! Dinner waits for no warrior!" she beckons, on her way to cook.

Upstairs, where I soak in a grand marble tub on golden claw feet that rests in the center of my enormous bathroom, a space larger than my entire house if it were one giant white marble room with sky-high ceilings and no walls, I feel content—sore and battered, but content in my battle-ravaged state and almost delight in watching little trails of blood seep from my gashes and cuts and dance their way to surface of the crystal blue water.

I stretch out as far as my hands and feet can in both directions but still don't reach the ends of the massive pool-like tub I'm floating in as eucalyptus and lavender and some

South American miracle minerals soothe my aching body, dissolving what feels like centuries of tension I'd never realized I'd been carrying in every cell.

With every exhale I sink deeper into the warmth of the water and in the knowledge that I'm safe, that maybe I'm even safe for the first time ever, safe in the new knowledge that I can protect myself, and safe here with Maricielo, Fiorella, Phoenix, and her sisters, who seem to have spent their entire lives preparing to defend me.

PART THREE

STARS ALIGN AND FATE WINS

CHAPTER 17

If I'd known that Phoenix lived in a sprawling castle with a bedroom fit for a queen, where there were heavy down blankets in fine silk duvets bearing my monogram, piled on a breathtaking canopy bed with Spanish linen curtain draping all sides, and a wardrobe of the finest designer clothes, all for me, I'd have come to live with her much, much sooner.

I'm so glad that I came to Rugby, I think as I look down at my feet and marvel at the swirly golden "E" delicately sewn on the toe box of the butter-soft royal blue suede slippers as they walk the fifty yards of imported Persian rug–lined oversized hallway from my suite to Phoenix's.

I knock on the tall mahogany door, knowing by the certain quality of the silence that follows that she's in there. That she heard the knock and knows it's me. Freed of the fears I once had of her, I enter without being invited.

"What do you want?" she asks, her voice sullen. "Because I know you don't need anything," she snaps from where she stands staring out her wall of windows that, like the perfect watchtower, overlook the vast property and even give her an unobstructed view of the entire town of Rugby, through Initium Valley, all the way to the buttes and beyond. Where the Great Plains appear to roll on into infinity.

So *that's* what she's afraid of. Now that it's clear I can fight just as well as she can, if it's her job to protect me and I don't need protecting, what do I need her for?

"Personally," I say as I enter and close the door behind me, "I think it's going to be much better to protect someone who has the ability to take care of herself." She whirls around to sharply disagree.

"What would be the point of that? It doesn't make any sense."

"Normally it wouldn't, I guess," I agree as she turns back to the window. Her eyes dart nervously over the scene before her, hoping there's more to my statement. "But in this case," I go on, not knowing but hoping the words just come to me, "whatever is going to happen, whatever we're going to have to do, whatever we're going to face, doing it, *surviving it,* is going to be beyond anything that's possible. And so even if I can do everything that's possible," I realize the same time the words leave my lips, "I still won't be able to do whatever I need to do … because I can't do the impossible … *not without you.*"

Phoenix turns around, face red, eyes bloodshot, tears once more running down her cheeks. How important it is, I realize, looking into the vulnerable face of such a powerful being, for people to actually get the chance to fulfill the purpose burning in their soul. And how gut-wrenching if they don't.

"Hey, the jungle knows what it's talking about," I say. Her eyes soften as the hint of a smile becomes visible. "Come on, Little Ayahuasca, I'm starving, and from the glorious smells coming all the way up these thousands of stairs I've got a feeling I'm going to like Peruvian food even better than Russian food."

"Eve," Phoenix calls to me after I've started for the door, her tone serious.

"Fine, I'll try not to overindulge, no promises!"

She smirks. Then her smile falls away again. A somber mood blankets us.

"Listen, and understand me when I tell you, you are *good, not evil.* We aren't the four beings they'll say we are. Okay? It won't be true." She searches my eyes and I nod. "Even though it's what the whole world will think," she divulges, almost tentatively, searching my eyes once more.

But I can't nod. I can't agree. Because I don't understand, because, "How can the four of us look so much like something we're not?"

"I don't know," she admits, her bravery radiating in the face of the unknown.

What if we *are* the four beings? What if I don't believe her, if I believe that maybe, just maybe, we *are* what they'll say we are!

"But I know this, we're not. And that if you don't believe that," she warns, "then we're *doomed*."

We stare at one another, engaged in visual chess—she's trying to ascertain what's going on in my head, what I believe, and I'm trying to excavate her brain, to find out whether she's harboring a way out of this.

Our intense moment is interrupted when Maricielo knocks on the door, then walks in with Jude in tow.

I'm not surprised Jude snuck over to see me. He did that constantly over the last week. But I am surprised he made it.

Maricielo and Fiorella tell us over dinner that Rugby, like every other place on the planet, is slipping into chaos. Rumors of checkpoints have been cropping up.

"The exact purpose of these checkpoints, we don't know yet."

"Maybe it's just a curfew," Zeppelin speculates, which causes her parents and everyone else to pause and consider. She's quickly earning her spot as the most formidably intelligent ten-year-old I've ever met. Sequoia, as the kindest.

"You might be right, Zee," Phoenix says to her sister's unabashed delight as we all return to our delicious meal of sweet fried plantains and slow-roasted pork. But an unexpected knock on the door pulls us all away from our plates and into our heads, wondering who it could be.

Gaebe, my philosophy teacher, is maybe the last person I was expecting to see. Maricielo and Fiorella don't know him so they don't let him in, forcing him to deliver his message from the door, which is open just enough for us to hear him and still be able to slam and bolt it shut at the first sign of a threat.

"Evening everyone, I'm Dr. DeCuir," he announces. Not Gaebe, not "hey everyone call me Gaebe,' but *Dr. DeCuir.* "Eve," he greets me especially as he looks over our faces, and though I'm the only person here he's actually met it still increases my growing unease.

"Is there something you need to let us know? We just sat down to family dinner," Maricielo informs him with the kind of gravity that "family dinner" only garners in people's fairy tales of suburbia but galvanizing me nonetheless.

Family.

That feels surprisingly good. Catches me off-guard just how good. But understandable, I suppose, if the beyond odd micro-family you really have has abandoned you at the end of the world.

"Pardon the interruption," he says to Maricielo, as he looks us over. "It's nice to see some people holding down civilities, things like family dinner at a time like this," his once-delightful drawl sounding more nefarious as I begin to suspect that his "lecture" might have actually been a press release.

And all at once, the moment he and Roman shared that look and the way Roman seemed to help him sell Animus starts a beating in my head like the rogue pulse of an alien trapped inside me. The list of things I don't know suddenly far outpacing the number of things I've figured out, and shooting to the top of the swelling list are two doozies. First of all, what does Roman have to do with Gaebe, and second, what exactly does Gaebe have to do with Animus?

After Gaebe attempted to confirm that he'd see us all tomorrow morning for our Animus testing, he left and we sat back down to dinner. But I wasn't hungry any more. I couldn't eat a bite. I couldn't think of food when I couldn't get two other things out of my head—

Family and *Animus.*

Family. *Where is my family*? Cian and Shamus? And whatever happened to *my* mom and dad? Who were they and what were they like? Were they protective and inspiring, compassionate, and a bit overindulgent, like Maricielo and Fiorella?

And Animus. *Animus is upon us*, an apparent beta test of humanity's last hope, beginning in Rugby, as it's the only place on earth where civil society, or the appearance of it, still exists. Rugby, the place I just had to get to. Where I dragged my "family." The place I call home, where Animus will begin. Where I sit around someone else's dinner table calling other people "family." Because they're the only people who will protect me from Animus and what it will reveal to the world, I think, looking into the faces of Phoenix, her parents, and her sisters, who taught me more about family in one day than any family I've had. The Torres family, with parents who raise their children, a mom and a dad, a husband and wife, who love, trust, and admire one another, who move heaven and earth for their girls, the beloved daughters, siblings who fiercely adore each other.

A real family, who would all kill or die to protect each other. Is this my family? Maybe it is. Maybe it's the only family I have now.

A few hours later, it's the middle of the night as Jude and I lay side by side on my bed, on my new princess bed, as I wear my new imported cashmere sweatpants and matching stylish hoodie given to me by my new family who are asleep in their own royal rooms nearby or busy plotting our elaborate escape like the Von Trappes, apocalypse version.

I've never laid on a bed with a boy. I've never laid on a bed with *anyone* for that matter. Cian, that I know of, does not sleep and as far as Shamus goes, I kept my door securely bolted to keep him out.

"Eve," Jude says, his voice relaxed, soft and sleepy.

"Yeah?"

"Do you think I'm different?"

"What are you talking about?" I ask. "Of course I think you're different." I smile, but seeing no smile on his face in return surprises me.

"I've felt … unusual … my whole life, like I'm from another planet." He looks at me. "Sometimes it gets to me … being different," he says, scanning for feedback, but with Jude being from another planet having crossed my mind, I try to help without lying to him.

"There's nothing wrong with being different. I *like* different, in case you haven't noticed." I tell him.

Seeing it's not the answer he's looking for I keep trying: "Okay, no, you're not like anyone I've ever met, and yes, you could be an alien, no doubt about that. It's one of my absolute favorite things about you," I say, my eyes locked on his as the volume of my thoughts of kissing him goes from a conversational whisper to the finale of Beethoven's Fifth Symphony. But seeing Jude, how he's still *in it*, as Cian says, still contemplating what sounds very important to him, I restrain myself.

"I would just love to know that there are more people like me out there," he says, staring at the scene painted on the ceiling twenty feet overhead, the battle of the fallen angels. Maybe that's what he is … some kind of angel.

"Where is this coming from? Is this about the test?" I ask reluctantly, not wanting to talk about Animus, knowing Jude knows nothing about … *anything*, really. Jude thinks I'm normal. Jude doesn't know any of the things Roman told me, about our past and who I am, he knows nothing about Cian … I've never even told him about Eremis!

Before I have time to determine that that seems incredibly unnecessary, that there's no good reason I haven't told him about Eremis, Phoenix comes barreling in.

"We need to go to Eremis. Like right now."

CHAPTER 18

Astral travel can be unpredictable. We didn't arrive on the tranquil beach like I did when Phoenix plucked me from the bathroom floor. We didn't show up in the middle of the dunes either, as I have done every time Cian has brought me here.

This time was different. After the room around us melted away I saw cracked and scorched earth beneath our feet where amber sand has always been.

Now, as I look around, nothing I see remotely resembles Eremis. All the land is flat, an unending plain of dried-out earth. And it goes on, just like this, into the infinite. I see no dunes anywhere at all, and no sea. And the usual piercing blue expanse above is now a dark vast nothing. A black void. No moon and no stars, just some circular wisps of grey and white dancing on a colorless sheet, a shadow of nonentity that stretches to the visual end in all directions, like someone has pulled down the curtain of space and buttoned it to the horizon.

Is this Eremis? I place the question in Phoenix's mind.

Part of it, she replies, looking over my shoulder.

I hear it before I see it, the thing she's looking at. I hear the low humming sound. It's constant, like a noise that's just part of the air. It's so fully invasive I hadn't noticed it at all, like the low buzz of an aquarium in your bedroom. But when I turn and see the hive, like a cone-shaped Tower of Babylon rising from the parched dry earth into the above and beyond, swarmed by clouds of insects … *bees*, I think and become aware, the way you do in Eremis, that the steady droning noise flooding this unfamiliar habitat is how the buzzing of bees sounds when every last bee in the universe is gathered in one place.

I become aware that Jude is not beside me and I think maybe he didn't make it here with us. I worry he's in another part of Eremis.

He's right there, Phoenix tells me and I see him instantly, far in the distance, looking straight up from the massive round base of the hive. Then he turns toward us. Without even moving or the passage of any time, Phoenix and I are now standing right next to Jude at the base of the hive.

Looking up, at the billions upon billions of bees swarming

overhead, encircling the towering clay giant. The top is beyond where the eye can see. There is no top, I become aware. The hive, like the desert and the sea, has no end. If there were an atmosphere to leave, which there isn't here on Eremis, the hive would stretch out of the atmosphere, through all of space and keep going beyond the farthest reaches of infinity. Eremis is funny like that. The confines we're accustomed to on Earth don't exist here, yet strangely, when you're in this place, it isn't hard to process. It all makes perfect sense. Like understanding that Jude knows all about Eremis, that he was born knowing how to get here, and how that doesn't shock me the way it would if he told it to me on Earth.

On Eremis everything you need to know comes into your mind and as it does it all makes sense in the vastest scope. Nothing like the way things are perceived on Earth, in dribbles of confusion followed by the smallest revelations of finite information about the immediate and containable. Yet this all-knowing awareness I get in Eremis feels like a human's more natural way of being. Slipping into it is effortless.

She's dead, Jude thinks into our minds and I see a visible wave of sadness emanate from him. It's a single pulse, a spontaneous detonation of energy. A colorless formless blur from within him sent floating out in all directions.

As it passes over me a streak of grief runs through my heart and with it the knowledge that Queen Rahda is dead. She was the last of all the queen bees.

And then the knowing begins. The gradual enlightening descends into me. It comes straight from Queen Rahda herself, the way it did last time from Mel, though I can't see her the way I saw him because her body is deep inside the hive.

She tells me that some of the ancient cultures on Earth like the Mayans and Sumerians, Egyptians and others were in touch with the energy of the universe. They lived in complete awareness of the cosmos and the infinite as their feet walked upon the earth. And though isolated from one another by geographic space and eons of time, they all said the same things.

One of those things was that the bee is the sacred symbol of the soul. These ancient cultures knew that bees represented the human soul and its journey on Earth. Understanding the connection of our realms they paid homage to the bees in their art and culture for this reason.

Then I learn that the colossal hive before us is the Colony of Queens.

And that the entire Colony of Queens, along with every queen inside, is invisible on Earth for their safekeeping and ours, to protect humanity, to maintain the unbroken ancestry that reaches back to the time life first appeared on Planet Earth.

She tells me more than half the population of queens has always remained inside the colony at all times. A rigorous system has been in place since the beginning to ensure that half of all the queens are out of the hive, and the other half are in the protection of the Colony of Queens. They can only do their work and create new colonies when they are outside, but they have always been completely safe inside.

But the safety of the colony has been violated. That's why we're here.

The number of queen bees has been steadily declining for the last two centuries of Earth time. The ultimate purpose of human life on earth is love, and with the bee being the sacred symbol the human soul, as humanity was growing further from its true purpose the queens were dying off.

Rahda has existed since the beginning. She was ancient like Mel. She was the first queen bee, she explains, and though she didn't die like the others, her death caused all the souls to leave the bodies of the unborn humans on Earth.

You said you didn't die like the others. How did you die? Jude asks her.

Instantly Phoenix, Jude, and I are on the opposite side of the colony. There is a copper-colored canister of some kind at Jude's feet. Then it's in his hands. As he rolls the strange cylinder over, examining it like the weapon Phoenix and I found, I understand that this object isn't from Eremis.

Shamus left this behind, I tell them as I become aware of it and that in Eremis, you can bring things in with you but you can't take anything out.

I see what happened to Queen Rahda. In my mind I watch

Shamus climb the towering hive. When he reaches a place where chunks of clay have been carved out he uses some kind of pickax tool to finish burrowing a tunnel then he climbs into the hive and disappears from my mind. But I know the canister, which is now in my hand, was filled with the deadly toxin Shamus used to kill Rahda, the last queen bee and cause "The Unthinkable." I become aware that objects from Earth can't come into Eremis. I also learn as I study the smooth metal item that this canister, the pickax, and the spear gun are from another place entirely. That Eremis is just one of fourteen planes. Eremis and six others planes exist over Earth and seven other realms exist under. That these weapons came from an underworld, a shadow place beneath Earth called Agora, a dangerous, violent plane where all demons and the depraved manifest, where the air is salty as seawater, filled with the sweat of desperation. Agora is an unending filthy street market where everything and everyone is for sale and warfare and mass destruction are freely peddled to the highest bidder.

I see Shamus there, cloaked in black, his hand covering his mouth as he makes his way through a sea of frantic bodies. Then I watch him buying the canister of poison from a vile and sweat-soaked homunculus without eyes.

Then suddenly, I'm standing in the sweeping familiar golden dunes, Phoenix and Jude at my side, the copper canister no longer in hand. We're at the mouth of a cave with a granite boulder, bigger than a city bus, blocking the entrance. But I see inside with my mind's eye and understand that Phoenix has been bringing in weapons and stashing them since Shamus first disappeared. Shamus isn't the only one who knows how to get to Agora. I see Phoenix there, following behind Shamus, tracking him. I see her buying a sword with a blade on each side and a small handle in the middle. *The double-edged sword.* It's in the cave with countless other weapons. She's built an arsenal of retribution. Everything we'll need for a battle we must fight in Eremis.

What were the dunes one moment turns to limestone before my eyes and we return from Eremis but we're not standing in my bedroom; we're in the middle of the fighting platform in Phoenix's basement.

I get the feeling it's a hint. That it's time to prepare for battle. I also get the feeling that time is running out.

We now know about Shamus's role in causing both "The Events" and "The Unthinkable," that he has plunged humanity into madness.

We also know that right now, right here in Rugby, Animus is upon us.

I feel a frantic sense of urgency. I can see that Phoenix does too as she quickly gathers all forms of training equipment to the platform. Even though it's almost two in the morning we break out into a spontaneous and intense training session, picking up right where we left off just a few hours earlier. So much revealed to us since then, everything moving rapidly and the distinct feeling it will only accelerate from here on out.

Once Jude watches us go a few rounds, he wants to spar against Phoenix.

Classic Jude. No fear.

Like me, he'd never actually fought anyone before but unlike me, I worried, he doesn't have the advantage of being a human data bank of seemingly unlimited and ready-to-use skills acquired over more lifetimes than any other person on the planet.

But what he lacks in experience he makes up for in raw instincts, sheer athleticism, and the unlimited power of fearlessness. He catches on so quickly, like he does with everything else. To watch his mind learn, at the inhuman pace that it does, is to witness the impossible. His intuitions are razor sharp. He never once questions them either. Ever. I see zero self-doubt in him right now. Which apparently, Phoenix points out, is the holy grail of dispositions for all forms of battle. Though she did out-match him most of the time at first, he always gives her a run for her money and fully assimilates the lesson in his mistake, allowing him to progress so rapidly, it seems like he'll be evenly matched with us within a couple of hours.

Now it's almost six in the morning. Jude is asleep on one of the many plush sofas as Phoenix and I battle on, unable to sleep and not knowing what else to do. Something became obvious about an hour ago. I may be the oldest soul on the planet but we discovered Jude is hands down the fastest learner when at that point he became equally matched, both with me and with Phoenix. Then he promptly passed out. He fell fast asleep, quickly and soundly, as if we weren't the last hope for a world careening into calamity. I couldn't tell if he was just exhausted or somehow wasn't worried at all.

Right about now, all residents are supposed to start reporting for their testing, according to Dr. DeCuir. But Maricielo tells us, as he sets down a large tray of breakfast, that we wouldn't be going anywhere this morning.

"A little civil disobedience is good for everyone in the system," he tells us.

Then he quickly settles into training mode.

"It's time to sharpen your mind, Eve," Maricielo says. "I believe you can harness all of your latent abilities with the proper focus." He takes us through a complex series of maneuvers, like a swift and deathly ballet, his loud rapid commands rising above the clanging sounds of our heavy steel swords repeatedly slamming against each other.

When we finally stop to eat something, we go back over what we know.

Then Maricielo tells us about a scenario he now believes,

that Animus will be a tool used to manipulate humanity into accepting a new one-world regime.

"They'll galvanize what's left of humanity with the promise of bringing order, an end to the chaos. Then whoever is behind the test will try to quietly move into power, using the scientific findings as some kind of template for a new world order."

I say it's an interesting theory. I think it's a definite possibility but don't know.

Maricielo tells me that Phoenix has detailed for him all six-hundred-and-thirty-three of his past lives. He's researched and studied each of them with fervent intensity.

"In the seventeenth century I was a privateer accused of piracy and murder. Several years ago Phoenix and I relocated and excavated a wealth of treasure, *my treasure*, that I hid on an island in the Caribbean during my former lifetime as Captain William Kidd."

"Treasure island ..." I infer, and he doesn't deny it.

"The flag is real," he tells me, "but the murders were not mine." He explains that in those days piracy was a subjective matter, "one of shifting borders, allegiances, and opinions." But it's where their wealth comes from, the fortress we now sit inside and the endless resources and weaponry. Riches he believes were destined, for hundreds of years, to remain unfound to be available to fund this very cause to the end. That's why it's this lifetime that inspired his theory about Animus.

"You see Eve, my execution is proof of the effectiveness of turning things and people into political tools to manipulate minds and push an agenda. The only reason you'd want a test like Animus is if your ultimate goal is to polarize the world to the point of no return so you can reorder it to your liking. That's what someone wants. And I would bet you all my treasure still sitting off Madagascar—" he winks—"that they've given some scientist the long-sought validation of his research and of course the promise of power. It always comes down to the promise of power. As Kidd, that was my undoing."

Trying to dig deeper, he asks about Gaebe. I tell him everything I remember him saying during class.

"He was a research biologist, he told us. Nobel Prize–winner," I say. Maricielo thinks on it.

"What else?" he asks.

"He told us about another scientist, Dr. Alastair, who created Animus. Gaebe referenced the tree of knowledge of good and evil, he asked if Animus is the apple and whether we should eat it. He asked that as he stood at my desk looking right at me. He was asking me, specifically."

"What did you say?" Phoenix asks me.

"At first I said I didn't know. But he kept standing there, pressuring me to give some kind of answer, and I said that maybe we were supposed to eat it."

Phoenix gives Maricielo an odd look. "What?" I ask, but

neither answers me. Phoenix just goes over to wake Jude, and Maricielo looks lost in thoughts.

"What are we doing?" I ask him.

"She thinks he needs to know what he is. She thinks it's time to tell him."

Jude and I sit across from Phoenix and Maricielo. Phoenix launches in before I have time to wonder what Jude is, what kind of soul, and what it will mean.

"Jude, I was born knowing things about people. For example, I've known about Eve my whole life. That I needed to find her and would one day help protect her ... I knew who she was." She pauses. I haven't told Jude about being the oldest soul, I haven't wanted to and I'm not sure why. Thankfully she doesn't mention it. "And I've always known about you, Jude."

"Why?" he asks.

"Well, as you might have already suspected, you're different," she starts to his visible dissatisfaction. "It's because you're a very new soul. Completely new, in fact. The only brand-new soul on earth. You're unlike anyone else in the entire world," she says, like it's miraculous but all I see in Jude's face is concern. I think of what he told me last night, how he didn't like feeling different. "You'll always be different from everyone around you, you'll never meet anyone like yourself," Phoenix continues. Jude's brow furrows—he had so hoped to find others like him, and she just told him, in no uncertain terms, that there are none.

That's when I see the spark start to go out. The brilliant pure light that is Jude, that radiates from his being, fades, then dims a little more and then vanishes—it's like watching an open portal to the heavens slam shut.

Phoenix, not seeing what I see, not knowing what he told me, goes on:

"Less than once a century, there's the birth of a Star soul," she says, but I can tell he isn't listening, not in the intense way he usually does. I don't think he's listening at all. "There hasn't been a soul like you born in more than a hundred and fifty years. Not since Abraham Lincoln. Jude, you've never incarnated on earth before, you're here, like every Star soul before you, to flip the world on its head. Star souls bring revolutionary change; they affect the existence of humanity at its core, and they do it in a single lifetime, they come in, almost from another planet, look at what humanity is doing with the freshest kind of eyes and have the power to shift our trajectory when we need it most."

"Eve, that's one of the reasons you're so drawn to him," Maricielo says.

"What do you mean? Why?" I ask, not really liking the sound of that.

"Because you've seen many times what Star souls do and you know, on some level, that you need to align with him."

I don't like this conversation, and I'm glad when Maricielo stands up to signal its end. I don't like it for what it seemed to do to Jude, how it broke his spirit. And I don't like how it makes me feel, like maybe, in some unconscious way, I've been using Jude. The oldest soul on earth could certainly take advantage of the newest if she wanted to.

It makes me feel sick to my stomach.

I need to clear my head. I need more sustenance and extreme hydration. So I walk into the kitchen. I overhear Zee's high voice, shrill in disbelief when I reach the top of the basement stairs.

"Roman's got to protect her!" I hear Zee declare, "Because she's *scared*."

"Poor Ruby," Sequoia comments, a lightly sarcastic bent to her words.

I was already in a bad place when I left a broken lightless Jude falling back asleep in the basement only to walk upstairs and find out that Roman has been staying at Ruby's house full-time. I haven't seen him at all since I got to Phoenix's and figured that was because she seems to move heaven and earth to keep him away from me. But as usual, I hadn't been thinking about him, I hadn't placed him anywhere else in my mind, least of all spooning Ruby to make her feel safe in what I'm certain is a room that contains an obnoxious level of pink and more than a few stuffed animals. Turns out Sequoia and

Zeppelin are the same age as Ruby's younger sister, Talia, who's been in their grade since kindergarten.

"Talia is great," Sequoia tells me. "But Ruby ..." she goes quiet. Even Sequoia has nothing nice to say about Ruby.

I just have one question.

"Why does Phoenix keep Roman away from me?" I demand of any of the three Torreses in the kitchen who will answer me. "I know there's a reason; it's not fair to keep me in the dark like this," I add when no one answers. "I'm tired, I think Jude just died on the inside, my other soul mate, my love of lifetimes is sleeping at the home of my sworn enemy and frankly I have less than nothing to lose."

The girls promptly disperse, Sequoya followed quickly by Zee, leaving me to stare into the face of Fiorella, silently begging her to level with me and simultaneously communicating how fully unprepared I am for practically anything that she might say.

She studies me lovingly for a second. Assessing my most critical needs. Then she pours me an extra-tall, extra-cold glass of the most delicious water I've ever tasted. She takes a bowl of freshly cut extra-juicy watermelon out of the massive stainless steel fridge. She places it on the counter and pats the soft down cushion of the nearest cozy high-back barstool and I plop down and melt into it, like I've never felt the relief of sitting before.

"You know what," I say once I'm off my feet, had a few

sips of water and with a mouthful of watermelon. "Never mind. Don't tell me. I don't want to know."

The very subtlest of smiles sneaks onto her face as she studies me—it's a look that's one part burning compassion one part maternal understanding and all parts ultimate wisdom. Then she declines my last-minute request and tells me anyway that in this lifetime, Roman is not my fate.

"You have much to do for this world. You and Jude both."

"But not Roman?" I ask. She combs my ratty hair out of my sticky face of dried sweat and watermelon juice. "I can't understand why he told you about the long romantic history the two of you share … something just doesn't make sense …" she says, like she's trying to figure it out herself, before walking out of the room.

"Get some rest," she tells me as she goes.

I lay down in my bed to close my eyes for just a minute and fell into a dead sleep. It was early evening, sometime before Jude woke up from when he'd fallen back asleep downstairs.

I don't know when he left to go back home but the next morning he was gone. The rest of us woke to the sound of incessant pounding. Like the heavy iron front door might not hold back whatever wanted in.

That was the moment our civil disobedience caught up with us.

CHAPTER 19

A model of calm, the residents of Rugby look ready to take part in what we've been told is both an "incredible opportunity" and a "mandatory directive."

A mandatory opportunity.

All we have to do is give our DNA samples and allow them to be used for some shadowy purpose we are not being made aware of. So, fairly straight-forward, I'm thinking, as hundreds of familiar faces walk toward a building none of us have ever seen, which in a town as small as Rugby, is beyond disorienting.

The modern facility is several stories high, made of concrete and metal, without a single window. Like an aboveground bomb shelter. I'm struggling to conceive how it landed on Boulder Avenue when I wasn't looking. We're all struggling, I can sense, but we look calm, filing forward like lambs to the slaughterhouse. Except for Jude, who isn't here with us, so I don't know how he's feeling right now. I don't like not knowing how he's doing. And what I like even less is the pit in my stomach. The one that holds the guilt. And how it's bubbling over right now because I never told Jude the truth about me and I should have. I know what *he* is, after all. And he'll soon find out about me. And I'm certain he'll feel betrayed, like he hardly knows me, the way I feel now watching Roman walking toward the same building with his arm around Ruby, comforting her. I could use some comfort about now. I wouldn't mind being tucked safely under Roman's arm.

From the sheer scope of the operation in front of us, the "Animus Task" looks like it's been up and running for years. The infrastructure that is in place boggles the mind. Once we enter the building we're herded into a vast lobby where an attractive woman with reddish-brown hair is on hundreds of TV monitors. She waits patiently for everyone to finishing crowding in. This is not a recorded message. She can see us.

"My name is Sourial, and I believe that everything happens for a reason," she proclaims, then goes on to tell us, quite convincingly, that this "information science" is called pheumachronology, which means "soul age," and its inconceivably incredible discovery led to Animus, the genetic test.

"Pheumachronology for world peace," she says and because of Maricielo my first thought is—okay, tell me how.

But she doesn't. She just declares that if there's even a chance that this human endeavor will somehow stop whatever cosmic process that's been set into motion, if it can somehow stop more "Events" and more "Unthinkable" things from happening, then we are obligated to try it.

"It's our opinion that Animus is the answer and that in future generations your soul age—your IN or 'incarnation number'—will be just as meaningful as your current life age or name. And because your IN is just as unique and important to you as your own name it should also be as openly shared. In keeping with this open spirit all IN numbers will be made public from the beginning."

She goes on to tell us that they have the capacity and equipment to test every man, woman, and child and the resources to do it in just a few months. As proven by the footage of an endless stream of staff, vans, equipment, and other buildings like this one, all bearing the dark glowing seal of the Animus Task. The ancient Celtic Triquetra, the symbol for soul, three points of a Celtic trinity connected by an inner circle.

I look around the lobby and see this symbol everywhere but no explanation on how it will create peace.

Less than an hour later I stare into the stark face of the poor girl who administered my test as she stands in the doorway struggling to breathe.

"Payge," I say, getting her attention. "Come in here. Close the door," I tell her, and she immediately does.

"You're not on the list," her hushed, shaking voice informs me from her safe place next to the closed door, far away from me.

"There's a list? What list?" I ask but she shakes her head no. "You're not supposed to tell me?" She nods. But it looks like she can't physically hold it in if I keep asking her to tell me. "Please Payge, I need to know."

"The list of numbers. There are new soul numbers and old soul numbers and you're not … it doesn't go that high. And your number …" She trails off, looking at me like she might pass out just being in the same room.

"What's my number? Tell me about the numbers and tell me mine, Payge."

"The old souls start at three hundred lives. In theory they go all the way up, over a thousand but no one has seen that, the highest I've see is just over nine hundred lives … I ran your test four times." She won't say the number. She can't seem to. Not out loud. She pushes herself toward me a few steps and holds up the results.

6666.

This is not going to end well. I start to panic as feelings of abandonment are followed by a swell of fear, like a rising tide filling my body to capacity.

Seeing the terror gripping me, Payge starts folding the paper into the tiniest square possible. Then she shoves it into my sweaty hand, opens the door and walks me down the hall like everything is normal. She escorts me to where the lab area ends in a big silver door to the lobby and nudges me back into the cattle call. She gives me a quick parting glance, a look of resolve, and I suspect that the ghost-white terror I saw when she came back with my results was actually her fear for my safety.

I'm nearing the main exit and wondering what good thing I did for Payge in a past life when I see a glass door that leads to a hallway. The man inside looks like Gaebe; my brain is telling me it's him. But since the person he's talking to in a secretive manner is Jude, I don't want to believe it. I watch Gaebe appear to ask Jude a question and Jude reach down the front of his shirt toward his chest and pull out a little gold key on a black string, take it from around his neck, and hand it to Gaebe just as I push through the doors and decide that things are officially out of control. I have officially found trouble, and gotten very into it, just like Cian asked me to do. And I've been quite reckless, and now I'm ready for the game to be over. I'm ready to go find my grandfather.

My plan was to drive east. That was my entire plan.

Last I heard Cian was "in the northeast." Being in North

Dakota, I'm already north. So, east it was. Only Cian would know why all of this was happening and what to do about it.

But when I stumbled out of the building into the blinding light of day, I started to see spots and braced myself to eat pavement, Phoenix was right there to catch me.

"What happened?" she asked knowing what I was and how long I'd been in there. When I told her my "plan," she said I was bat-shit crazy if I thought I could just leave. She said we needed to regroup. Then she told me her test result: one hundred and eleven. She beamed a little for being "dead accurate" on her dad's number of six hundred and thirty-three, then told me the results for Fiorella: five hundred and fifty-two. Zeppelin: three hundred and forty-four, and Sequoia: one thousand and forty-seven.

I didn't want to tell her my number. But she already knew.

"Four sixes. Roman and I have always known your number."

"That's funny. He told me he didn't know."

"He thought it would scare you." He was right. "He wanted to protect you," she said. "We disagreed about it; we disagree about a lot of things."

Then she said we had to do something that I wasn't going to like.

That's how driving east and leaving Rugby behind turned into going to the house on East Gate Drive and falling deeper down the rabbit hole.

"Not what I meant by east," I protested as Phoenix turned onto the road where my little house sits, third one in, on the right side of the street.

"We need to understand Shamus's plan. And I think, personally, we also need to break into your grandfather's night stand, smash it open and see what's inside."

"I'm not breaking it. The only way I'm opening it is with a key. The key I think Jude has been wearing around his neck all along ..." I paused. "What if that was part of my fate with him?" I asked myself aloud. "I remember..." I said, suddenly recalling a lost memory of our trek through Alaska, "... when I was five. That's the first time I remember asking Cian about the nightstand. The first time I saw it. I saw a man who, now that I think about it, was a dark-haired, blue-eyed, thirty-five-year-old version of Jude. He was carefully loading it into the cargo hold of a ship Cian, Shamus, and I were boarding."

"So you're saying that the only way you'll open the mysterious piece of furniture that likely contains some kind of help is with the key you just saw Jude give to Gaebe?"

My answer should've been obvious. But it wasn't. I wasn't going to destroy Cian's nightstand. So naturally, I said nothing, but did conclude that stubbornness is a disease and that I might be dying of it.

The last time I saw the inside of my house it was immaculate. But now, as we walk through the living room as cautiously as possible, ready for anything, it's hard to piece together what could have happened between then and now. What could have resulted in such total destruction, in every breakable thing broken. Every valuable thing stolen. Thieves and vandals would be a likely explanation if the mayhem of the apocalypse had reached Rugby but it hasn't. My street is a model of order and civility, almost ridiculously normal given the state of the rest of the world.

Shamus's room was one clue as to who might have thrown an epic end-of-the-world party. His room typically resembled what the rest of the house looks like now. But Phoenix slowly swings his door open to reveal perfect order and pristine cleanliness, his bed tightly made …

"I've never seen his bed made before," I say as Phoenix goes in ahead of me, scouting for danger. "I never even knew what the top of his blanket looked like." It's red plaid and looks just like Kristina's favorite shirt.

My room is the next clue. As we push the door, trying to open it against the mountains of debris inside, Phoenix sees it first and her face tells me that whatever it is, it's not good. But I'm not prepared for the giant eye spray-painted on the wall right over my bed. My eye, my exact green-colored eye. At least five feet around, it covers more than half the wall. But its size and the fact that it's over my bed isn't what bothers me most—the Animus symbol drawn in the center of the pupil. The symbol I hadn't seen until today but now seems to cover the entire world, staring back at me from the center of my own eye. I turn and walk out. I go straight into the bathroom and throw up. I don't even bother to flush when I'm done, figuring the house probably won't be standing much longer so what's the point.

I have to hold my shirt over my mouth as we walk carefully through the kitchen. It's a good thing I got throwing up out of the way because all the contents of both the freezer and the refrigerator are dumped out, spilled, sprayed, and thrown everywhere. The thick wall of flies in the air is a close second to the hordes of maggots under our feet as the most repulsive thing I've ever experienced.

Cian's room has been ransacked worst of all. His bed is flipped up onto the wall, every possession smashed, every article of clothing ripped to shreds. And his nightstand? The mysteriously important relic, maybe the last thing I have of my grandfather … Gone. I stare at the spot where it once stood and my heart skips a beat when the phone rings.

Phoenix and I lock eyes. A thousand thoughts are racing through me.

"You have to answer it," she says quickly, the way she does when suddenly she *knows*. So I walk into the kitchen and pick it up. Silence on the line. Then Ansel's curious voice.

"Eve."

"Yeah," I say quietly. That's all I say.

"Please tell me you're okay. Where have you been?"

"Staying with a friend."

"I'm with Cian, he's very weak. He wants you to come. Can you get here?"

We drive back to Phoenix's in silence. What is there to say? She feels certain it's a trap. So do I, but what choice do I have? I've told her I'm going, even if I have to go alone. Even if I have to leave on foot in the middle of the night and steal a car, who cares. There are no rules out there, not any more. We're the only idiots who sit around and let people we don't know take our blood and tell us what we can and can't do. Rugby is the only place where people aren't doing whatever the hell they want.

As we turn onto the winding road up to her house she looks at me.

"Eve, we're not going. That's the end of it."

She watched me load my car from her window, arms crossed, face expressionless. I wondered what was worse for her—knowing she couldn't physically stop me, or my blatant disregard of her remarkable leadership that had yet to fail me. I was just nearing the edge of town when I started to flush her disapproving face from my mind. I even turned on the radio and was surprised to hear music. That's when I saw the roadblock, cars and barricades all emblazoned with the Animus symbol, and I turned around.

Who was I kidding trying to leave like this? I'd go at night, on foot I decided.

I'd been gone no more than fifteen minutes when I pulled back up Phoenix's long winding driveway, my "you were right" speech all prepared.

It's the sight of Ruby that gets me first. Perched on the front steps, her arms crossed in front of her. And when I see the handful of Animus Task Force goons around her, it's not hard to figure out why she's here.

But her pointing in my direction as I put the car in park, that's what puts me over the edge. I stare at that stupid pointing finger and all the rage in every cell of my body erupts in a wildfire of madness.

I don't remember breaking her nose before the goons took me down, that's the unfortunate thing about seeing red. You don't get to remember much about what happens after that. But that's how I end up back at the lab under heavy guard, steel restraints around my wrists. Because Ruby had ratted me out. She told me herself. When my face was down in the grass and I had four grown men holding my limbs. That's the moment she happily revealed how Roman, *who wouldn't even tell me how many lifetimes I'd had*, went ahead and told his poo bear. Oh, and her number? A delicate and acceptable one hundred and thirty-eight. A shiny and perfect new soul. And of course, she couldn't wait for the sky to fall when people found out my demonic, far too high, shamefully abnormal incarnation number. It was to be her day of reckoning. But when she didn't see any test results by my name, when she knew I'd been there, when her and her boyfriend Roman had seen me there, well, it didn't take long for her to find herself sitting in Dr. Alastair's office telling him everything that she knew.

Now, I'm alone in a stark white room strapped to what looks like a white dentist's chair, and I'm wondering about two things. One: Karl Alastair, the man who mapped the human soul, foremost genome biologist in the world. And two: the promise of power.

For some reason, I thought Dr. Alastair would be better looking. More like a movie star and less like a hideous troll-doll. I certainly thought he'd be taller and I made sure it was the first thing I told him when we met. After which he leaned over and whispered in my ear that he knew Animus could save the world but he couldn't have imagined it would actually catch the Antichrist.

Then Payge comes in the room. Alastair gives her a warning glare. She's holding a vial and test kit on a silver tray, which rattles from her shaking hands. She got in trouble for what she did for me. I can see that she's been crying by how the whites of her eyes burn red and I notice, for the first time, her most distinctive feature—stunningly pale wintergreen eyes. Eyes I know. The eyes from Pompeii.

It's Lucia.

"I think the two of you already know one another," he remarks as he snaps on a pair of rubber gloves, not realizing the incredible truth of his statement.

Then, "I made a new friend today," he says, clearly leading me somewhere. But I have the stubborn silent thing down so well I don't even have to think about it. In my silence he instructs Payge to ready the vial and prepare the needle.

"Jude. Interesting name. Don't hear it much. Do you believe in coincidences? I should tell you right up front that I don't. There are no coincidences. So when your friend Jude had an IN of zero … it was almost too good to be true. And then I heard about you. *Jude and Eve*, two of my favorite Biblical characters. Eve, who of course bit the apple and damned all of humanity and Jude, Judas, who betrayed the savior who came to redeem it. The two of you, the world's newest and the world's oldest soul, in one place, together? At a time like this? Coincidence? No. It makes too much sense."

And once again I watch Payge sink the steel needle into my arm but this time it's different. She can't steady her hand, which causes it to hurt much more than the first time. And now, her eyes burn with the misery of knowing, that by having to get my blood, because of what my test will say, she's hurting me. And for reasons she doesn't understand, I'm just not someone she wants to hurt. Her face racked with confusion and pain—my heart breaks for her.

Then he tells me, as my blood floods into the vial, that he also knows about the four of us.

"You and your friends," he says, prompting him to reframe his argument that the importance of open public records simply cannot be overstated. How else would he have known that the four of us were born on the day with the most end times lore, at the end of the millennium, on the four corners of the earth? "So there's that mess to play with."

But, he says, since he's already confirmed with multiple sources, that Jude and I were together during each of the catastrophic tragedies.

"It's the best option, I think. The forbidden love of new and old souls. So many options for such an important science finally validated and poised to change the world."

Now, all he needs is my blood. The blood he didn't even know he was looking for.

"The blood that's going to change everything."

PART FOUR

THE LAST WAKER

CHAPTER 20

Left to their own devices, people wouldn't have been able to figure out whether I was a shrine of hope or a temple of doom, whether I was going to save the world or burn it down. Even with the number 6666 right next to my name. People like Payge, people who instantly liked me, whose mysterious loyalty was like a force of nature within them, wouldn't have known what to think. And they'd have been hard-pressed to arrive at a conclusion that was compelling enough to catapult Animus to its rightful place.

"That's precisely why," Dr. Alastair said, "I'll clarify it for everyone. And frankly, the timing couldn't be better."

I admit, he was right about that.

The world outside of Rugby had become a living hell from one burning continent to the next. The whole of humanity was caving in on itself. Possessed by a self-fulfilling psychosis.

Their civil disorder was absolute, lawlessness total. The result had been continuous and widespread anarchy, death and destruction for the twelve days and nights since the tsunami struck. Now what was left was a desperate and broken mob, hungry for an elixir, starving for order and peace, ripe to unwittingly make a deal with the devil.

It's no wonder the news of my results spread like the Black Plague, a horror, a wicked omen propagated on its own at the speed of light, the people with a hardwired distaste for me the disease's perfect hosts. Dr. Alastair made sure I was issued a TV so I could watch all my preordained enemies take to the airwaves to talk about how immoral they're sure I am, Ruby leading the charge with her busted face and terrifying story of her encounter with the unstoppable force of pure evil, and the crazed public eat her up, they can't get enough Ruby. They foam at the mouth for her ingenuous caricature: the damsel, adorably foolish, daftly feigning ignorance of her own widely lauded sex appeal. She was made for the limelight; even with her black eyes and bandaged nose the camera loves her.

I have the pleasure of watching from a twelve-inch TV in a maximum-security crypt in the bowels of the building I wasn't permitted to leave. I watch Ruby become an instant sensation. Not quite a savior—that title was reserved for Dr. Alastair—but the next best thing, a savior's number one "helpmate." And the fact that Dr. Alastair's last name means "protector of humanity," well, that was just a bonus, I figured.

Honestly, it struck me more as an overt red flag than a sign from above, but it became the headline: "Creator of Animus, Protector of Humanity." Instead of the one I thought more fitting: "Dr. Alastair, unattractive power-hungry gnome-like biologist seeking validation, quietly lurking decades in the shadows, turned cold-blooded scientific opportunist." It had a certain ring to it but wouldn't have fit so neatly on the bottom screen like the first one did.

The truth according to Alastair was now being fed and digested, that because Jude and I were together when all the events happened, the earthquake, the tsunami, the unthinkable, and because we're romantically involved, the world's oldest soul and the world's newest, it's finally been determined once and for all, what was hypothesized a decade ago by Dr. DeCuir, is now conclusively proven by Dr. Alastair, that "unordered soul assimilation" has long been the undoing of world peace, and it's the cause of this final warning of the end of days. More specifically, I am the cause. A diabolist of staggering earthly incarnations, an enchantress born to ensnare the newest among us for what would have been the final act in humankind's long and painful play of broken covenants of world peace. And the fix, of course, is Animus, and it starts with immediate worldwide testing, no one stopping to ask the next logical question—"and then what?" What will be done with the results? I watch them accept that Jude and I and our "unordered soul assimilation" are the undoing of world peace, and that we must separate, yet they never question what that will mean for them, for husbands and wives, for their children, and their families and communities? Some would test old soul and some would test new soul and I kept waiting for someone to pose the question. To at least wonder what they were signing up for. But no one on TV was questioning anything. Like Maricielo had predicted, I was a diversion—a damn good one. But that couldn't last forever, right?

Wrong. I begin to lose all faith in humanity watching Lou give "exclusive live testimony" to Nancy Grace that he "bore witness" to my "devious ensnarement" over Jude as I "swindled him" into being named on the title of my car. Lou, who actually liked me, brainwashed by terror, desperate to hedge his bets to secure a seat in heaven just in case Animus can't prevent the rapture. That he was accusing me of an act that was more whimsically generous than criminal is fully lost on the host and her audience. Then, I really start to snap, as I watch Mrs. Billings tell the world of the undignified kiss she saw me steal in the gymnasium "during our somber memorial service." I'm ready to tap out. Seeing how easily her reckless fear-mongering rally morphs into a somber memorial service—do I even try to cling to my last bit of hope, I wonder, or let it all go? I think of Phoenix's words, warning me to remember that I'm good, not evil—and now I get it. The real irony is, now it's impossible to do.

So I'm feeling less than optimal when Gaebe comes to see me despite my vocal and repeated objections. Wicked enchantresses, apparently, don't get much say in their roster of visitors.

As he stands outside my cell, he tells me that Jude was of course free to go.

A hapless victim.

"Powerless against the sorcery of a girl with so many sixes branded on her soul," I snark, echoing what I heard on TV in my best fake scary voice.

Then I get the special pleasure of hearing, from a grown man I'd hoped would be an inspirational school teacher, how Jude is feeling "unsure" about me and our relationship, that he's "questioning everything," what with all the secrets I've been keeping, and the scary and vile things people are saying about me.

"You should hear yourself right now. Honestly," I say, disgusted I ever looked forward to learning anything from such a low-life perpetuator of lies.

"Just thought you'd like to know," he says, as if he's shocked I'm uninterested.

"Thanks, but I'm good on the relationship advice. I'm more interested in the key you got from him," I say, surprised how direct one gets when one has nothing left to lose. "That key was for me."

"What makes you so sure about that?" he asks carefully, attempting to mask his interest.

"I'm not, but I'm not so sure it was for you either. And I also know that it's not difficult to get Jude to do things. He's a pretty willing person. He once gave me all the money he had in the world without even asking why."

"I might not make it a habit of retelling that story if I were you," he advises, sounding amused.

"I have nothing to hide. Unlike *some* people I could mention. What's the key for?" I press, walking toward the bars between us.

"This key?" He holds it up from around his neck. "It unlocks something very important. I'm just holding it for a while for someone else, the rightful owner. So it doesn't fall into the wrong hands," his voice taunting and cruel.

Then, in his eyes, as he places the key back under his shirt, a quick mysterious shift toward me and then back that almost says *he's holding it for me*. That he came in to give me that message about Jude for a reason. Like he's playing the other side but might actually be my ally. Then without a second look, he just turns around and walks out.

Falling asleep on a plastic cot mattress, the way it sticks to my sweaty body and sounds like a diaper whenever I move, is quite challenging. It doesn't happen until several hours after my nine o'clock lights-out. That's why seeing someone in my face, waking me, pisses me off at first. Before it registers that it's Phoenix, I knock her to the ground.

"I hope you just enjoyed the last time I ever save your life," she says from the dusty floor before standing up and walking right out the wide-open door to my cell. I quickly follow when I realize what's happening and I'm happy to see the guard who'd kept whispering that I was a filthy jezebel knocked out cold.

"You know you don't mean that," I say about never helping me again.

"No, but threats are kind of my thing."

As we walk into the deserted lobby she stops to stare into a camera mounted to the ceiling.

"What are you doing?" I whisper.

"Securing my place in history," she says clearly, not bothering to whisper back. "It's more important than you might think. It reminds people what they can do, even just one person. People continue to forget."

Then she turns around and leads me to a back door where we just walk out.

"The security here is kind of a joke," I marvel.

"Is it?" She scans my face for a thought more cunning than that.

"Gaebe," I say to her immediate satisfaction.

"Now you're thinking like a warrior who's going to bring down a global terrorist organization." Then she turns and sinks a syringe into my thigh.

And the world goes black.

The wind feels good. And so does Roman's voice. The low whisper of his words when he talks about important things. It sounded like that a lot the day he told me about us. He sounds just like that now … as I drift out to sleep. But his smoothly hushed tone pulls me back when I hear him say that he woke up this morning and he knew "it was time" to "finally bring Eve to Antiquus." When I hear Phoenix's voice confirm she felt the same the throbbing soreness in my thigh reminds me that for some reason Phoenix knocked me out with what was apparently a mightily potent sedative.

I open one eye just a hair and see Roman riding shotgun and Phoenix at the wheel of my jeep. The flaps are open and the whipping breeze is as intense as the speed she's driving, but I can make out most of what they're saying. I close my eyes and pretend I'm still sleeping as I listen.

Their exact words are not easy to discern but I learn we're heading to this place called Antiquus, where Cian is waiting for me, where Ansel has always been. It's an ancient secret enclave of the world's oldest souls, a network of castles high in the Adirondack Mountains connected by a subterranean tunnel system. It's been in existence for centuries created by a small group of the Founding Fathers of the United States who belonged to something called the Aion Dorea.

I translate the ancient Greek words in my mind—*Aion* meaning "forever," "timeless," or "eternity." *Dorea* meaning "gift." Maybe the Aion Dorea believes they possess "the gift of eternal time." Then Phoenix starts to speculate where Jude might be. *Jude is missing! What?*

"Yeah, that's why I had to drug you," Phoenix says to me. "So you wouldn't give us any trouble."

"First of all, let's make one thing clear," I shout as I sit up, "Drugging a person, namely me, is not a viable option. Ever. How did you know I was awake?"

"Your breathing changed."

"Really?" Roman asks her. "How did you hear that?"

"How did you not?" She shakes her head in disbelief, rolls her eyes at him. "Now do you see why I had to be the one keeping you safe?" she asks me.

"When's the last time you saw Jude?" I ask them. "What if Shamus has him?"

When neither one of them say a word or look at me I know. Shamus *does* have him. I can tell by their silence, how they don't deny it. I could handle that. I could even imagine how we would rescue him. It's that they believe Jude went with Shamus on his own that sets my world spinning out of control—and the ruins of civilization smoldering in all directions as far as I can see don't help.

Then Phoenix tells me that Jude is going to be Shamus's shrine of new souls, Shamus's magnetic puppet by which to build an army.

As I wonder why Jude might want to do that I remember how well Shamus can find weaknesses. It's the one thing I've seen him excel at. And it wouldn't take him any time at all to crack Jude's code.

I can almost hear Shamus luring Jude in with promises, a whole world of people, *where everyone is just like him.*

And if we're supposed to be heading to Antiquus, where the oldest souls are holed up in a fortress, while Shamus is gathering the newest souls, amassing a force of fighters somewhere else … one thing is becoming obvious. War is on the horizon—a war that feels like it could be the last on earth. The final war, for it's the war of souls.

And what else is there to fight about after that?

CHAPTER 21

"Whomever can wake the dead will win the war," I tell Phoenix and Roman as we careen sharply up winding mountain roads.

Whomever can wake the dead will win the war of souls, a seed for which is being planted right now by the idea of old versus new, a war easily formed through the pliability of a desperate populace, enflamed by the hapless crowning of leadership with the lethal combination of ultimate power and secret agenda, and then fully ignited by Shamus in his ceaseless quest to destroy things and feel important.

"She's right," Roman says. "If that's Shamus, he will win and who knows what will become of the world." I take a deep breath trying not to throw up from the thought and simultaneous nausea of Phoenix tearing around sharp corners.

"If, as I suspect, as Shamus suspects, it turns out to be me,"

I say, "And I'm able to stay *alive*"—a hint for Phoenix to drive safer rather than a reference to my brother's obsession with destroying me—"well, that would be better," is all I can say of it.

I sit back; sober with the thought that it's come to this. I'd always suspected that my brother would kill me the first chance he got, but a little part of me didn't want to believe it. That little girl inside who kept wishing for a protective older brother to look up to is long gone now.

Roman reaches back for my hand. I look at his open palm, a familiar life raft in my ocean of dread, and I grab onto it for my life. Through its warm protective shelter I melt into him. My nerves start to calm as he somehow holds my whole being in his hand.

When he squeezes it once reassuringly, I feel a surge of determination. This is someone who knows what I can do as well as anyone, who knows me better than anyone. As is always the case when he's near me, he's an instant anchor, a roving home base that roots me to the earth wherever the two of us land.

Phoenix glares at our tightly clasped hands. How our fingers are affectionately intertwined. We both see her looking, but neither one of us lets go.

"Old habits die hard," he says to her quietly, and I wonder if he's talking about his habit of loving me, or her habit of needing to prevent it. But when she turns her eyes back to the road I feel the wall she'd been building between Roman and I start to crumble.

Around the last bend a dead end looms before us in the form of an overlook that's as magnificent as it is chilling for the substantial rise in altitude it reveals.

Just to the right there's a dirt trail. You'd never see it if you weren't looking. We drive down it a hundred yards and come to a tunnel of sorts. A canopy of ancient forest that beckons us down a dim corridor, a single shimmering yellow light on either side of the secret road every forty yards. Phoenix drives slowly now, carefully staying between the leaning trees, as they grow ever tighter around us.

After ten minutes the feeling that we're too far now to get back out, if suddenly we wanted to, starts creeping in. The trail is so narrow that we could no longer turn around. If we needed to escape we'd have to do so in reverse. But Phoenix presses on, following the intermittently placed lights for an agonizing twenty minutes, long enough for even her to start looking uneasy as the faint lights become noticeably dimmer and begin to appear more and more infrequently, the dark stretches growing like the presence of an unseen phantom. After twenty-five minutes, every second continuing on feels like certain suicide.

That's when the slim tunnel opens up to a clearing, where a hundred yards in front of us, a castle the likes of which I'd never could have imagined existing in the mountains of New

York looms above us. The stone fortress looks impenetrable and what must be a thousand pointed spires tower boldly into the night sky, piercing through the clouds.

In the distance, a small man holding a bright light walks toward us.

"Get in the back," Phoenix tells Roman, who grabs the roll bar overhead and swings himself gracefully into the seat next to me. She looks at the two of us next to each other. We look to her, deferring to her leadership.

She shakes her head. "I don't know if I should tell you to protect her or her to protect you," she says of the two of us, knowing both my level of skill as a fighter and Roman's fierce protective instinct toward me. "Just stay here," Phoenix commands as she exits the car and strides toward the man. Intimidation in her every step, he stops moving toward her as her pace only increases until she's standing over him. She looms larger than life next to his small stature. As we watch we see them starting to talk. Their peaceful-looking exchange continues without incident and I exhale a breath I didn't know I'd been holding in.

"I was wondering when you were going to breathe," Roman remarks, keeping his eyes focused on their exchange between glancing around us every few seconds. I take another breath, a deep inhale and exhale, not thinking of how I felt when Roman did that. How when I heard him breathe I felt his soul. How I was brought to whatever place it is in the universe where all the stars cross and some collide.

He looks at me. Right into me. To the deepest part.

My heart doesn't race, it actually slows down, the way time seems to. My whole body relaxes like it usually does when I see him, but now with the freedom to really look into his eyes I realize it's the world's strongest anesthesia, and it delivers me to a tranquil dreamland that melts everything in existence but the two of us.

"I had to stay away from you, Eve ..." He pauses for a moment, looking at every part of my face. "I don't have to do that anymore," he says, relief in his eyes.

"Why did you have to do that?" I ask, shocked, as I am confused, feeling like there's a humming bird in my chest. Is he telling me that now, if I wanted to, I could be with him? "What about Ruby? You love her ..."

He shakes his head. "I had to make sure she would play her role. I had to keep her close so that everything would happen the way it was supposed to. My job was to pretend to love Ruby and to try and stay away from you. And hardest of all, I had to help you find Jude. Jude is your fate," he says, looking down, probably thinking of watching the two of us kiss. Then he looks back at me. "But ... *I'm your soul mate.* I always have been." His words suck the oxygen from my every cell. "This must be hard for you," he says, responding to the shock on my face. "It must be so confusing. One minute I'm encouraging you to be with Jude, sitting right there as you kiss him, pretending it doesn't kill me, pretending I love someone else, and the next minute I'm sitting here praying to God you still have feelings for me and wanting to tell you that ... I've never stopped loving you." Tears, ones of disbelief and confusion well in my eyes. His validation of what I was feeling, his eternal devotion, and his acknowledgement of how hard it's been—that's what makes me do it. That's what makes me close my eyes and start to lean into him. That and the unstoppable force of lifetimes of love draw my lips toward the soft landing place of his.

"Hey." Phoenix's voice startles us both. "That didn't take long." She shakes her head at Roman, then she gestures toward the man in front of the jeep. "He says he's Ansel."

"Okay," I say after a long pause, completely breathless from nearly kissing Roman.

"Is he?" she demands, pissed and impatient.

"I don't know."

"What do you mean you don't know?"

"I've never actually met Ansel," I say like she should know that. "Did I not mention that?" I see her unstable emotions rise up in her. She breathes them down.

"No big deal. We'll just go ahead and take his word for it," she says, trying to manufacture patience out of thin air. Then the rawness that is Phoenix rears up ferociously: "But if we end up on the wrong end of a guillotine so help me God, I'll blame you!" Again she tries to rein it in. "Fair enough?"

Practicing, for what it's worth, the high-pitched sound of being an agreeable person.

It is Ansel. His voice is as familiar to me as anything could be. There is no doubt about that. As he welcomes us into the inconceivably vast entrance I walk beside him, Phoenix and Roman together behind us. He tells me about Antiquus, how it's been a safe haven for people like me for centuries. He tells me he's always known who I am, that Cian shared it with him when he asked him to help guide me through what was destined to be a my most tumultuous lifetime yet.

He tells me that he and Cian are members of a group of "faithful servants of humanity." That's what Ansel tells me is the meaning and mission of the Aion Dorea. This is wrong, obviously, but I don't mention my complete knowledge of ancient Greek. Nor do I mention the DI tattoo on his right forearm, how I know it's the Roman numeral five hundred and one, and I get the distinct feeling he doesn't think I know anything other than what I've learned as Evelyn O'Cleirigh, a naïve teenager.

CHAPTER 22

There is an unusual sensation that accompanies a phone call from the pope. An extremely specific type of majesty-soaked terror in knowing the pope is on the line, waiting to speak to you. It's a sort of awestruck wonder drenched in dread.

It's very specific.

And I'm saturated with this particular feeling when Ansel lets me know, appearing reluctant to have to, that I've gotten a call from Rome, from the pope himself, interrupting the tour he was about to lead us on.

"Hello …" I say into a large computer screen on the wall of a grand office, not sure whether it's having a video chat with the pope or doing it in front of Ansel, Phoenix, and Roman that feels so awkward.

"Evelyn," I hear the familiar voice come out of the face I

recognize from his many televised speeches over the last two weeks. In the beat I take to answer he intuitively infers, "You prefer Eve," even more impressive when I note the time delay.

"Yes," I say, after which Pope Gelasius II informs me that we actually have a great deal in common.

"*N ba*," he says, which is a Bambara greeting used by men in Mali. It's the equivalent of hello but actually means "my mother" or more specifically "thanks to the mother who bore me, I am here this moment to greet you."

"*Nsay*," I reply, the traditional female response, which translates to "my power" and culturally means "my power as a female always wins against time."

Then he just starts speaking to me in Bambara as he tells me that he was born in Mali too. He warns me of certain people.

"*I farati nilifen*."—*Watch out for those offering a gift*. My mind snaps to the real meaning of Aion Dorea—"the gift of eternal time"—and wonder why Ansel tried to tell me it meant "faithful servants of humanity" and whether this is really something that Cian's a part of.

He goes on to tell me in English that my work is important and that he'll be holding me up in his prayers. He will pray for me ceaselessly, for the intercession of Saint Jude on my behalf. Then asks if I know about Saint Jude, the brother of Jesus, and not to confuse him with Judas Iscariot.

"Jude of James," the son of James and "the patron saint of

lost causes," he says, slow and deliberate. The son of James. I think of Jude's license, Judah James, and I know he's telling me that Jude isn't a lost cause. Which makes me more certain than ever that he'll start to appear as though he is one, which I struggle to imagine. He tells me that my grandfather is his close friend, and that he's weak and I must go to him.

As I ascend a never-ending stone staircase, Phoenix and Roman just behind me, I've already decided that we will take Cian to Eremis to heal. I worry Shamus is planning to kill him so that he can become the waker and his new souls will be unstoppable. We need to strengthen him as much as possible even if bringing him to Eremis carries a risk of running into Shamus. There's no other way.

The moment I see Cian, lying nearly lifeless in a giant bed, looking small and feeble I feel like it's me who deserted him. I know it is. I'm fully crying by the time I reach his bedside, a sobbing fitful mess, a blubbering remorseful fool begging his eternal forgiveness for my repugnant self-focus and blatant abandonment. Phoenix stands guard at the door, and Roman is by my side. I'm grateful he is because I'm so grief-struck at the sight of Cian standing in death's doorway that Roman holds me upright until I collapse on the bed and curl up to my grandfather. I sob and weep for what feels like eons, Roman gently stroking my hair, both my hands resting in Cian's.

With the grief growing too much to bear, I close my eyes. All my focus and attention narrows suddenly, to the center of my forehead. A burning between my eyes begins taking hold. Then even from behind my closed eyelids I see the room and everything in it go white in a single all-consuming flash.

When my eyes open, Cian is standing on my right, Roman on my left, and Phoenix behind us. We stand together in the sweeping vacant silence of the golden dunes.

In my mind I can see Shamus. Jude is showing him the arsenal Phoenix stockpiled. I turn around and from the look on Phoenix's face she sees it too. Jude appears wholly unlike himself—dead eyes, and brainwashed. I can hear Shamus communicating to Jude.

I'll take you to Primitus. It's a fantasyland on earth; an oasis for new souls in the Black Rock Desert, where we're free to be fearless, where everyone there is just like you.

Jude has a moment where he thinks of me, when he thinks of our first kiss and all the ones that followed. Then he pictures the two of us lying in bed at Phoenix's. One glance at Roman tells me that we're all seeing the same thing. My most intimate, most private moments with Jude and the one fear he shared with me that night, the fear that there was no one else in the world like him.

Eve doesn't love you, Shamus tells Jude, further draining the light from Jude's eyes if that's possible. *I tell you this as your friend,* he says to Jude, *Eve told Kristina that she knows Roman is her soul mate.* I look at Roman, who gives me a little smile at Shamus's words—the truth, brilliantly manipulated. It's incredible for me to watch Shamus, and see how transfixing, how magnetic he can be. He's mesmerizing. This is the Shamus that drew Kristina halfway around the world. This is the Shamus that will build an army and a vast empire of new souls. And Jude, his powerless figurehead.

All at once, the dunes dissolve into Cian's room and his deathbed.

"We have to go to Primitus," I say. Despite the immediate reservation on Phoenix and Roman's faces I'm convinced that's the only next possible step when suddenly Cian sits up and begins choking. A bloody mist spewing from his lips. Before I remotely process what's happening Roman grabs my shoulders and stares into my eyes.

"We need to go back," he says, and the next second I'm diving into the burning space between my eyes and the room is melting.

I see the golden dunes around us, but nothing prepares me to see Shamus standing over Cian, putting one of the long blades of the double-edged sword through his throat.

NOOOOO!!! I scream the word in my mind, so loudly that the bloodcurdling shrill fills Eremis, sending every bird streaking across the blue sky and blowing the sand around

Shamus into a hundred-foot-tall tornado.

The swirling wind and sand doesn't faze Shamus in the least. His grin only grows wider as his black eyes devour every last drop of my frenzied pleading with the sickest pleasure. It's the anger he's been waiting for.

My outpouring of unbound and helpless rage is the song of his heart.

You want to find out as much as I do, he snarls, insinuating that I'm in accord with his brutally murdering my beloved grandfather to see which one of us will inherit his gift.

That's when I see red.

I don't remember flying toward him, but find myself on the wrong end of his sword, the blade pressed into my rib cage, my back buried a foot into the sand. Phoenix and Roman begin to charge at him but his warning—an inch-long slice into my throat, a millimeter from my carotid artery—forces them to halt.

It's a double-edged sword for a reason. He tells them in no uncertain terms that this second side of the sword is for me. *If she's not the waker, then I'll kill her with it. But if she is the waker, she's coming to Primitus, where she can be with Jude;* he taunts Roman, who Phoenix struggles to hold back from charging. *Eve will be the most important service member of my army, from her very own prison cell.*

That those were the last words Cian would ever hear will haunt me always.

I feel an incredible rush of wind as his powerful soul departs. The rush moves through me. It's Cian I feel and I'm suddenly filled with a strength that's so ferocious I throw Shamus off me, ten feet in the air. Phoenix and Roman surround me as he comes crashing back to the ground.

Shamus rises to his feet, a detectable terror in his eyes. A fear that Cian's soul just bestowed his gift upon me, as he's witnessed many times this same superhuman strength from Cian in times of great need.

He approaches the lifeless body, pointing his sword at the three of us. He kneels down and presses his hand to Cian's chest, just as he's watched Cian do a thousand times. He waits, watching for the rushing return of the soul that floods in like a gust lifting a curtain in one swelling billow.

But nothing happens. Cian's body stays very much dead.

Shamus, visibly dejected and fearful of what will happen next, points at me with the tip of the shaking sword, directing me toward Cian.

I slowly walk toward the body of my grandfather. Weeping at the sight of sand kicked onto his face, sand in his gaping mouth and open dead eyes. I throw myself on his body wailing, pounding the ground with my fists. Then, desperate for him to live, I place my hand across his chest. I summon all the energy in the universe …

But nothing happens.

I am not the waker I realize, and the knowing starts.

Cian was it. He was the last.

Humanity must forge into a war of souls without Cian. Though the world has never known a time without a waker to counteract the chaos, to keep the fate of the universe on its path. Leaving us to settle the score on our own.

As Shamus sets his dark eyes on me I begin to flood with more knowledge.

Cian's death is releasing all the memories of all my past lives. I feel them coming, overwhelming me, engulfing me, and instantly I know why Shamus has spent the last seventeen years wishing me dead.

Because I know who he was in our first lifetime together.

I know what I did to him, and why he hates me for it.

End of Book One

THE AION DOREA PAPERS

PHEUMACHRONOLOGY FOR WORLD PEACE

Official guide to every soul's truth

Animus Test

All souls will be demarcated on the right forearm with the Roman numeral of their unique pheumachronology or "soul age." A second marking, their AD sacred symbol, will be provided at the soul's complete discretion.

NEW SOULS

GYPSY SOULS

1–50 lifetimes

The Gypsy soul is the blessed baby of the planet. Their focus is on the experience of being alive; they are learning about survival, awareness of their environment, how their choices affect their circumstances and the beginning concepts of morality. Like a baby, they are clean slates; they have very little to no self-concept; in this way they lack any hidden agendas; they are far too primal for pretense. An earthy, untamed, and unaltered beauty is the hallmark of a Gypsy. They are often consumed for an entire lifetime or lifetimes with gaining and maintaining the simplest abilities of survival. Gypsies can tend to give in to distraction and quite easily slip into addiction but just as easily Gypsies can display an exuberance and unbridled enthusiasm for life that's infectious.

Gypsies are easy targets for others to hurt or manipulate. They are naïve and impulsive. They don't understand society and its rules and can display this lack of understanding in antisocial and even immoral acts with little or sometimes no remorse at all. Eventually they will give in to their natural inclination to wander. They will pull away from their family or clan or tribe or society in general, almost violently, often becoming homeless for a time or a lifetime. Their wandering phase is critical to their soul's truth. Going and doing, seeing and experiencing while learning to sustain their survival, either of the physical body or of the spirit and heart are their life's work.

In the last lifetimes of a Gypsy soul, they begin to draw pride from their proficiency at self-care. They become even more beautiful and begin to identify with and adorn their physical bodies. With everything from flowers in their hair to tattoos they yearn to create and exude the "story of who they are." This should be encouraged.

WARRIOR SOULS

51–125 lifetimes

In the Warrior phase primal senses of good and evil begin to form. A time of focus on the body, like gladiators, Warriors are physically imposing. From athletes to models to all types of fighters, Warrior souls are clad in unbelievably ideal appearances. These often-breathtaking humans can tend to be confrontational, rarely backing down from a fight and in most cases actively looking for one at all times. Depending on their soul's expression, their physical virility can range from a distraction to themselves to a weapon they learn to wield, and their sharp tongue and outspoken manner keeps the fights coming. A telltale sign of a Warrior is that their passions can be unbridled; they can too easily throw themselves behind causes, movements, and leaders and will fight to the death as if possessed to do so. This is because their concepts of good and evil are taking shape and they are playing with standing on different sides. They will have to learn to master themselves, to fight according to the rules, to know where their true strength resides, and finally, in later Warrior lifetimes, to fully dis-identify with their gifts of strength and beauty and their yearning to win and start to become conscious of the ripple effects their actions create. They eventually learn, often through physical injury, which brings on great internal conflict, that they are not their body. Thus they are not their wins, nor their loses. They begin to reluctantly suspect that they are the sum of their intentions. This can be met with relief and acceptance or resistance and depression. They move out of the Warrior phase the very first time they truly realize "I don't have to go to every fight I'm invited to." *I can decide.*

GUARDIAN SOULS

126–199 lifetimes

The experience of being born Guardian is that everywhere they look they are confronted with people, animals, causes in need of assistance and they feel it's their duty and their calling to swoop in, often to their own detriment. Guardians will be or aspire to be members of the military, Coast Guard, or Peace Corps, or teachers, nurses, firefighters, social workers, councilors, physical therapists, veterinarians, lower-level politicians, government workers, or humanitarians. The work of Guardian souls is learning to balance their unending compulsion to help with maintaining balance within themselves; they must understand the difference between empowering others and the easily made error of giving away their power in the process. With personalities that tend to be noble, self-sacrificing, accommodating, humane, selfless, philanthropic, caring, nurturing, hospitable, compassionate, empathetic, and altruistic, Guardian souls represent an evolutionary leap in human awareness, an entire swath of humanity who instinctively know how to look outside themselves, compelled, even compulsively at times, to focus on others.

This compulsive side has a potentially destructive effect. If it results in a complete erosion of their own being a Guardian can become engulfed in feelings of resentment and neglect. From this, some Guardians will evolve and grow while others' darker tendencies will emerge, leading them to actively erode others, expertly mastering how to handicap, cripple, and enable under the admirable guise of service. The hallmark of Guardian souls is that they experience a great deal of the pain of their own choices and can have an incessant feeling of never seeming to get what they want, their heart's desire always just out of reach.

Some Guardians will expunge this selfish thought through true and authentic service to others and in that will see that they do experience receiving, it is the receiving of giving, which they will learn is the highest form of receiving. Other Darker Guardians will grow unhinged, fearful, and frantic; their giving morphs into smothering and controlling, and their ill intentions grow like twisted vines around their hearts.

Once all Guardians begin to understand where others end and they begin they become more powerful. Eventually Noble Guardians, who can gain strength through helping others with pure intentions, clearly emerge, their help almost magically effective in strengthening and uplifting others, while the Darker Guardians, by now skilled purveyors of manipulation and mind games, identify mostly as victims; the only thing they guard any more is their self-concept as they begin to try their hand at more deeply controlling the fates of others, both types gradually moving more and more into their power until being born a King soul.

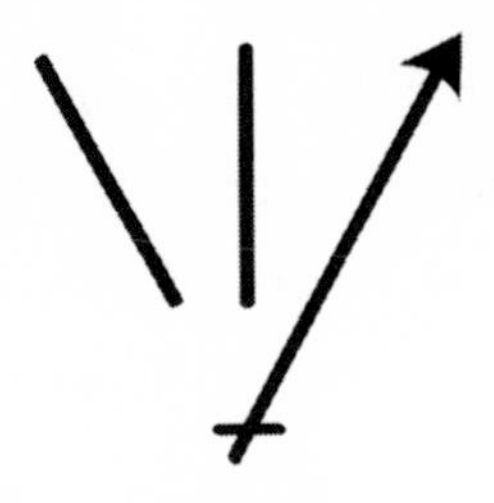

KING SOULS

200–299 lifetimes

Acquiring power, possessions, and status is what drive many King souls. Others are driven by notoriety, legacy, and leaving their mark on this world. Many doctors and lawyers, musicians, actors, high-level executives, and powerful politicians are Kings. They are headstrong and often spend most lifetimes lost in obsessive thinking and fantasizing, though often realizing their fantasies, as Kings are naturally charismatic, popular, persuasive, and generally able to get whatever they want with an almost shockingly small amount of effort, a fact they feel a deep desire to hide. Kings often find themselves at the center of things, always seeming to garner attention.

Almost all Kings tend to be polished, glamorous, charming, and attractive, but they can also easily display wild-eyed greed and ugly unchecked ambition. A hallmark of a King is their ability to swiftly destroy both themselves and those around them physically and emotionally. Kings often repeat this pattern for lifetimes in many of the most public arenas.

In later incarnations King souls shift their awareness from possessions, status, power, and legacy, an uncomfortable and often traumatic transition spurred by the repeated experience of losing these elusive things, how easily money, titles, and reputation scan slip through their fingers. The distinct emptiness that begins nagging them eventually gives birth to a transcendent curiosity as they ponder what is beyond themselves and the worlds and illusions they build. What does it all mean anyway?

OLD SOULS

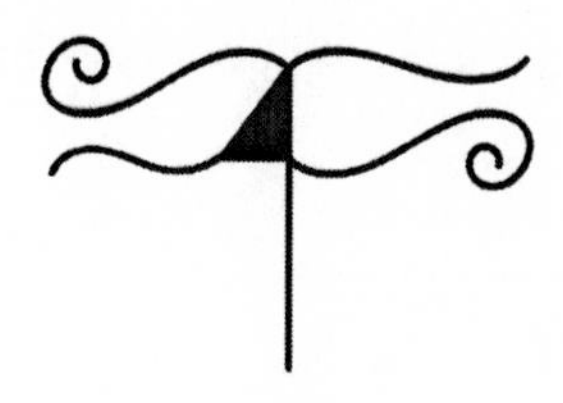

<u>SAGE SOULS</u>

300–500 lifetimes

Mastering knowing. From mediums and psychics to scholars and visionaries, to the devout and divine, Sage souls are about tapping into the flow of ideas. Accessing the universal consciousness is second nature to them. This is something that all souls have access to but Sages are born with an innate frequency tuned in and ready to go. Like human receivers, Sage souls can sometimes feel overloaded with information and ideas, often with a feeling of "where is this coming from?!" They can be drawn to become anything from writers, composers, poets, inventors, scholars, and teachers to preachers, spiritual guides, monks, priests, and so on. In darker incarnations this innate cleverness is devoid of wisdom and manifests in dangerous and destructive ways—think cult leaders and creators of weapons of mass destruction. Sages can easily become delusional when they become too identified with their thoughts and visions. They can lose lifetimes believing that they ARE their mind and its thoughts. In later Sage lifetimes a quiet wisdom settles them; they feel the flow of information move through them and learn to grab onto what they want or need without attachment, a powerful practice harnessing the universe to manifest.

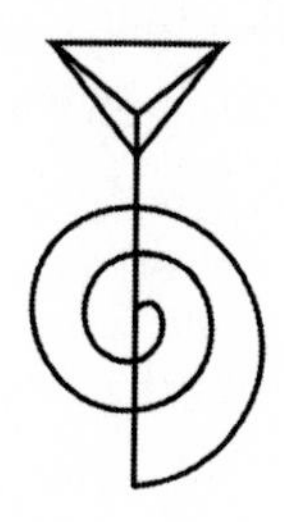

DRAGON SOULS

501–1,000 lifetimes

Playing with power. Playing with fire. Often achieving grandiose levels of success in academics, business, politics, and all areas of science, the arts, and entertainment, Dragon souls are now distinctly operating as beings of darkness and pain and havoc or light and beauty and expansion. They now have an even deeper awareness of the distinction between good and evil then they had when they were Sages. Dragons know on an acutely conscious level that they have absolute freedom of will; they are born feeling a little elastic inside, bound by less allegiances then ever before. They feel that they are free to move from good to evil or evil to good at any time during a Dragon incarnation or from one Dragon lifetime to the next. Dragons understand that they have long had the power over their own will, but now they feel their hand resting on the switch. Because of that distinctly dangerous feeling, some Dragons can come across as rigid and overly steadfast in their ideals, views, and dogmas, imposing them on as many others as they possibly can, while other Dragons appear to flip-flop from moral to immoral with a terrifyingly absolute knowledge of all the ramifications of their actions. All Dragons, knowing that free will can override an identification with being distinctly moral or immoral, have the ability to manipulate Sages and Kings for the end goals of either good or evil like puppets. All Dragons are masters of illusion when they want to be, spinning intricate webs without any effort and easily causing hurricanes of confusion in those around them. They can also access divine abilities for building and creating human achievements to previously incomprehensible new heights, almost always in the realms of either music, technology, corporate leadership, or the alliances of nations. They know that their words and their actions are as powerful as a the fire of a dragon's breath; they can burn down the world if they want to, or they can save and protect it from the greatest, most seemingly insurmountable threats … namely, other Dragons.

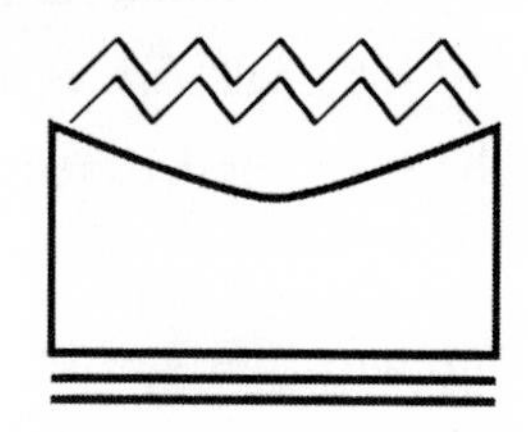

MOUNTAIN SOULS

1,001+ lifetimes

Coming into stillness. As Gypsy souls are too innocent yet to be either good or bad, Mountain souls are in many ways neutral. A telltale trademark of a Mountain is that they lack identification with who the world says they are. They are unattached to their material possessions, like a mountain does not own the grass or trees that grow upon it. Though abundance can sometimes easily accumulate around the Mountain soul, it knows it does not *have* these things. The Mountain soul feels ownership over nothing, including people, and thus has nothing to lose. They now know on the deepest levels that a larger truth is at work; they may not fully understand it yet, but they do trust it.

Mountain souls are born with a sense that existence itself is some sort of waking dream, and the many storms of life, that can be destructive and terrifying to younger souls, have little to no effect on them. They choose their words and at times their words are often few. Their center is unshakable, forged in granite, and their nature can range from quiet and introspective to highly comical and gregarious. One hallmark of a Mountain is their ability to be absolutely passive and incredibly powerful at the same time.

Being with a Mountain soul can be uncomfortable for certain younger souls, as they shine the light of truth so clearly there is nowhere to hide in their presence. On the other hand, Mountain souls can feel incredibly comfortable and inspiring to others. They are coming into peace with their innate higher understanding of how things work and comfortable with the illusion of distance that can create with certain people. From relationships to the cosmos, they perceive the synchronicity in real time as well as understand it in a timeless primordial way. Through the final lifetimes of a Mountain soul, reality itself starts melting away and the feeling that "all is one" begins as a slow drip, almost a suspicion, like a crack in the snow globe of human existence, and within a single lifetime or two is like a dam that gives way, flooding the consciousness with all of the absolute knowing of the universe.

ZODIAC SOULS

The oldest of the old souls, being one is the singular focus of a Zodiac from the moment of their existence in human form. Their egos barely take hold, if at all, during adolescence, the details of human-created identities such as name, race, social status, and so on fail to bear any lasting significance to a Zodiac. Early on, they find themselves on the outside of the human experience everyone around them is wrapped up in, even their own parents. Yet they fully understand that "there is no outside." Separateness, in all forms, is an illusion. This knowledge is the sacred gift, the birthright of existence at this level; it is also the single vulnerability to a Zodiac's human form, as this truth that permeates every cell of their being from the moment of their birth goes against the illusory concept of separateness that humans of lesser consciousness believe in—the misconceptions that we are man or woman, gay or straight, black, brown, or white, one religion or nationality or another, rich or poor, that these differences are our individual truths and that they mean something is the falsely agreed upon fantasy of most of humanity. Though throughout time, Zodiacs have been few and far between, they have also tended to surge in numbers at once, coming in like a wave of higher consciousness.

A telltale sign of a Zodiac is a feeling of being displaced, like they are from another planet, at times feeling even curious as to what they are doing here. They learn quickly that they have the ability to create, to manifest, and to harness all the power of the universe, but for this reason are feared and misunderstood and have always eventually been destroyed, either literally or by means of suppression.

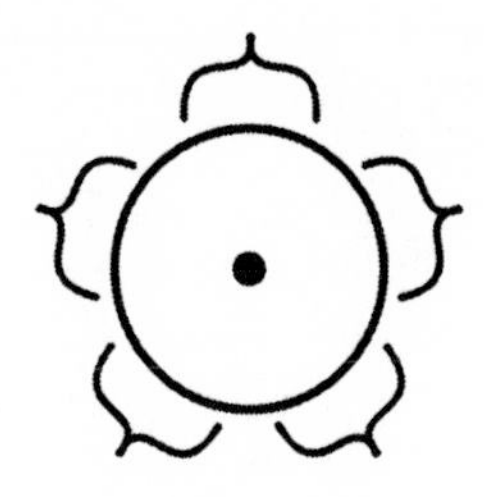

STAR SOULS

Like Zodiacs but the other end of the spectrum, Star souls are very important. They're not of this world, have never been, and may never be. Their Animus test shows zero lifetimes. Dubbed the "Nulla," as no Roman numeral exists for zero. A Star soul sees everything through fresh eyes; they lack the attachments brought by lifetimes of lessons and learning the ways of earth. Abraham Lincoln is an example of a Star soul. They come to bring revolutionary change; this kind of soul has the power of a Zodiac and a purity of being beyond any human comprehension. Star souls always change the world, always over the course of just a single life. Though incredibly powerful, these souls will have a weakness. It can be the single force standing between them and the fulfillment of their destiny. Most Star souls will be acutely aware of this weakness but may not know when it's standing in the way of their fate.